STOCKMAN'S STOWAWAY

THE STOCKMEN SERIES

MEL A ROWE

Also by Mel A ROWE

THE STOCKMEN SERIES:
Stockman's Sandstorm
Stockman's Stowaway
Stockman's Stormcloud
Stockman's Showdown

ELSIE CREEK SERIES:
The Art of Dust
Diamond in the Dust
Caked in Dust
Xmas Dust
Muster in the Dust
Rolled in Dust
Written in Dust
Doctoring Dust
Buffalo Dust

OASIS OF THE OUTBACK DUOLOGY:
The Station, Volume One
The Station, Volume Two

STANDALONE STORIES:
Avoiding the Pity Party
Unplanned Party
The Football Whisperer
Winter's Walk
Run Beautiful Run
The Sister Trip

Receive exclusive insights, and news on upcoming releases by joining:
https://melarowe.com/newsletter/

COPYRIGHT

***Caveat: As a courtesy, since there may be some sparse language choices in this story that may represent an obstacle for the reader, I am offering this warning. Please note this language and cultural references are purely for fictional purposes only and not designed to offend any individual persons, culture, or religions implied.*

The following is written in Australian English

To those who may
see imperfections within themselves,
know you are imperfectly perfect.

CASCADE SPUR
DINNER CAMP TREE
WOMBAT FLATS
STONEYS
WAIT-A-WHILE WATERS
STARVATION DAM
EMU PLAINS
TOMBSTONE TERRITORY
BRINK A STURGIE DOWNS
MALUS BREAKAWAY
CATTLEMAN'S KEEP
BULLOCK'S BATH
STOCK ROUTE
SCARY FOREST
DRAFTING YARDS
LEVIATHON CREEK
DROVERS REST
HOMESTEAD
ELSIE CREEK STATION
W
E
N
S
EST 1910

Zero

Elsie Creek Station - October 1962

'**M**ind your manners, Harry Splint. I'm a married woman.' Penelope Price swatted his hand away.

Harry chuckled. Leaning a shoulder against the pole on the farmhouse verandah, he poked up the brim of his Akubra. His saddled stockhorse grazed on the grass behind him as he inhaled the scents of a roast cooking, a welcome reprieve from sucking bulldust all week. 'It doesn't stop me wanting you any less, Pen.' His eyes slow-crawled over Penelope in her pretty summer dress.

'It's wrong.' Even if she did give that skirt of hers a bit of swing.

He grinned, putting one hand on her hip to drag her into his chest. 'What's wrong is that you're not married to me.'

She pushed against his chest as his arms snaked around her body. 'We shouldn't—'

'Shh, let me kiss you.' And he did, pressing his lips to hers, savouring the flavour of this woman who had become his whole world.

'Harry, someone might see us.'

Reluctantly, he let her go, admiring how her lips were all red and shiny from his kisses. 'You look beautiful.'

She dropped her head as a pretty flush made her cheeks all rosy. But her latest bruise peeked out from her collar.

That mongrel. 'What happened?'

'Nothing.' She plucked up the collar on her dress to hide

the bruise, dropping her head in shame.

He frowned, stepping back off the porch to give her space. 'What do you want me to do?'

'Leave.'

'I'm not leaving without you.' His frown deepened. 'I'm not leaving you with that mongrel who hurts you. If I ever catch him raising another fist at you, I will return the favour.'

Penelope wrapped her arms around herself. 'I'm not worth the fuss.'

'Believe me, you are worth it.' Harry tenderly stroked her soft blonde curls, lowering himself to meet her eyes, but she wouldn't look at him.

He stepped onto the verandah, so close that their noses were just touching. 'I love you, Penelope Price. We can't fight what we both feel. It's fate.'

Yet she still wouldn't look at him.

'Have you found your marriage certificate yet?' He asked her. It was the last piece she needed to be free.

'I'm looking. And I won't stop looking.' Her eyes were filled with determination. 'How about as soon as I find that paperwork,' her voice dropped to a whisper, 'we pack up that monstrous green car of yours and run away together?'

Harry could barely contain his grin from cracking wide open. He wanted to toss his hat in the air and let the world know their story.

But they couldn't.

It was a dangerous business being in love with the head stockman's wife.

But he just couldn't help himself when it came to Penelope Price. 'Do you really mean it?'

She gave a shy shrug.

Pulling her into his chest, once more snaking his arms around her waist. 'We'll go to a place where we can reinvent ourselves, where no one will know us. We'll be free.'

'What about your brother?'

'Charlie's his own man—'

'Who'll thump you as soon as he finds out you're having

an affair with a married woman. Stockmen have traditions, you know.'

'Oi. This isn't some affair. This—you and me—we're meant to be together forever. Right?'

Her sweet smile spread like pure sunshine. Gosh, she was pretty.

'Together forever, you and me, Harry Splint.'

'Too right, we'll be together forever. I'll start getting the car ready. You pack, and find that paperwork, and we'll disappear before anyone misses us. Say in a week? Everyone will be busy mustering along the stock route to beat the rains.' He peered back at the horizon, the sweltering weather teasing them with thick inky clouds that had yet to break the drought.

'Where will we go?'

'To a place where we can be husband and wife, and where no one will know who we are.' They'd make it. He believed it. He just didn't know how to tell his younger brother, Charlie.

One

Present Day

'I'd like to report a missing person.' Charlie's gravelly voice was as crusty as the lines etched deep into his face; the face of a man who'd lived a long life under an outback sun. Holding his hat in hand, with its crocodile hatband belonging to the beast that dared to bite him, Cap Riggs had never seen the old stockman looking so gloomy.

'You're not talking about your brother, are you?' Cap closed the driver's door of his old Toyota *Tojo* that he'd parked outside the town's local pub, beside the police paddy wagon.

'Was I talking to you? I'm talking to him, Policeman Porter.' Charlie hoisted the heavy bundle of freshly made cattle brands over his shoulder.

'It's senior constable—'

'Whatever. You're wearing the uniform, aren't ya? Driving that paddy wagon like you stole it.' Charlie waved his tanned, callused hand at the officer. 'So, I wanna report a missing person. It's my older brother, Harry Splint.'

Porter flipped open his notebook and clicked his pen. 'How long has your brother been missing?'

Charlie stuck out his chin and said, 'Sixty-two years.'

Porter's pen paused, his eyes flicking to Charlie, then to Cap, who could only shrug.

'Is there a time limit for reporting a missing person?' Cap didn't expect this out of his simple trip to town for supplies.

'No. But, sixty-two years.' Porter rubbed the back of his neck. 'Why do you want to report it now, Charlie?'

'Because we found *the car*.'

'What car?'

'A 1957 FJ Holden, stashed deep in the Stoneys. We dragged it back from our last muster. The Riggs brothers,' Charlie said, tossing his thumb at Cap, 'helped me restore it. Even got it freshly painted in the original Brookmere Green.'

'To sell?'

'Nah. So my granddaughter, Bree, can drive me to the pub on Fridays.'

But it wasn't Friday, and Charlie had covertly asked Cap for a lift into town.

Cap narrowed his eyes at the sneaky stockman. 'Does Bree know you're doing this?' Because no one wanted to upset the redhead back at the station.

'Listen, Porter...' The elderly stockman sniffed hard, ignoring Cap. He lowered one end of his long, heavy packages to land with a thud on the red dirt. 'There must be something you can do to find my brother.' From the back pocket of his dusty jeans, Charlie dragged out a booklet. 'Here's Harry's bankbook, coz we never had no smancy bank machines back then.' He flipped open the thick, lined pages. 'See...' His stubby finger tapped at some numbers on the page. 'It shows here that Harry took none of his money. He wouldn't leave this behind.'

'How did you bank back then?' Porter flicked the pages of the old bankbook, which was a little smaller than a passport.

'At the post office.' He waved towards Elsie Creek's main street. 'I talked to the postmistress, and she said it's legit. She just couldn't tell me anything else, coz it's in my brother's name. Laws, she said.' He nodded at the lawman.

The cunning old bugger.

'I like to avoid the post office.' Porter clicked his pen and scribbled down some notes. 'Where did you find the bankbook?'

'Inside Harry's old car. I also found his favourite footy guernsey and the family branding iron. Things my brother treasured.'

'Why would Harry go missing? And again, I'll ask, why hadn't you reported this sooner?'

Charlie dropped his head, shuffling his boots' thick Cuban heels in the red dirt. 'Coz of the murder.'

'What murder?' Porter leaned in closer.

Charlie gave a sad sigh. 'Someone accused my brother of murder. But Harry didn't do it. Harry's not like that. And if he'd done a runner, why leave his most precious items in his car and stash it in the Stoneys? And—'

'Okay, okay.' Porter held up his hand. 'Look, mate, how about giving me an approximate date of Harry's disappearance?'

'Around the time Harry made his last bank deposit.' Charlie pointed at the ancient bankbook Porter held.

'Back in November 1962?'

'Yeah, that's right. It happened just before that big wet buggered up Christmas, but it broke the drought, for sure. Does this mean you'll take a gecko's gander at it, mate?' Charlie's eyes lit up with hope.

'I can't promise anything, Charlie. But if you leave this bankbook with me, I'll do some research. How's that?'

'You're a champion, mate. Thank you.' Charlie shook the officer's hand vigorously. 'I'd appreciate it if you didn't mention any of this to Bree. I wouldn't wanna worry the girl.' The sly old stockman winked, as he hoisted the heavy cattle brands back over his shoulder.

'Oh, man.' Cap dropped his head, hoping Bree didn't bite his head off, too.

'Right, my business is done. I'll be dropping these brands off and havin' a coldie in the pub.' Charlie sauntered off.

'We can't be long, Charlie. I've got the dogs with me.' Cap tapped the mesh cage that covered the entire back of his old Tojo. Today, only half of his muster dogs had come for the trip into town. Now lazing around the large sacks of dog food he'd just picked up, enjoying the breezy shade.

'Before you go, Cap?' Porter removed his sunglasses to peer at the cattle dogs resting in the back cage. 'I have a favour to ask. A big one.'

'Go on.'

'Well, it's about this dog I found on a wallaby track in the middle of nowhere. I think she fell out the back of a ute, or something. She was in pretty rough shape, and I've spent thousands on her vet bills just to get her well again.' Porter shared a sad smile. 'But she's a working dog, I can see it. And you being who you are, I'm hoping you might…'

The air became still, no birds flew, not even a car cruised down the town's main street to distract them. Did he really need another dog?

'Please? Just take a look at her.'

Cap sighed. 'Like you said to Charlie, I can't promise anything.' Not when he had yet to talk to his brothers about his plans for the muster dogs on Elsie Creek Station.

'Thanks, Cap, I appreciate it. I'll bring her out to the station. You'll fall in love with her, with just one look. You wait and see.'

'You know I could never turn away a stray.' It was a soft spot that was sending him broke.

'So I've heard.' Porter nodded, yet there was no sign of the easy-going smile that he normally wore, as he tapped the brim of his police cap before driving away.

It seemed like giving up that dog had to be tough for Porter, so it must be for a reason. Cap already had a few rescue dogs living it up at the station, so what did one more matter. Right?

Cap shook his head as he turned to face his muster dogs. Some were strays he'd found; some had been rescued from the bullet. Funny thing was, after the time he'd spent training them, he could now sell those same dogs back to those farmers as brilliant muster dogs—if he wanted to. 'Well, it looks like we may have a new addition to the pack. Watch the Tojo, I'll be back in five if I can drag Charlie out of the pub.'

And then he'd front his brothers and tell them his plans.

Two

ia Dixon cowered behind the dilapidated stables, her heart hammering in her throat. Sweat stung her eyes as her cheek thumped with raging hot pain. Using the sleeve of her crusty work shirt, she wiped away the blood from her nose.

She'd spotted the police van and had wanted to cry out for help. But she just couldn't risk it. Instead, she remained rooted to the spot, desperately trying to control her trembling.

At least she was safe while that police car was in the pub's car park.

But then it moved, the officer driving off with a wave to the stockman he'd been talking to.

The stockman checked over the large cage on the back of his mustard-coloured Toyota ute. It was old, and full of cattle dogs. 'Back in five...'

A bird whistled nearby.

Mia clasped a hand over her mouth to stop her squeal, squeezing her eyes shut, forcing out the tears. Her heart ka-thumped heavily in her chest, but the pulse pounding in her ears made it almost impossible to listen for footsteps.

It felt like it took forever to find the courage to look around her. She had ten metres of empty space to get to the car park. The pub was even further.

Behind her stood a barren field with nothing to hide behind. She'd been lucky to have the trees and long grasses filling the roadside ditch as a cover to get her this far.

But where was he?

She craned her neck to peer through the hole in the corrugated iron that made up the stables. There were assorted chunky utes and trucks parked in the pub's dusty car park, but she couldn't see any people.

She took her shot. Crouched low, with her backpack to her chest, her steel-capped workboots scuffed over the dust as she weaved between the large four-wheel-drive work utes. Her breath ragged, the adrenaline coursing through her, she was almost there. She was going to make it.

Then she heard male voices.

Mia dropped and rolled under the nearest truck tray. A string of sharp stones dug through her shirt. Dirt clung to her hair as a pesky ant crawled over her hand. She didn't move, except to keep her eyes glued on the two sets of boots walking right past her. They were cattleman's boots, not miner's boots, and thankfully not the pair she was hiding from. But she couldn't risk it.

Mia wriggled along the shady underbelly of the truck, through to the other side.

Nearby stood the mustard-coloured Toyota, belonging to the stockman who'd been talking to the policeman like mates. It gave her hope.

Mia crept up slowly. '*Shh…*' she said to the dogs through the cage's wide mesh. One of them sniffed at her. Then another. Then another.

She then did the most daring thing in her life, and slid back the latch, opened the cage, and climbed inside.

'It's okay, puppies, it's okay, I just need a ride out of town.' She slid the latch shut, then squeezed against the cab to hide behind the large bags of dog food.

And the dogs never made a sound, except to sniff at her tears and blood.

Three

The Tojo bounced along the dirt track as Cap changed its gears to enter the deep floodway bearing the sign *Leviathan Creek*. Large rocks made up the wide creek bed, where towering ghost gums lined the banks. 'Have you ever seen this causeway flooded?' he asked Charlie.

'Plenty of times.' Charlie leaned his elbow on the passenger door and poked his head out of the window. 'There's a spring around the bend, you can let the dogs take a dip.'

'Could be crocs in that.'

'Them snapping handbags are everywhere, it's why I don't swim, but in the dry it's clear enough to see the bottom. Bree lets our stockhorses swim there.'

Cap pushed the accelerator, and the old ute chugged up the hill, never missing a beat as it made the slight incline. Hitting one of the deep ruts, the Tojo bounced, the dogs barked, and something screamed in the back.

He glanced at the rear-view mirror. *'What the fates!?'*

Cap slammed on the brakes. The red dust swirled around them as he peered through the back window to the cage meant to hold only the dogs.

'Is that a girl?' Charlie rubbed at his hat. 'Cor blimey, she's gotta have guts of forged steel to climb in there with all those dogs.'

'What are you doing?' Cap asked the stowaway hiding in the dog cage, as he opened its back door.

'Trying not to die.' On her hands and knees the woman

crawled to the door. 'That last bump was a killer.'

'Sorry—No, wait. Why are you in the back with my dogs?' He held his hand out to help her climb free. Her tiny hands were filthy, but her grip was strong.

But when she flung her hair back, he was sucker-punched. All the air left his lungs as if he'd forgotten to breathe, while feeling seriously ill at the same time.

She'd have to be in her late twenties, with windblown knotty hair that brushed her shoulders. Her honey-hazel eyes held a mixture of determination and vulnerability only heightened by the bruising from a whopping black eye, along with the swelling of her bloody nose and split lip.

'Please tell me I didn't do that, did I?' The mortifying thought turned his guts into hot lead.

'No.' She hung her head low, brushing her hair forward. Her knuckles were red raw, as if she'd put up a fight.

Charlie hissed in air over his teeth. 'You alright, girlie?'

'I...' With glassy hazel eyes she gave them a meek shrug.

'Did your house door get ya?'

'What?' Cap glared at the old man.

'That's what the women would say, back in the day, when their fellas got heavy-handed. I hope you kicked his hiney—'

'Here, I've got an icepack in the first-aid kit.' Cap dug around behind his seat and pulled out the kit and cracked open an icepack. 'My brother swears by these for his face. He's a professional fighter. You?' Because she looked like she'd just done ten rounds in a boxing ring.

'I wish. Do you have anything for a headache?'

'I do.'

She took the icepack with her dirty hands and short nails. They were working hands, and she was dressed in miner's clothes—a long-sleeved high-viz shirt, blue work pants and steel capped boots.

'Where are we?' Holding the icepack to her cheek and split lip, she peered around the deserted road where only the breeze rustled the leaves of the nearby trees.

'Near Elsie Creek Station,' replied Charlie, as Cap dug

around in the first-aid kit. 'Why did you climb in there with them dogs?'

'I needed to, um…' Her words became a whisper, 'get away.'

Cap had guessed that, recognising a stray when he saw one. 'I'm Cap Riggs, this is Charlie Splint. You are?' He held out the paracetamol and a bottle of cold water.

'Mia Dixon' Her hands trembled as she took the pills, washing them down thirstily.

'Hi, Mia.' The poor thing. 'Do you want me to drive you anywhere? The hospital?'

'I'm okay.' She didn't look okay, bunching up her shirt to hide the splatters of blood.

'Have you got anywhere you need to be, girlie?' Charlie asked.

'I don't really have a plan.' She wiped her bloodied nose with the sleeve of her work shirt, which was covered in dirt and dog hair.

Cap held out the roll of toilet paper he'd stashed behind his seat. 'I don't have a box of tissues, but this'll come close.'

She was such a short thing, with a tiny smile, yet her hands trembled, as she took the toilet roll. Her fragile condition was enough to give him ulcers.

'Well, girlie, this is your lucky day.' Charlie stepped in closer, wearing a big smile.

'Oi!' Cap arched his eyebrows at the insensitive old man.

'It just so happens I've got a couch you can crash on, and a granddaughter near your age. I reckon she'll take one look at you and become your instant best friend.'

'Why?' Mia asked warily.

'You can ask her when you meet her.' Charlie opened the passenger door. 'Come on, girlie. If we get a wriggle on, we'll get you settled in for dinner. Bree always puts on a good spread.'

'But…' Mia hesitated, her thick lashes shading her eyes as she peered up at Cap.

'I can't leave you on the road like this.' Not when Cap

wanted to bundle her up and keep her safe. 'Come on, this road only goes one way. And Charlie's right, Bree will help you.' Cap trusted the brassy redhead.

'Where are you going?'

'Elsie Creek Station. Home.' From inside the dog cage, he dragged out a small backpack. 'Is this yours?'

'Yeah, thanks.' She hugged it like a security blanket.

Inside the cage lay large sacks of dry dog food. Nearby, his dogs sat watching, no tails wagging, no barking. Nothing. All of them looking at him with guilty eyes. 'Where were you hiding?'

'Behind the dog food.'

He shut the cage door on his abnormally quiet canines. 'Good dogs.' That got their tails wagging, because usually no one got within six feet of the Tojo without the dogs going ape.

They must have known something was wrong. And Cap always trusted his dogs' instincts over humans any day. 'We'll take you home, so you can work out what you want to do next. You'll be safe there, I promise.' It's what he promised all the dogs he'd rescued, and he'd never turned away a stray—but this was his first time picking up a human stray, when he did his best to avoid people.

Tucking the first-aid kit back behind his seat, he started the truck and waited. Would she climb in? Or run?

Four

Mia searched the road for a sign, but there was nothing but red dirt and dry paddocks surrounding them. She had wanted a lift out of town, and she got that, but it didn't leave her with much choice of where to go.

Yet, Cap seemed like a friend to that policeman, earlier in town, and the old guy seemed harmless enough, and she had—

'Come on, girlie.' Charlie took off his hat and held it to his chest, his eyes sombre, as he held open the passenger door. 'We're the good guys. Swear it on my precious wife's soul we are.'

'Yeah, all right.' She gingerly climbed into the cab. It was old and dusty, but well taken care of. Assorted trucker caps lined the front dashboard, while a sun-faded red dog's collar hung from the rear-view mirror. Stuck in the middle of the seat, she tried to make herself smaller to avoid touching the two men's shoulders. 'Is your name Cap from all the hats?'

'You could say that.'

'I like your truck. You don't see many of these around.' But she saw Cap's big hands, callused and strong, on the steering wheel. His wrists were thick, and his forearms were muscular with thick veins hinting at this guy's muscles, that could do some damage, if they wanted to.

'I don't like trucks that are full of computers and electric gadgets. If you have a problem, you can't fix them when you're out in the middle of the scrub.' Cap put the beast into gear, and it began rolling towards what she hoped was a good thing. Even though her face pounded, the icepack was a true blessing. But what was she doing, squeezed into the front, between two strange men?

Cap casually gave her a side glance. His eyes were a rich malt-whisky colour, the kind of colour that evoked thoughts of warm malted milk drinks before a winter fireplace. 'You know, I'm happy to drive you back to town.'

She shook her head, only to wince at the headache. 'I'm good.' If she kept telling herself that, she might wake up from this nightmare any second now. 'So, um, what do you guys do?'

'Me, I'm an old stockman who's pretending he's retired.' Charlie gave her a playful nudge, enough to make her smile, even if her fat lip hurt. 'Cap there, runs the station with his brothers.'

'How many brothers?'

'Four of us. Ryder is the oldest. Then there's Dex, me, followed by Ash, who has his partner, Harper, with him. They've got a boy, my nephew Mason there, too.' Cap shared a grin at the mention of a child.

'A family station.'

Cap nodded.

'Do you live in the same house?' she asked Charlie.

'Nah, me and my granddaughter have the caretaker's cottage.'

'Which is better than the farmhouse, where two of my brothers live.' Cap cracked a grin. 'And then there's Dex's situation.'

'Dex is squatting in the stockman's shack.' Charlie chuckled at some in-house joke.

'And I'm renovating a demountable near the kennels.' Cap then cleared his throat. 'So, you're at the mine?'

She plucked at the dirt and dog hair off her work shirt. 'Was. I just finished my contract today. I was having knock-off drinks with the team.'

'Team for what area?'

'I'm…' She gathered her courage to reveal her job title, which regularly made miners scowl at her. 'I'm a mining revegetation specialist.'

'For real?' Cap eyes lit up like he'd struck gold. His hint of a grin made her look at him, like really look at him.

Cap was a rugged but stunningly handsome man—which was not what she needed right now.

But she couldn't stop herself from taking in the details of how the sun and wind had etched lines of experience over his weathered face where a shadow of a beard complemented his strong jawline.

'What sort of job is that?' Charlie asked.

'Basically, I plant trees.'

'So that'd make you a specialist in digging holes, eh?' Charlie cheekily winked at her.

'Charlie's old school. You'll have to explain it to him.'

'Well…' She jutted out her tender, bruised chin. 'I'm a tropical native botanist who specialises in soil repair. I love dirt so much I help repair mining site landscapes, which means planting a lot of trees.'

'So, you're one of them eco-thingies like Cap.'

She shrugged.

Cap shifted behind the steering wheel. 'I might have a job for you, if you want?'

'Doing what?'

'I'm trying to work out where to create wildlife corridors to protect the soil. Last muster we had a killer sandstorm, and we lost topsoil.'

'Worst one I'd seen in all my years,' said Charlie.

'Besides rehabilitating some areas on the station, I want to try some no-tilling, self-seeding feed crop methods, too.' The excitement was evident in Cap's voice, as he rested his thick wrists on the steering wheel of the Tojo that plodded along the dirt road.

'But aren't you a cattle producer?' In her experience they were very protective of their carbon monoxide–producing cattle that accelerated climate change. But she wasn't going to mention that to the guy helping her out of a jam.

'It's all gobbledegook to me,' mumbled Charlie.

'I'm trying to reduce our carbon emissions,' said Cap.

She whipped her head around to face him. 'Are you for real?'

Cap gave a curt nod. 'Absolutely. My younger brother, Ash, is using his drone for certain jobs, to cut down on fossil fuels, while I'm focusing on using muster dogs and stockhorses to do the same. I'm always looking for the best ways to reduce our carbon emissions, and I've also been researching regenerative agriculture practices to increase our biodiversity.'

'What the hell did you just say?' Charlie asked.

Cap spoke so passionately as he sat higher behind the steering wheel. 'It's all about farming for the future by looking after the soil today. I know the changes are coming fast, where the market will be demanding carbon-neutral beef on their shelves, and I'm hoping Elsie Creek Station will be there, front and centre.'

'I still don't understand all that.' Old Charlie shook his head. 'Was that English?'

'It means that the methane created by the cattle won't hurt the environment, because we're balancing out the amount of stock among the landmass in the way we create our crops, use our water, and maintain our trees.' He grinned at Mia. 'It's possible, right?'

She just stared at him, nodding like a fool with wide eyes, while her mind tripped over: *Where have you been all my life?*

'So, do you want a job? I could really use your input.'

All she could do was nod. Normally, men would baulk at her job, especially those in the mining and cattle industry. The mining execs ignored her, because she was there as part of a government policy, and most of them would call her a misplaced hippy. Some cattlemen were so set in their ways they'd rather ignore anyone telling them what science had proven, but this… 'I'm in.' Sweet sassy malassy she was in.

'Great. You can help me explain it to my brothers.'

'Eeerh—um…' She sank back into her seat trying to make herself small while twisting her fingers. 'I-I-I don't like public speaking.' She avoided all forms of public speaking. 'And I—'

'How about we let the girl settle in first?'

She gave Charlie a small thank-you nod.

'No worries. When you're ready, I'll show you the property and I'm happy to pay for your time.'

Right now, all she wanted was to get rid of her headache, to stop her face from throbbing, and feel safe again.

The dogs started yapping as they drove through an enormous set of gates, then under a huge archway where a sturdy metal sign made of intricately woven metals like old lace proclaimed: *Elsie Creek Station*.

'Dex did a good job grading the driveway, eh?' Charlie nodded at the wide dirt track.

Cap nodded, his grip loose on the steering wheel. 'Harper is happy she can get her car in and out for work. It won't be long, and we'll start shipping out our first load of fats, after we've done the drafting—where you'll give us our cattle brand back.'

Cap side-eyed Charlie, who was mumbling under his breath as they travelled down the smooth track that ran alongside a dried-up dusty paddock. The track took a sweeping left bend, where rising from the dust was a weatherboard house. It stood on the right of a large clearing with a group of sheds at the far end.

'Is this the homestead?'

'Yep. That's the farmhouse.' Cap waved to the woman holding the hand of a small boy, who was eagerly waving at Cap. Beside them stood a seriously strong-looking shepherd, with a plump cream labrador, and a tail-wagging beagle.

'You'll have to introduce Mia to that police dog,' said Charlie, also waving at the boy. 'Swear that boy grew an inch overnight.'

'You have a police dog?' Mia guessed it had to be the dark shepherd, who was bristling with muscles.

'Sarge is an ex-riot dog.'

'Aren't they dangerous? And you have that child.'

'He's well-trained, and he had nowhere to go. Sadly, his owner was killed on duty. No one else trusted the dog.'

'But you do?'

'I trust all my dogs. Never could say no to a stray.' His malt-whisky eyes softened, displaying a deep level of kindness she hadn't seen from anyone in a long time.

'And that's my place there—the caretaker's cottage.' Charlie spoke with such pride in his voice as he pointed at the stone cottage, with a large assortment of flourishing flowers in the front.

She wriggled out of the seat, only to discover her body ached all over. Her thighs and calves hurt from running, and her back was a massive cluster of thumping aches and bruises. She was a mess.

'Oi, BREE. You round?' Charlie whistled as he followed the stone path down the side of the cottage.

Cap opened the back cage, and the dogs spilled out like water gushing from a tap. Eight dogs, and all of them stocky cattle dogs.

She gasped at the realisation of what she'd done. The sheer desperation that forced her to her climb inside a cage full of strange dogs.

As Cap filled their water bucket, the working dogs sniffed at the soil, or found the nearest fence to do their doggy business. 'That'll keep them happy for a bit.' He patted a few of the dogs, all of them wagging their tails.

'The flowers are so pretty.' She brushed her fingertips over the soft velvety rose petals that peeked through the iron fence. They blended well with the vibrant clusters of other assorted flowers, many of them not normally found in this part of the outback.

Cap pushed open the wrought-iron gate that had to be as old as the house. 'This is nothing, wait until you see the backyard.'

They followed the stone pathway down the right side of the house where a tall wall of corrugated iron hid them from the outside world.

'Sweet sassy malassy.' Mia stopped on the edge of the backyard, her fingertips hovering over her swollen lip. She'd completely forgotten about her pain. 'What is this place?'

'I'd say it's one of the oldest permaculture gardens in the region.' Cap grinned, hooking his thumbs through the belt loops of the dusty jeans that hugged the man in all the right places. She shouldn't even be noticing him like this, tearing her eyes back to the garden.

'Amazing.' The garden that is.

'My wife started it, and now my granddaughter manages it.' Charlie nodded at the yard filled with an assortment of vegetables.

'I've never seen squash like this.' Mia pointed at the strangely shaped summer squash that grew alongside luffa squashes and gourds, even some tri-coloured winter pumpkin shaped like a bell. 'How? It's winter with summer crops?'

'I'd say they've adapted, considering they've been using the same seed stock for half a century, which would make them heirloom vegetables,' explained Cap. 'What do you think?'

'This is incredible.' Mia wanted to pluck at the vegetables she'd only seen in books. An oasis in the outback that filled the air with astonishing scents. It had her stomach rumbling.

'BREE?' Charlie hollered.

Mia jumped in fright. Swallowing hard, she looked back for an escape.

But Cap was there, holding out his hands to calm her down with his soothing tone. 'It's okay, Mia. You're safe here. I promise.'

'I'm not normally this jumpy.' Even if her heart was hammering in her chest, with her throat so dry and tight.

Cap said nothing, just giving her those sad eyes. She had to turn away.

'I'm coming, Pop.' The woman's voice came from the left area of the back sheds. Horse stables stood on the right end of the corrugated fence line, and in the middle was a spectacular view of horses grazing in a paddock, which led to a group of trees and the rocky red escarpment. What a view.

Movement caught her eye and she turned to discover a meshed dome covering a raised garden bed. Inside it three hens were busily digging like tractors in the richest dark soil. It was so sweet, her dirt-loving fingers itched to dive in there.

A gate shut, and footsteps came down the stone path. 'Where have you been, Charlie?' The woman was hidden by a high trellis of sugar peas and snake beans.

'I went to town with Cap to see a bloke about a dog.'

'Is that your knitting circle where you blokes make jumpers you'll never wear?'

'I left you a note.'

'Where?'

'Kitchen. Wind must've blown it away.'

'Uh huh. Which reminds me to update my spam filters, and to spray the house for note-stealing spinifex fairies.'

'Anyhoodle, we picked up a stray.' Charlie pointed at Mia. 'Bree, meet Mia. She's gonna crash on the couch for a bit.'

In a thick leather apron, Bree ripped off her long leather gloves, pulling off her skullcap to release a shocking spill of red curls. Mia had never seen so much hair.

'Uh, hi, Bree.'

Bree said nothing for the longest time, while her green eyes took in the details. 'Are you okay?'

Mia nodded, then shook her head, her eyes hot with tears. 'This has never happened to me before.'

'Aw, come here, precious.' Bree swallowed Mia in a big sisterly hug.

Normally Mia didn't hug anyone, but something inside her broke as she lowered her face into Bree's soft hair, gently scented with lavender and vanilla. Or was that pecan?

'I've got you. You're safe now, precious.' Bree rubbed her back in a soothing manner.

'Told ya my granddaughter would be an instant friend.'

Charlie nodded. 'Come on, Cap, let's leave 'em to it. Mia's in good hands now.'

'I'll check on you later, Mia. If you need anything, let me know.' Cap nodded at her, clearly concerned for her, before he followed Charlie.

Strangely, Mia didn't want Cap to leave. She wanted to say thanks. She wanted to stop blubbering, but was helpless as her shoulders slumped, and the adrenaline leached out of her to leave her a hot thumping mess.

Five

Mia wept, while being held by a woman she'd just met, still spinning over the reason that brought her here. She'd never felt so lost.

'Um, sorry to impose like this.' Mia wiped at her tears, but the dirt scratched like sandpaper against her swollen cheek.

'Come on, let's get you cleaned up in the best shower made for women.'

'Huh?'

'I made it myself.' Bree giggled. 'I'll dig up some clothes for you. Do you prefer dresses or pants?'

'I'm not a dress kind of girl.' She was always the tomboy.

'I've got plenty of welding pants. They might be long in the leg for you.'

'I'm used to that. Working on a male-dominated mining site, my clothes were always too baggy for me.'

From the nod, it was obvious Bree understood, and she was wearing heavy boots and welder's trousers, so presumably she worked in some metal trade.

'I could run you a bubble bath, put in some soothing herbs that'll do wonders for the skin.' With her arm gently around Mia's shoulders, Bree guided her towards the cottage.

'I'd hate to put you out.'

'You're not a bother at all.'

Inside, it took a moment for her eyes to adjust to the large room. The temperature dropped at least ten degrees, but there was no air conditioner running, nor any fans in the low ceiling. Vintage pictures hung on the walls, and a large couch stood under a stained-glass window, near what was obviously the front door. A solid wooden table sat near the kitchen that took up the entire back wall, with a large island bench made from one solid piece of timber. It was gorgeous.

'What is all this?' She pointed at the large jars resting on the kitchen bench, they smelled of vinegar.

'I pickled some cucumbers and eggs for Pop, earlier. He likes them with his beer.'

'And the chillies?' She pointed to the assorted green and red chilli varieties spread out on trays, along with crates of plump red tomatoes sitting in the corner.

'I'll be making a batch of chilli sauces and some chilli cooking oils.' She grabbed some glasses and a jug from the fridge. The scent of fresh mint soon filled the air. 'Make yourself at home.'

Mia caught her reflection in the mirror that hung above the vintage hat rack loaded with assorted coats, cowboy hats and stockwhips. It was the first time she'd seen her face. 'I shouldn't be here.'

Bree gently touched her shoulder, as she held a glass of water complete with sliced cucumber and mint. 'It's okay. Pop did the right thing bringing you here. Drink this, it's filtered rainwater. Do you need anything for the pain?'

'Cap gave me something earlier.' She gulped the invigoratingly fresh water down in a matter of moments.

'Top up that glass anytime.' Bree nodded at the large office-style water cooler that stood by the hats.

'Thank you.' Mia refilled her glass.

'Want a cup of tea? Sorry, there's no coffee in the house.'

Mia shook her head.

'Do you want to call someone?' Between grinding with the mortar and pestle, Bree nodded at the desk crammed into the corner with its silent PC and phone.

Mia shook her head again, drinking more water, as an unexpected wave of shame smothered her. Putting the glass down on the kitchen bench, she tucked her dirty hands under her armpits, her head bent, desperate to hide her face.

'Will anyone be worried about you?'

'I-I…' Her body gave her away, shivering with fear.

'Are you hiding from someone?'

'He used to be so…' Tears blinded her, and her lip hurt as the bruises on her face pounded. 'I-I should go.'

'Hey, stop that, it's fine. Listen, what I'm going to do is set you up and give you some space. I'll get you some clothes, so you can take a long hot shower, and then I'll leave you alone to recuperate, unhindered, on the best couch on the planet.' She pointed to the large couch.

'It looks comfy.'

'It is.' Bree led her to the couch, helping her to sit. 'The problem is if I sit on that couch, I can kiss the rest of the day goodbye because I won't move again.'

Even though she was sore all over, the couch was cool and seemed to hug her body in the perfect way. 'I see what you mean.'

Bree handed her a light linen bag that smelt of flowers, and an open tin of what looked like wax. 'You can put this bag over your eye. It will soothe and help reduce the swelling. And you can rub this ointment on the areas that hurt, too.'

'What is it?'

'It's a natural magnesium salve for muscle aches. Pop swears by it. Just dab it on the area that hurts the most. Or I can get you a lump of steak?'

'This is fine, thank you.' The cloth was soft, and the ointment so cool on her skin. 'I'm so sorry to bother you.'

Bree leaned in closer, to tenderly capture Mia's hands. 'I want no more saying sorry to me. No more thinking you're bothering us, because you're not. Charlie and Cap brought you here for a reason, and you can trust us. There is no hidden agenda here. We will keep you safe.'

Again, her eyes teared up at Bree's open kindness. 'But you don't know me.'

'Well, then, don't be shy in telling me your story. Starting with, are you in any danger?'

'I honestly don't know.' Mia hid her face in her hands, only to wince. 'Ow.'

'The salve will help.' Bree ever so gently brushed the hair away from Mia's face. 'Your wounds show this happened today?'

Mia nodded.

'Do you want me to call the police?'

'I don't know?' Why couldn't she think straight?

'I bet the whole incident is so fresh that you've got all these fragments rattling around in your brain that haven't had a chance to soak in yet.'

'How did you know?'

Bree gave a mild shrug.

But her patience in waiting for a response made Mia want to speak. 'I'd been at the pub having lunch with workmates, that went longer than I thought. Then my boyfriend, Gavin, showed up to drive me home.' *What the hell, Gavin.* She tried to get angry at him for what he'd done but could only shiver.

'You worked for the mine?' Bree nodded at her work shirt, as she dragged over a soft blanket for Mia.

'We'd finished our contract. I wanted to stay and party longer with everyone before we scattered across the country. But Gavin snapped. I don't know what happened.' For the life of her, she had no idea what she had done that was so wrong for Gavin to lash out at her like that.

'Was he jealous of you with your workmates?'

'I don't know.' She dragged the blanket over her legs, hiding her cold hands under its soft edge where she twisted her fingers to stop them trembling. 'One minute we're in the car, the next Gavin's elbow slams into my eye. I was so stunned.' She swallowed hard, pulling the blanket up to her chest, while staring at her fat tears splattering on the floor. 'He stopped the car, dragged me out, and...' She squeezed her eyes shut and the tears fell down her cheeks as the horror replayed in her mind. No one had ever hit her, until today. 'I fell back and hit the fence, and I rolled under it.' She inhaled a shaky breath. 'That's when I ran. But he chased me down in his car.'

'Arsehole. How did you get away?'

'I hid in the long grass and ran for the pub.' At times she'd heard him, in some places so close she could hear the crunch of the grass, and his laboured breathing. 'That's where I climbed into the back of Cap's ute—'

'With all of those dogs?'

Mia nodded.

'You poor thing.' Bree rubbed her back in soothing circles. 'Well, that idiot won't want to come near me or this station, that's for sure. Just know you're safe and you're welcome to stay as long as you like.'

Could Mia believe them about keeping her safe? Yet with the recent events that brought her here, she might not be that lucky.

Six

'We've got dingoes.' Dex dragged out his chair at the outdoor table that occupied the corner of the farmhouse's front porch. It's where Cap and the rest of his brothers had gathered for every sunrise and sunset since they'd moved in. 'Mongrels got one of the calves.'

'Which means they'll be back,' said Ryder, passing out a round of cold beers to his brothers.

'Can we bait them?' Ash asked as he spun his chair around to sit on it like a saddle.

'Not with my dogs around, thank you. Besides, they're a native animal that was here first.' Cap patted Sarge, the guard dog, before dragging out his chair.

'Not for long, if they keep this up. They'll have a belly full of lead if they take any more of our calves,' said Dex.

'I may have a solution.' Cap scrubbed at his hair, hidden under his cap, unsure how to broach the subject with his two older brothers, who weren't as open to change as his younger brother, Ash.

'We could put up an electric fence,' Ash offered.

'They're too smart and cunning for that, when a box of bullets will do.'

Cap frowned at the bully, Dex, who provoked his violent streak for a living. 'We don't need to kill them. We can share the space with them as they're an Apex hunter that will effectively manage the roos from destroying our crops, just the way nature intended. And I have some ideas.'

'Well, you're the dog whisperer. Let's hear it.' Dex rocked in his chair while chugging on his beer, but his dark steely eyes kept watching. But they weren't nearly as cold as Ryder's.

'I'm thinking of getting some nanny dogs.'

'We've got one; it's Ruby who looks after Mason.' Ash pointed his beer at the plump labrador lying next to the child playing in the lounge.

Dex tilted his head. 'Is it me or is that labrador getting fat.'

'Stop fat-shaming my son's dog,' said Ash. 'Ruby's retired, leave her alone.'

'Harper has ruined those police dogs, she's turned them into pampered house pets. Look at what she's done to that beagle.' Dex pointed at the beagle, flat on her back inside a very plush dog bed, wearing a neckerchief, snoring.

'I'm thinking of getting dogs for the calves,' blurted out Cap to stop his brothers bickering.

'Eh?' Dex raised an eyebrow.

'Do you mean guardian dogs?' Ryder asked. 'Like they do with sheep?'

Cap nodded. 'Yes, it's the same concept. I can get us some maremmas. There's a station up near Broome that's had some luck with that breed in protecting their calves.' Cap scrolled through his phone and brought up some pictures. 'They'd live with the calves to protect the herd. Eventually I'd love to establish a breeding program here and sell the pups.'

'You'd give up a dog?' Dex chuckled. 'You, who is forever bringing home strays?'

'Sure, if they're going to a good home. I'd check out the owners before they left, and I'd ensure they had proper training. I'd also like to train local farmers on using muster dogs, or help them with any problem dogs they have to help build their mustering teams.'

'That's a lot to take on. When we're flat out fixing this place up.' Ryder looked annoyed, which was normal.

'Talking about strays…'

'What did you bring home now?' Ryder arched an

eyebrow at Cap.

'Porter's bringing out a dog.' Cap then spotted Bree coming towards them from the caretaker's cottage. It was enough to make him rub the bridge of his nose to push back the headache that was about to form. 'And I brought back someone else.'

'Who?' Dex followed Cap's line of sight to turn in his seat. 'Uh-oh, incoming.'

'She's staying at Bree's.'

'Friend of Bree's?'

'Nah, she snuck into the back of the ute.'

Dex swivelled back to face Cap. 'Were your dogs in there?'

Cap nodded. 'She made it all the way to Leviathan Creek before we found her.'

'We?'

'Me and Charlie. Hey, did you know he's put in a missing person's report with Porter over his brother?'

'Does Bree know this?' Ryder's deep voice was lower than normal.

Cap shook his head as Bree approached. 'How's Mia?'

'She's asleep.' Bree stopped by the steps. Her red hair shone in the sun, but it did nothing to dampen the smouldering temper that made her green eyes darken. 'That bastard did a number on her.'

'All right, you two, what the hell is going on?' demanded Ryder.

'It's what I was trying to tell you...' Cap waited a beat, hoping Bree would step in, before he continued

But Bree arched her eyebrows at him to speak.

For fate's sake. 'I found Mia hiding in the back of the ute with the dogs. She's pretty banged up, got a black eye, a fat lip and I'm sure there's more bruising on her back.' It made him sick to think of someone doing that to a woman. He turned to Bree. 'Did Mia tell you who did that to her?'

'Her boyfriend did.' Bree plonked her fists on her hips. 'As this is your station, you boys have a right to know, so I'm telling you this now, so none of you demand twenty questions out of her later. Her name is Mia Dixon. She used to work at the mine on the far side of Elsie Creek. And, she's grateful Cap gave her a job.'

'You what?' Ryder spun around in his chair and glared at Cap.

'Mia's a botanist who specialises in soil. I told you I want us to become carbon neutral with our beef and creating wildlife corridors is an important part of that.'

'Only for the dingoes to come in and pick off our herd.' Dex was such a dick.

'There is enough wildlife around that they don't need to touch our herd, and the guardian dogs will watch out for them.'

'Pfft, at this rate we'll just be producing pet meat to feed *your pack!*'

'*For fate's sake,* I'm suggesting all this to put us in front of the competition, and to stop that neighbouring mine stealing our water by proving how environmentally sound we are. But you're still stuck in the boggy bulldust—'

'*Oi!*' Ryder slammed his beer on the table like a judge hammering his gavel in court. 'First thing, is Mia okay?'

'She's going to be fine.' Yet Bree's jaw twitched with anger. 'Nothing's broken, but he put the boot into her, so she's bruised all over. That sociopathic scumbag had better not come near me and my stash—'

'Bree.' Ryder raised his hand, cutting off her tirade. 'How many shotguns do you actually have stashed around this place?'

She shrugged.

'How many are registered?'

Again, she shrugged. 'Let me put it this way, cupcake, if that degenerate shows up here, he won't get within six feet of her before I'll have a double barrel locked and loaded.'

'Jeez, Bree, you're scaring me,' said Ash, poking up the brim of his hat.

'It's a good thing she's on our team.' Dex chuckled,

rocking back on his chair.

'Do we need to be concerned about this guy showing up?' Ryder arched his eyebrows at Cap.

Cap shrugged. He hadn't considered that. This was the first human stray he'd ever brought home.

'No,' replied Bree. 'Mia said she lost him at the Elsie Creek Pub, where she climbed into the Tojo's cage of dogs—and that shows how truly desperate she was.'

'And brave,' mumbled Ash, shaking his head. 'But she must be alright for the dogs to let her in like that.'

'How could you not see her?' Dex asked Cap. 'I know you're always checking that cage.'

'The dogs must have shielded her while she hid behind the bags of dog food. And she's such a tiny thing.' Pretty, even. But he wasn't sharing that with his brothers.

'Oh, as an FYI, Mia talks just like Cap about the garden, soil, and stuff. All eco-friendly.' Bree gave Cap a wry grin, her eyes all sparkly, which was a sure sign of trouble.

'I see.' Ryder gripped his beer, as his scowl deepened. 'You're not trying to save another stray, are you, Cap? When everything went to hell with the last mystery woman we had out here.'

'Oi, leave Harper out of it.' Ash frowned.

Cap gritted his teeth, his hands curling to fists on his thighs. 'I don't care what you say, Mia is staying as long as she wants.'

'I vote we let her stay.' Ash raised his beer. 'If this Mia knows her stuff, she could offer ideas on fodder and how to improve our pasture grasses. Right, Cap?'

'Exactly.' Cap nodded at his younger brother, so glad to have him on board. 'You gave me a paddock to run my own trials, and I'm hoping Mia can advise me on the best plant stock we can use in the best possible way to improve our soil.'

'But only when she's ready, Cap.' Bree lowered herself to meet his eyes, there was a heavy protectiveness laced within her voice. 'Mia is going to be sore for the next few days, so I'd appreciate it if she had no visitors to let her heal in peace.'

'Thank you, Bree.' The relief was enormous that the redhead was on the job.

'Do you think Mia should call the police?' Ryder asked.

'Hell, yeah.' Cap's scowl was low over his eyes, as an unexpected rage began bristling within his chest. 'Porter's bringing out a dog later, we can talk to him then.'

'Mongrel.' Dex frowned as his chair thumped hard on the floorboards. 'If anyone laid a hand on one of our sisters, I'd kill the bastard. We all would.' Dex's voice was loaded with grit, coming from a man who never backed down from a fight in and out of the ring. 'But as I'm so good-looking, I'd hate to steal Cap's thunder of being the white knight—'

'Leave off.'

'Tell this girl—'

'Her name is *Mia*.' Cap ground his teeth and sneered viciously at Dex.

'Did Mia say this man's name, to keep a lookout for him?' Ryder asked Bree.

'Gavin Rikers.'

A name Cap would never forget.

Seven

'You're welcome to flick through Pop's cowboy books or magazines. I've got an e-reader if you want to read anything else.' Bree led Mia out the front door to the small verandah where a set of comfy cane chairs, a small table, and a sparsely filled bookcase created a cosy corner with a view of the front yard's flower garden. 'It's a good spot here in the mornings. The flowers are at their most fragrant then.'

'Did you plant this?'

'Me, no. Pop grows them in memory of my grandmother, Beverly Splint. Granny Bea loved this part of the garden.'

'It's beautiful.'

'It is. And you should tell him that and watch ol' Charlie blush. It's the sweetest thing.' Bree giggled as she plumped up some cushions on the comfy cane chair.

'Where are your parents?'

'Gone. Yours?'

'They live with my brother on the family farm.' Mia lowered herself into the chair, the plump cushions cocooning her sore ribs.

'Where?'

'Nildottie. On the river, near Swan Reach?'

Bree shook her head.

'Not far from Murray Bridge.'

'Oh, I've driven through there. Feel free to call them anytime.' She pointed to the open front door.

'I don't want to worry them.' Again, she dropped her

head in shame.

'Hey.' Bree dropped to her haunches, her eyes level with Mia's. 'You have nothing to be ashamed about. But your ex sure as hell has a lot to answer for. He's the one who did wrong by you.'

'Gavin's never done anything like that before.'

'Once is too many times, Mia. But I bet it's been building up for a while.'

Mia shook her head. 'Not true. But he was drinking.'

Bree narrowed those green eyes at her. 'That's no excuse.'

'He was—'

'Stop sticking up for the guy.'

Mia gasped at the realisation that Bree was right.

'Hey…' Bree grabbed her hands, holding them to her heart, as her voice softened. 'You are so much more than that. Don't let this one incident define you, when you deserve only the good, living in a world where no man hits you. Unless you're a boxer like Dex.'

'Is that one of Cap's brothers? I haven't seen Cap today.'

'I told Dex and his brothers to stay away and let you heal in peace.'

Aw, bless Bree for being so considerate. It had also surprised Mia when Bree had asked permission to share her story. 'So, you told them I'm here?'

Bree nodded. 'I gave them the brief version. And Cap told them you're staying as long as you need and they're okay with that.'

'What are they like? The brothers.'

'Oh, is this where I get out the good crockery to drink gin from teacups while we pretend we're high society, gossiping about everyone as we spill the tea on all their inappropriate family secrets?' Bree grinned, plonking herself down in the next chair, leaning back, to casually cross one leg over the other.

A giggle slipped out of her. If it wasn't for her fat lip, Mia could almost match Bree's wolfish grin. 'I meant—'

'I know what you meant, because I'd want to know too, if

I were in your situation.' Bree inhaled deeply to peer over the bobbing flower heads towards the farmhouse that stood in the distance as if dumped onto the red dirt like a forgotten child's toy.

'So, who is the oldest?'

'Ryder. He's hot to look at—all the Riggs' brothers are in their own way.'

Mia didn't want to think about Cap and his good looks, she couldn't. Yet…

'Ryder's hard and cold as steel,' continued Bree. 'Some days I swear he's got ice in his veins, he's that cold. He's also the business brains who can spot a con within a millisecond, and the bank out of their little quartet of brothers who own Elsie Creek Station.'

'Bank?'

'Ryder paid for this place with cash, and the others put in their deposits. I think he's a self-made millionaire or something?' Bree shrugged. 'And then there's Dex.'

'The boxer?'

'Bareknuckle boxer. Dex does the hardcore street fights.'

'Oh, that sounds scary.' Mia wriggled in her seat uncomfortably, thinking of hiding back inside. Which was so wrong when she lived for the outdoors as a soil sister. Maybe the sooner she got back to work, the sooner she could forget this nightmare of bruises. 'Is this Dex, um…' *Safe?*

'Dex is cool. We share the same weird sense of humour—but we will never ever tell him that.' Again, Bree shared another wolfish grin, helping to distract Mia from her issues. 'Then you have Ash, who used to love the game of chasing skirt and playing computer games all night. Until the little snowflake grew up overnight when his son, Mason, arrived, along with the perfect lady to suit Ash.'

'And her name?'

'Harper. She's only been in the Territory a few months, knows nothing about cattle, but is a whizz with politics and office stuff. She works part-time at the vet surgery in town, which is handy because she loves to shop—so it's like dial-up delivery service. You'll meet her soon. Harper visits for cooking lessons. Can you cook?'

'Basic stuff. You?' Mia had been spoiled with flavoursome soups, smoothies, and lots of comforting cupcakes. Food that was easy for her to eat with her sore jaw. The level of care these strangers provided for her was heartwarming.

'Well, me and my curves like my food, and my gin.' Bree patted her healthy curves. Bree not only had the height and a stack of red hair, she also had a generous bosom that Mia would kill for.

'Which reminds me, I've got a new batch of gin to test.'

'You make your own gin?'

'It keeps me out of trouble.' Bree winked with those green eyes all sparkly. 'We'll have to find a flavour you like when you're ready. But I noticed you haven't asked about him yet.'

'Who?'

'Cap. Don't you want the dirt on him?'

Mia swallowed hard, desperate to fight her blush. 'I—'

'Don't worry, precious.' Bree waved her hand in the air as if shooing away a bug. 'There is no dirt on Cap, except the dirt he wears at the end of the day.'

'So, um, he's…' Trying not to make it too obvious, but she had to learn more about the guy who'd offered her a job. 'Nice?'

Bree tilted her head at Mia, sharing a wry grin. 'Cap is a rare unicorn.'

'A what?'

'He's very much a masculine male who is in touch with his sensitive side, but it's not a weakness in him, it's a strength.'

'Cap helped me.'

'And Cap will continue to help you, because that's what Cap does.'

'For everyone?'

'No.'

'Excuse me?' Mia's eyelids fluttered as if to blink away some imaginary grit.

'Cap only rescues stray dogs. Working dogs are his specialty.'

'I noticed he has a lot of dogs.' Having been up close and personal with the pack in the cage.

'Cap's either found those dogs on the side of the road, saved them from some farmer's bullet, or people have sought him out to care for the dog—like Sarge, the ex-riot dog.' Bree leaned closer, resting her forearms on her knees. 'But you're Cap's first human stray. Which is rare because Cap doesn't do people. He'd rather hang with his dogs, or his brothers, than deal with people. So, he may struggle to say what he means, especially when he likes someone.' Bree's green eyes locked onto Mia's for a long beat, as if sending a message.

'VISITORS!' Charlie's shout came from the back sheds, as a dog gave a deep bark from up at the farmhouse.

'I have to tell Charlie to stop doing that!' Bree peered over the garden and watched as a white car roof, topped with emergency lights, parked nearby.

'It's the police. What are they doing here?' Mia jumped out of her seat, pushing past the flaring pain from her bruises with her heart hammering in her chest.

'It's only Porter.'

'I can't. He'll see my face and ask too many questions.' Bree had told her to call the police, but Mia didn't want to cause trouble, or for her family to find out. Most of all she never wanted to see Gavin again. She hated confrontations, avoiding them at all costs. It was right up there with public speaking.

'You can hide inside. I won't say anything.' Bree held the front door open.

'Thank you.' Mia hobbled inside then positioned herself to peek out from behind the curtain at the open window. Were the police here for her?

'Are you lost, Porter?' Bree asked, as the wrought-iron gate creaked.

'Morning to you too, Bree. I'm looking for your grandfather?'

Mia recognised him. It was the policeman Cap had been talking to in the pub's car park yesterday.

'What did the old man do now?'

'Nothin' that concerns you, kid.' Charlie rushed up the stone path from the back of the house. 'What brings you here, Porter?'

'I brought your brother's bankbook back.'

'Pop, you didn't!' Bree crossed her arms over her chest and glared at Charlie.

'Leave off, kid, I had to know.' Charlie snatched the bankbook back. 'And I thought I told you not to tell Bree.' Charlie wagged a plump finger at the police officer as if scolding a child.

'Do you want to find out if your brother is still around or not?'

'Too right, I do. I'm an old man who wants to know what happened to my brother, because I know Harry is no murderer.'

Murderer! Mia raised her eyebrows, peeking over the window's ledge, their voices so clear.

'It's the family trade, right? Murder before breakfast,' said Bree in a snarky tone.

'Stop saying that, will ya.' Charlie wagged his finger at Bree.

'Er, hello, police officer here.' Porter tapped at his uniform. 'Please tell me you're talking about a murder of crows.'

'Relax, sugar bear, no need to flash the handcuffs as part of your foreplay.'

The policeman blushed, dropping his head.

His reaction had Bree grinning. But she soon sobered up as she spoke to her grandfather. 'Do you think your brother is still out there, Pop?'

Charlie sighed, his shoulders sinking. 'I don't know what to think. I have too many questions and I'm hoping Policeman Porter—'

Porter cleared his throat. 'It's Senior Constable—'

'Whatever. He can help me find some answers.' Charlie then lifted his chin to the officer. 'Anyhoodle, what did you find out?'

'Nothing yet. I've put in a load of queries and I'm waiting for their replies.'

'So, you drove all the way out here for nothing, besides getting me into trouble with the granddaughter?' Charlie screwed his nose up. 'We have a landline, you know.'

'I came out here to give Cap this dog. Is Cap around?' Porter went back to his police vehicle, opened the back door, and out jumped a glossy chocolate-brown kelpie attached to a lead. She was such a dainty thing.

'She's gorgeous.' Charlie went to pat the dog, but it flinched and cowered behind Porter. 'She's a bit bullwhipped, isn't she?'

'The vet says Willow's not too sure around men. I suspect her old owner hurt her.'

Inside the house, Mia gasped.

The dog tilted her head in Mia's direction as if she'd heard her.

Bree held out her hand to the policeman. 'I'll take—'

'Willow.' Porter handed the lead to Bree.

Bree crouched down to the dog. 'Hello, Willow. You can stay here until Cap comes in from the paddocks. They're fixing the drafting yards out the back.'

Porter dragged out a box from his vehicle's front seat. 'Here's Willow's gear.'

'That's a lot of gear for a stray dog.' Charlie started poking through the box.

'I wanted to keep her.' Porter leaned down and patted the dog.

'Your working hours won't let you keep her?'

'I was thinking about letting her stay in the car with me while on patrol. But that's a lot of hours sitting inside when Willow is an outside dog. I'd go jogging with her in the morning, and then after work I'd let her run alongside the car. I clocked her doing fifty clicks once, and she still had steam to run. But she's a working dog.'

'Of course she is. Look at her build.' Charlie pointed at the dog. 'She's made for speed and agility and the way them eyes move, she's a smart cookie, for sure.'

'Not wrong there. Once Willow recovered from her injuries, she worked out how to open the cupboard for the dog food. Then she destroyed my yard, my garage, and my couch from boredom. Willow needs to run, she needs to live on a station and not in a police house.'

The police officer looked so sad to see her go.

'You be good, Willow.' Porter tenderly patted the dog, nodded at Charlie and Bree, adjusted his hat and climbed into his police car and drove away.

Charlie went around the back as Bree, carrying the box, led the dog inside. She unclipped the lead and left the dog by the shut front door, while she rummaged around at the sink. 'Know anything about kelpies, Mia?'

'My dad had them on the family sheep farm.'

'Good. You can babysit this one until Cap comes back.'

'What do I do?'

'Just chill. Both of you.' Bree put a water bowl down by the door. 'I'll be in the smithy's shed if you need me.' Bree slipped on her leather apron, plucked a skullcap from the hat rack and began tucking her curls away. 'Oh, and her name is Willow. Use the lead when you take her outside for toilet breaks.'

And just like that Mia was left with a dog.

The dog tucked her tail between her legs and trembled as if cold. Just like Mia was only yesterday.

'It's okay, Willow.'

Willow's ears twitched at her name. Her moist nose wrinkled as she sniffed at the air.

'Did someone hurt you, too?' Mia sat on the floor with her back pressed against the cool stone wall. She felt safe there, keeping a watch on both the front and back doors.

Willow sniffed around the room for an escape, drank some water, then did another lap of the room. Finally, her soft dainty paws whispered quietly over the slate floor to sit beside Mia, her back to the corner wall, her eyes on both the front and back door, as well.

'Hello, Willow.'

The dog sniffed at her.

'Nice to meet you.' Mia gave her a gentle smile that grew when she could pat Willow's soft fur. Then when the dog curled up alongside her leg, the warmth was soothing. Hidden from the world that normally ignored her, she finally felt safe.

Eight

Cap knocked on the door of the caretaker's cottage. The faded red paint blended well with the small squares of colour that made up the stained-glass windows. 'Mia? You in?'

Even though it had been a few days since Porter had dropped off the dog, Cap had agreed with Bree that Mia might need a companion, having unexpectedly found one in Willow, that he'd put off collecting the dog.

He also hadn't seen Mia since he'd brought her home. Yet he'd been dying to check up on her, even though he knew she was in good hands with Bree watching over her.

The wooden door opened, and it was a smiling Mia. Wow! Her eyes, a gorgeous honey-hazel colour, widened as he locked gazes with her. It was enough to have his heart hammering in his chest.

But then his eyes roamed over the rest of her delicate features. The angry-red swelling was gone, but the bruising was a horrific purply-blue.

'Did you come for Willow?' Mia's voice was so bright and cheery.

He hesitated. 'Bree was telling me you and Willow were doing okay together.' Sadly, the canine and female shared something in common, both recovering from a brutal past. Bree called it trauma-bonding. 'You can keep her.'

'As much as I adore her,' she said, tickling her nails across the dog's snout. 'Willow is yours and she needs a good run. I don't live on a property.'

'Where is your home?'

'Um…'

Hold on, if she was running from her boyfriend then she probably didn't have a home anymore. To run like that, with nothing, and to hide in fear like she'd done these past few days, he couldn't imagine it.

What sort of man hurt a woman like that? It only fuelled the anger bristling inside his chest. When normally, Cap was the peacemaker who never got angry over anything. But this was different.

Cap cleared his throat, shoving his hands into the pockets of his jeans. 'I was wondering if you're up for a drive?'

'Where to?'

'I'd like to show you the paddock I get to play with.'

'Seriously?'

'We all have one. Ash has one he's trialling for his water system and drone work. I've taken the paddock next to it to build the first wildlife corridor, which will also act as a windbreak.' To finally start on his dream was intimidating, but to have someone like Mia with her skill set practically land on his doorstep was fate. And he believed in fate working in mysterious ways.

'And you want my opinion?'

He nodded. It was rare that he sought out the company of strangers like this, particularly female ones, but this might help Mia too. 'You can just sit in the car. I've got coffee in the thermos and some lunch. Nothing fancy, like Bree makes when on a muster, but it's edible.'

'So, a day trip?' She took a few timid steps outside while still keeping within the verandah's shade.

From around her legs the kelpie surprisingly trotted towards him and sat at his feet.

'Hello, Willow. Let's take a look at you.' Cap squatted low to inspect the beautiful animal. He was never shy around animals—just women. 'She looks like a purebred.'

'I know.' Mia squatted next to him. Her aroma was a lively scent of summer mixed with exotic orange blossom. It matched the shine in her eyes, which he took as a good sign considering what she'd been through.

'My dad would kill for a dog like Willow.' Mia's gorgeous grin grew as she patted the dog. 'Look at her stance, it's so square and solid. Her muscle structure is sound. Her ears are perfectly pointed, and her coat is super glossy. Besides a few scars here and there, she's perfect.' Mia frowned. 'Bree told me that Willow was…'

'Hurt. Yeah.' He patiently let the dog sniff at his hand until she allowed him to pat her. Her fur was like silk. 'Porter did a good job in looking after this animal, it had to hurt to give her up like this.'

'The policeman looked like he really hated leaving her behind.'

'Sometimes you have to do what's right for the animal and what's in their nature, and Porter knew Willow is a working dog. Reckons she'll make a good muster dog.' He adjusted his hat to look over the dog's stance. 'How do you know about dogs and their stances?'

'My mother used to do the local dog shows for fun. Nothing too fancy. But she won a few trophies, some dog food and all of these canine accessories. But she was happy.' Mia sighed, dropping her head to let her hair fall over her eyes to hide her bruises.

'Well, come on then.' He stood, dusting his hands, as both dog and Mia flinched from him.

That hurt. There's no way he'd hurt them.

But he understood their trust had been broken, and that would take time to heal. With Willow, he knew how to help her. With Mia, he had no idea, but he was hoping this day trip would be a step in the right direction.

'Let's go. Willow can ride in the front until she meets the other dogs at our first stop.' He opened the passenger door of the Tojo. '*Willow. Up.*' He tapped the bench seat, and the dog jumped with ease. 'Hmm, you've had training.' So why was she dumped?

'I'd love to see what she can do.'

'Yeah, I'm keen to find out, too.' Especially all about Mia. 'Ready for a drive?'

'Count me in.' Her little button nose lifted, and her grin grew as she climbed into the passenger seat. Not only did it have him grinning as he closed her door, but his stomach was rolling with warmth, too. Fate was smiling today.

After a short trek down the rambling dirt track, Cap parked his trusty Tojo under the shade of some towering gum trees. On a small rise, the front window framed their view where the sun bathed the land in a soft buttery sunlight. Rolling open plains, red soils, and large clusters of strong gums were scattered across the landscape to share their long shade over assorted grazing fields, all beneath a dazzling clear blue sky.

Finally, he owned some country. A land he could work on the way he wanted to. Besides his dogs, this was what made him jump out of bed in the mornings, what drove him to all hours of the night researching for a dream that was so close he could taste it.

Now, licking his lips, he was finally going to talk about it. 'This is my paddock.' Turning off the engine, he patted Willow as she sat between them.

'How can you tell? There are no fences.'

'Not yet. Which is where you come in.' He climbed out of the driver's seat. Willow stayed with Mia, following her out the passenger side.

'Have a look, you mob.' Cap opened the cage door on the back of the ute and the cattle dogs poured out like beer from a pub's beer tap, to happily sniff around the area, giving the new dog, Willow some space.

The introduction to the pack would begin soon enough. Yet, Willow obediently remained seated beside Mia's steel capped boots, as if the dog had already bonded with her owner of choice.

'Well, here's the station's map.' He rolled it out across the Tojo's bonnet, using his coffee thermos and a travel mug to hold it in place. 'We have Starvation Dam there.'

'Seriously?'

'I didn't make the names up in this place, but if you ask Charlie, he'll tell you that each place has a story.'

'Is this cattle station that old to have some history to it?'

'It was established in 1910. Even though it's not a great name, Starvation Dam is a good dam. And we have over seventy bores on the property, somewhere. Haven't made our way around to them all yet, but I'm sure we will as the herd grows.' He pointed to the coloured marks on the map.

'So, plenty of water then.'

'Yep.' But it still niggled him that the neighbouring mine had tried to take their water.

'And you're looking at putting in some native corridors?'

'Just this paddock, to start with.'

'I should warn you, that even if this paddock is a much smaller scale than the work I did for the mines, it's still expensive. You're looking at seedlings. Irrigation. It all adds up.'

He could almost hear what she was thinking, *The Riggs brothers were running a family station, not a mining site that had a big budget with their billion-dollar profit margins.*

Cap might not have mining experience, or degrees in his pocket, but he had a solid working knowledge, and he knew what he wanted. To have someone with Mia's technical skills was pure icing on his dream cake. Thank you, fate.

'There's a stack of irrigation pipes behind the shed. And I'm thinking of using one of the kennel structures to create a nursery.' It was Bree who'd given him the idea, back when he first looked at the kennels.

He adjusted his hat to peer out over the land. 'I plan to use this paddock to show my brothers how big an impact my ideas can have on this place. If we can run a successful revegetation trial, they'll let me do it with the rest of the property.' It was enough to have the adrenaline racing through his veins, as he licked his lips, again tasting the reality of his dream coming true. 'If I can convince my brothers and get them on board, I can show other local cattle producers what we've done, to create an impact for positive change within this region.'

'It sounds like a lot of hard work.'

Didn't he know it. 'I want this place to flourish.' His words echoed around him, but he spoke from the heart. This was his passion. 'I've done the same kind of work on other properties for crop farms, sheep and cattle stations, and I've been a part of their many trials and errors, so I know what works. As this is our family's land now, it deserves to be treated right for our family to enjoy for generations to come.'

'I get it. But it's still a big ask. You're talking about how many acres?' She tapped on the map.

'The station is 5,334 square kilometres or 2,060 square miles. That's 1,320,000 acres.' He grinned at the numbers that made him rock like Dex on his boot heels. Sure, they might seem small numbers compared to some of the other stations he'd worked on, but it was prime cattle country. 'Don't let the numbers scare you, there are plenty of pockets on this property that are pristine.' He tapped on the map. 'Wombat Flats is one of them. It's paradise.'

'So, it's not all bad, then?'

He cracked a smile that barely contained his inner pride over his family's land. 'We've got lots of amazing grazing land that has been resting for a while now, because we've had no cattle. I think it's been over a year since the herds were sold, but even then, Charlie looked after the grazing lands.' Cap could see this station's future. Like his brothers, they all saw the potential of this land to produce a high class of cattle, it's what attracted them to Elsie Creek Station in the first place. And, as Ryder said, with all the cattle sold off the sale price dropped substantially.

Mia turned back to the map. 'So, where were you thinking of creating this wildlife corridor?'

'I was thinking either here or here.' Cap indicated the likely spots on the map. 'As well as the obvious benefits, it would also act as a windbreak to help improve our pastures, and potential dingo deterrents by putting something native between them and our livestock, to recreate that balance of nature.'

It was cute how she sucked in her cheeks while thinking. Yet he recognised that look of someone who was reading the land, just like he did. Only a thousand times prettier.

Focus, mate.

He shuffled his boots in the dirt, scratching the back of his head. 'I should mention that in just over a month there's a campdraft happening in town. And I'm hoping to sell a few native seedlings to buy dog food.'

Mia laughed. It was the sweetest sound. 'So, you want me to be your nursery hand?'

'And be my consultant for what type of plants go where. There's plenty of natural vegetation around, so I'm sure we can scrounge up plenty of native seeds. Hopefully we'll have excess to sell at the show. You could sweet-talk Bree into donating some of her soil—'

'It's gorgeous, isn't it?'

Cap chuckled. Her enthusiasm was stunning, especially the way the world reflected in her warm eyes.

'I know, I'm weird.' Again, she dropped her head, only this time there was a pretty red flush to her cheeks.

'I like that someone else gets excited over soil like I do.'

'Really?' She peered up at him with such hope it did something odd to his heart.

'My older brothers also think I'm weird, but I've converted Ash to my side. But I'm going to speak with Harper about doing up a something to promote the seedlings at the campdraft.'

'I haven't met Harper yet.'

'Bree said you needed space.' And time to heal.

'Bree has been amazing. So has Charlie, and you,' she mumbled shyly, while twisting her fingers.

'Me? I didn't do anything. I just want to use you for your brains, lady.'

Lifting that dainty chin of hers, Mia's smile just got bigger. Holy fates, it was pretty. He had to see more. 'Hey, what do you know about dog trials?'

'Not much. Only what my mum did for the show dogs. Why?'

'Because I want to show off my muster dogs.'

'Which ones? You have so many.' She pointed to the pack spread out under the trees.

'Fern. Atlas.' He whistled and two beautiful and proud-looking cattle dogs rushed towards him. It was time for the introductions to begin.

'The blue heeler is Fern. The red heeler is Atlas. He's the alpha dog of this pack, and my best muster dog. Fern is a close second. I want to use the upcoming campdraft to show them in the muster dog trials.' He patted his best mates of the pack.

'To win more dog food?'

'That's the plan. Willow, say hello to Atlas.' He let Atlas sniff around Willow. Fern, doing the same. 'You should tell Willow to play. You're her owner.'

'I am not. Will not, whatever.' Mia awkwardly crossed her arms at her wrists, barely containing her giggle. 'So, you want my opinion on planting?'

'Yes.' He gave the dogs a nod at how accepting they were towards Willow. After all, they'd all been in Willow's position before, either rehomed or saved, easily welcoming the newest member to the team. 'And I promise to not pay you in dog food.'

Again, he scored another sweet giggle. What would he do for a laugh?

'Bree feeds me enough.'

'Lucky you. Every night, we're arguing over who's cooking dinner at the farmhouse. We've only scored an invite to the caretaker's pizza night once. We're waiting to be invited again.'

'But don't you and your brothers own the station?'

'We do. When we bought this place, it came with a caretaker's caveat to protect Charlie. We can't evict him or charge him rent on his area, but we'd never kick him out.

We're meant to leave him be, because he's retired, but Charlie knows this place so well, it's his home, and he wants to work.'

'And Bree? She said she didn't work for you.'

'Bree is here for Charlie. She's said when Charlie goes, she's going to pack up her yellow Kombi van and find the nearest international airport to fly out and sit on some beach in Tahiti that doesn't have crocodiles, to drink gin and watch some ice hockey game.'

'But their yard is like a home.'

'To Charlie it is. I'm not sure how long Bree has lived here. She never stands still long enough for us to have a conversation that lasts more than ten minutes. We'd hire Bree to be a stockwoman straight up. She's highly skilled.'

'And she's a blacksmith.'

He nodded. 'Bree's a master brand maker. It's a family trade she learned from Charlie. But you, too,' he said, gently poking her arm, 'have a unique set of skills this station desperately needs to help steer it towards a new future. If you want in?' It was a big ask, and his biggest pitch ever to convince someone to take a job, but he was hoping it would help her heal. He knew that dogs liked to be useful, to be included, and working dogs were at their happiest when mustering. Would his job proposal be something that could help Mia?

'I'll do it.'

He blinked, unsure if he'd heard right. 'You will? I don't want you to do anything you don't—'

'I'd love to do this job. Seriously, this is major.'

'You're right, it is a lot of work.'

'I'm not scared of getting dirty, but you bet your sweet sassy malassy I'll have a crack.' She gave an affirmative nod, rolling up her shirt sleeves as if ready to dig in today. 'But I can't sleep on Bree's couch forever.'

'I can help with that.'

'How?'

'There's a spare room in the demountable, near me.' But

he hadn't opened it in a while.

'Sounds like the rooms you'd find at a mine site. How bad is it? Apparently, your brother Dex lives in a tent inside his shack? Is that true?'

'Dex has his camp bed tucked inside his tent inside his lounge room. Don't ask me why.' Cap chuckled. 'But if you don't mind barking dogs, I can offer you a room near the kennels and that nursery.' Yeah, he was laying it on thick, hoping to help her, which would help him and this station. It was a win-win all round.

'I'd hate to put you out.'

'No sweat, I've got the room. We could get Bree to check it out, she can then send Harper shopping for bedding and stuff. Harper likes to shop, and Bree's great at knowing what people need and where to find stuff in the sheds. Sadly, you'll be having meals up at the farmhouse and you'll get added to our cooking rotation.'

'I'm happy to chip in any way I can.' She nodded eagerly; it was promising.

'Do you want to get any gear from your place?'

Mia winced. Her joyous mood gone.

'I'm sorry I said that.' *Idiot!*

'It's okay. There's nothing I want there.' She turned away, twisting her fingers. Mia's change in mood was enough to have Willow nudging her leg.

'Are you sure?'

She tenderly stroked the dog's ears. 'I've got my ID with me. The rest were just mining clothes.'

'Were you a FIFO?'

'Short-term contractor. Gavin was the FIFO, a diesel mechanic for mining machinery.' She cleared her throat, crossing her arms tight over her chest. 'He was renting a farmhouse with the prospect of looking to buy.'

'And do what?'

'Exactly what you're doing here.'

Mia glanced over the wide field, her eyes became dreamy and soft, with a slight smile curving her luscious lips. She was a true natural beauty, with no make-up to hide her inner shine.

'It was actually my dream. Mine.'

It was as if those words flashed in his brain, like some savage animal wanting to imprint on her until she was his. He wiped his mouth, as if that would get rid of the flavour of desire so deep it travelled like an earth tremor all over him. He turned for the car. 'Well, how about you give me some ideas on what to do with this paddock.' He drank deeply from his mug, quenching his inner thirst.

Women never looked at him, not when he spent more time with animals than humans. Cap avoided people if he could, except for his brothers. Besides, someone like Mia wouldn't be interested in getting involved with anyone, not after what Gavin had done to her.

Pity, because she might just be the perfect woman for him. Or did fate have something else in store…

Nine

'I've always called this *the dogbox*.'

'Aw, come on, Bree. It's not that bad, is it?' Cap pointed at the long rectangle box of steel and ironclad sheeting that contained two rooms and one bathroom.

Hold on a second…

He tilted his head at the demountable. Bree was right, it was a dogbox. Especially when his muster dogs were sprawled underneath it, enjoying the shade from the mid-morning sun.

'It's fitting for the kennel master who hangs out with dogs all day, but you can't expect Mia to stay here.' Bree opened the door, waving her hand at the musty fumes billowing out of the spare room.

'It'll be fine.' Mia stood close enough for Cap to enjoy her sprightly summer aroma of orange blossoms. 'I've been in worse on mine sites. Really, I have.'

Cap gave Mia a grateful smile. After spending most of yesterday with her going over his plans for his paddock, he was hoping to give her a space to stay and be a part of something big — with him.

But who was he kidding. Bree was right, this wasn't good enough for Mia. 'This was a bad idea.'

'No, it's a brilliant idea.' Bree grinned at him.

'But you just said—'

'I know what I said, tiger. I don't have short-term memory loss. It may be a dogbox, but it has enormous potential.' Bree jumped down the rickety wooden steps that sat beneath each door. 'Do you have any ideas for this place?'

Cap shrugged.

'Don't you have some secret wish list on how your dream home should look?'

He may have dreams about the land, but for dwellings... Meh.

'I just want somewhere safe for the dogs and a view for my morning cuppa.' He pointed to the far end of the demountable. It was his favourite spot where he kept his camp chair near his billy on a tiny gas plate. It looked primitive. What was he thinking, inviting Mia here? She deserved better than this.

'Oh, wow.' Mia's jaw dropped as her eyes widened at the open landscape where the sun's rays peeked through the sparse clouds hovering above the wide valley that held nothing but open country. 'I'd live out here. I mean, right here, on this spot.'

Cap would too.

'Can't we spin the demountable around to face this view or something?' Mia's smile was so sparkly and sweet.

'Precious,' said Bree, tapping Mia's shoulder, 'we have buildings lying a certain way, so they don't take the full brunt of the outback sun all day long, to burn out the engines of our already overworked air conditioners. But, for that gorgeous view, it's worth doing something.'

He was stoked that Bree and Mia liked the view as much as he did. 'Such as?'

Bree hesitated.

'Come on, Bree, it's why I asked you over here this morning? I'm hoping for some of your magicking.' Dex called her a witch to tease the redhead.

Today, Cap was grateful Bree had downed tools to come over with Mia to check this place out. Because Bree, like her grandfather, was a master crafter when it came to metals. She could do anything with this place, plus give it the female's POV for Mia's sake.

Cap understood that mastery was picking a skill that you

worked tremendously hard at until you became one of the best. He wasn't a master, preferring to pick up several skills, working hard at each of those skills until he became fairly competent in all of them, to then combine them to create an entirely new style or form to suit his needs. It was handy when he adapted his skills to suit the individual animals he taught, and the lands he lived on.

Mia was also a master in her field, and that was an advantage for what he wanted. It was also a privilege to have these two strong women here; it was like breathing a rare air indeed. Especially when he never had much to do with women.

'Bree-*Bree*-BREEE!' A small boy's voice echoed in the air.

Cap grinned, turning to watch his nephew, Mason, run towards them on his little legs. The toddler was getting bigger every day.

'Hello, little big man.' Bree swooped Mason up in her arms, her smile wide.

It still pained him to know about the son Bree had lost. How Bree could smile like she did showed spirit. Or she hid the pain of her past well.

'Look who else is here.' Bree pointed to Cap. 'Go on, tell him your new word.'

The toddler grinned, looking just like his father. 'U-u. Unnn—cal. Uncle.'

'Uncle who?' Bree put the boy on the ground.

'Unnncle CAP.'

Didn't his heart just freaking melt! 'That's right, Mason.' He couldn't help but scoop up the boy and hug his nephew. 'Want to help us set up house for Mia?' Wait. Did he just say that out loud?

Ten

Mia smiled so wide it bloomed from her heart as she watched Cap play with the small boy, Mason. He was a truly kind man, who saved dogs, and had been so helpful to Mia, just like Bree and Charlie. Cap was not only sensitive to others and animals, he also had the body to create one stunning masculine package. He was a rare unicorn indeed.

But then a stabbing twinge of pain became that cruel dose of reality forcing her to turn away from Cap doting over his nephew. She didn't deserve those happy family moments, it's why she chose losers for partners, and in the last instance, a monster.

Cap was doing his best to help her, giving her a place to stay, and a job she'd always dreamed about. Technically he was her boss. And she'd hate for him look at her with pity like she was some broken animal.

The reality being she really was broken in a way that was hidden to the world.

'Hi, I'm Harper.' A slender woman with ivory skin and black hair approached, wearing a wide-brimmed hat, new jeans, and a crisp collared shirt. She looked fancy. 'You must be Mia.' Surprisingly, she shook hands like a man.

'You did the shopping for me. Thank you.' After Mia arrived at this place with nothing but the clothes she was wearing, Bree rang Harper to collect the necessities for Mia on her way home from work.

'I hope it all fits.'

'Absolutely, I must pay you back.'

'All good. You can pay in babysitting fees. If you stay… *here*?' Harper screwed her nose up at the demountable. 'Really? You'd give up Bree's comfy couch for this?'

'I've lived in worse. Mining companies make a point of putting the revegetation workers in the worst accommodations.'

'You should have seen the farmhouse when I first arrived. Bree called it a frat house.' Harper held out a dark brown, wide-brimmed hat. 'This is for you. Cap said you'd need one. Bree suggested the size and style, she's good like that. If you don't like it, I have others you can try, or I can swap it for a different size when I go in to work later. It seems I have a new obsession with hats these days. I've accumulated so many that Ash is making me a new hat rack for the hallway.'

'Because of your skin.' Mia slid on the wide-brimmed hat. 'This is brilliant.' It was a great fit. Same with the overalls Bree had found for Mia to sloth around in.

'You should hit up Bree for her sunscreen. It's the best. She makes it herself, and all sorts of home remedies. I think that's why Dex calls her a witch.'

'I didn't know that.' Mia watched Bree go through the demountable while Cap played with Mason. 'It's like being back home, hanging out with Bree and Charlie.'

'How so?'

'Bree had me helping her make chilli sauce, and tomato purees for pizzas. My mother did that too with jams and preserves.' Washing jars, sterilising them, then doing the bottling, to leave the kitchen bench covered with bottles, and the fragrance of fruit lingering in the house. Especially when Charlie brought in loaves of bread he'd baked that morning before sunrise, it was the best.

'I've been having cooking lessons with Bree. Can't cook, but I can make a salad. Cap said if you move in here, you'll go on the cooking roster for the farmhouse.'

'I want to be useful, because you guys have done so much for me.'

'They do that,' said Harper, sharing a soft smile at Cap. 'The Riggs brothers will drop everything to help when needed. You should've seen what they did for Mason. Now you.'

'I'm not putting them out, am I?'

'Are you kidding? Cap is like mega-excited to have you here. He can't wait for you to start. He really likes you.' Harper nudged her playfully.

'Cap is just being kind. Offering me a room so I stop taking up space on Bree's couch.' She wanted to get her independence back, to get her mind on her job and bury her past. Plus, this would make Cap her boss, and workplace romances rarely lasted.

'Oh, good, you're here, Harper.' Bree jumped out of the demountable, her boots landing squarely in the dirt. 'Have you two swapped recipes yet?'

'Getting there.' Harper giggled. 'I'm putting Mia on the cooking roster.'

'Brilliant. You won't need lessons from me then.'

'But…' Harper pouted as if to start fake crying.

'Oh, right. Sorry. Silly me.' Bree playfully rolled her eyes. '*Cooking lessons* is code for a girls' get-together to drink wine and gin while I try to teach you the ways to perve on men who play ice hockey. Not necessarily in that order. You're included, precious.'

'I've never done that,' replied Mia.

'What? Perved on ice hockey players?'

'I meant the girls thing. Not since school. On mine sites its mostly men. We'd get a few women on differing shifts, but not enough to plan things.'

'I can relate.' Harper shared a timid shrug. 'I worked in politics, always drinking cold coffee, too busy to eat a meal and savour it, until I came here. Bree's like my first female friend.'

'Really?' Mia didn't believe it.

'So, I'd better warn you, I suck at small talk and generally scare people away when I start talking about politics.'

'Pfft. You're doing fine. Both of you are.' Bree put her arms around the two younger women. 'Right, so now we have our little coven happening, I have a plan. Cap?'

He sauntered over, with Mason sitting on his shoulders. 'Please tell me you have some ideas?'

'Why? Don't you like this retro 50s horror movie theme you've got happening here?'

Cap angled his head at her, his Stockman's hat shading his sexy eyes. 'Mia, Harper, please help?'

Bree grinned, removing a tape measure, a notebook, and a pencil from the deep side pockets of her workman's trousers. 'My first suggestion is you ditch the rickety steps and build a wide walkway along this side of the demountable, with a roof to cover the doorways. I'd suggest you make that roof long enough so you can park your vehicles under it for the wet season. As for that spot, where you like to sit and enjoy the view, I'm suggesting you build an enormous outdoor deck.'

Pressing her back to the wall of the demountable Bree took long lunging steps and stopped about ten metres away. 'You can make it a long viewing deck—who doesn't love a long deck. It'd be a brilliant spot to put a Mexican heater in the corner for winter that you can use to boil your billy.'

Cap raised an eyebrow, intently listening, especially about the cuppa bit.

'And in the wet,' continued Bree, 'you can use shade sails to pull across, allowing you to watch the rain and still enjoy the sunrise and sunsets from this space. If it was me, I'd use this section to create an outdoor kitchen and put in a double sliding door in this wall.'

Bree walked and talked, leading them to the back. 'And, if you really want to dream big, tiger—which I'd totally approve of—you can turn your room into the lounge area, make Mia's room an office or extend your bathroom, then pick up a few shipping containers and whack them together like Lego bricks—'

'To build extra rooms.' Cap's eyes shone like delicious

dark diamonds.

'So you can see it?' Bree smiled at him with hands on her hips. 'The potential is there to make this into your family home, but one that would suit your ethical standards by using recyclable materials.'

Carrying the toddler on his shoulders, Cap took long steps, counting out the meterage. Then he turned and smiled. 'Bree, you're bloody brilliant. I can see it now.'

'You might want to ask Dex to do some grading first. He likes to play with the grader, so I can't see him saying no.' Bree pointed towards the kennels that stood further along, from where the house stood on the rise. 'This place cops the main run-off in the wet season. It's what Pop calls *Kennel River*. So, I suggest you ask Dex to channel the run-off away from the demountable and the dog kennels before you start building that—' She pointed to the empty metal structure with a torn shade cloth. 'What have you decided to call it?'

'Mia's native plant nursery.' Cap nodded at her and the rush of warm gooey goodness had her toes curling in her boots. Mia had to look away and face the dirt. Cap had given her permission to design it however she wanted, using whatever materials the property had available to her. And Bree said there was plenty of gear to use.

'Hey, we could build a pond for the run-off.' Mia blurted out, tapping into Cap's excitement.

'Is that a good idea? It'd be a breeding ground for mozzies.' Bree shrugged.

'I get what Mia is saying.' Cap stood beside Mia to face the dirt patch beyond the rundown kennels. 'We can re-use the run-off from the house and the kennels for the nursery.'

'Not wasting a precious drop.' Mia mirrored Cap's smile. For a hot second, her mind pictured the whole scenario, her plant nursery, sharing lazy sunsets on the deck beside Cap as they both watched over his dogs. She couldn't deny how much she liked the idea.

'Wow, you two speak your own language.' Harper covered her mouth to giggle.

'Told you so,' muttered Bree.

Mia felt the heat brush her cheeks, because she'd forgotten Bree and Harper were there. She had to stop this attraction to Cap, because she was nothing but a load of red flags for a guy like him—who deserved so much better. Besides, Cap wasn't interested in her, he was just being helpful, which was his nature.

No way would she take advantage of him. But she could help him with his land, which wouldn't be hard when it was her dream job. She also had to do something to forget her heated dreams of her and Cap—when she should be healing and forgetting all about men.

She needed to get back to work. And there was nothing better than a girl covered in dirt to scare away any man.

'With your permission, Cap, there's a stash of steel girders around the back shed we could use to make a start.' Bree extended her tape measure against the demountable.

'What about timber?'

'You'll have to order treated timber from town. But if we do this right, you could sweet-talk your brothers into a working bee on Saturday afternoon.'

'That's a lot of work.' Cap arched his eyebrows at Bree as she wrote down the measurements in her notebook.

Bree shifted to the next area, again extending her tape measure. 'I'm talking about building the deck and painting Mia's room. The rest you'll have to plan for, and Dex has the skills to be your builder.'

'We'll be drafting the cattle we brought back from Wombat Flats soon. My brothers and I are hoping you'll help us, Bree.' Cap shifted the toddler on his shoulders.

'Bree-Bree help?' Mason asked.

'Always, for my little big man.' Bree playfully tickled the little boy's knee, as he squirmed on Cap's shoulder. 'But I don't work for your uncles.' Bree stared at Cap for a beat before returning to her measuring.

'I already told Ash I'm in. But he said we won't need the horses this time. But I'm still in.' Harper raised her hand. 'I've never seen the drafting process.'

'Me neither. If you need my help, I'm in.' Mia was keen, too.

'I think that's why Bree had me get you that hat.' Harper playfully tapped the brim of Mia's new hat.

'If it's okay with you, Mia, I'd like to see what Willow is capable of.' Cap nodded at the kelpie sitting beside Mia.

'Me too.' Out of habit she tickled the fur on the bridge of Willow's nose. 'I can't ride a horse, but I can ride a motorbike.'

'We'll have to give you horse riding lessons in the future, as we're trying to use horses more if we can.'

'I have riding lessons,' said Harper, again playfully nudging Mia like a long-lost friend. 'Ash bought me a stock horse.'

'Oh, I'm definitely in.' She was in farmer's heaven.

'I know Charlie's keen to help,' he said, facing the redhead busily taking measurements and scribbling notes down in her notebook. 'We could really use your help, Bree.'

'I'm not a stockwoman.' Bree's tape measure wound back with a snap.

'Come on, Bree. You're a thousand times better than all of us on a muster.'

'Behave, buttercup. As much as you all may want me to drag out my Wonder Woman costume from the back of the cupboard, I'll be busy working on your new deck. Wait—' Bree narrowed her eyes at Cap. 'Are you using me to get to the brand?'

'The one your grandfather is holding hostage.'

'Are you talking about a cattle brand?' Mia asked.

Cap nodded. 'Somehow, Charlie has the Elsie Creek Station's cattle brand registered in his name.'

'That he does.' Bree laughed, closing her notepad and sliding it into her pocket. 'So, you've finished fencing the drafting yards, then?'

'They'll be finished today, and the paddock's fence, too.'

'It's Ash's paddock, he can't wait,' said Harper. 'He's got

his new tags he wants to test out.'

'I can't wait to see them myself.' Cap then faced Bree. 'But we need to re-muster the herd we brought in from Wombat Flats. We're hoping to have enough fats to make a sale.'

'Got a stock agent?' Bree asked.

'Not yet. Do you know of one?'

Bree shrugged. 'I might.'

'Do you have any idea what they're talking about?' Mia asked Harper. 'I only know sheep.' Mia tugged at the bib straps of her overalls. 'We'd bring in the sheep for shearing and do health checks.'

'No, it's all over my head.' Harper cleared her throat and waved at Bree and Cap. 'Hello, can you please explain to us in the private theatre boxes what you just said?'

'Well, aren't you two in for a treat, because a day in the drafting yards is something you'll never forget. Just be ready to jump some fences, protect your shins and enjoy the smell of—'

'Bree, don't scare them off.' Cap warned her.

'Fine. It'll be the stuff of stories, ladies.' Bree removed her hat, her locks spilling everywhere, to deeply bow to them like they were royalty.

'Please, Bree,' implored Cap. 'We need your help. It's our first draft at Elsie Creek Station, and Charlie told me you'd be an asset to the team.'

Bree huffed, crossing her arms over her generous chest. 'Fine. I'll help muster the mob to the drafting yards, and that's it. Then I'll start on the support frames for your deck.' She looked at the patch of parched dirt, bleached from the sun, and the old demountable with its walls covered in red dirt. But Bree looked at it with excitement.

'On your own?' Mia blurted out.

'Listen, precious, it's not my first building makeover, when I work with steel all day.' Bree then playfully poked Cap's arm. 'While Mia and Harper paint Mia's new room, your job is to get your brothers to screw the decking boards in place. But we need Dex to play grader driver first, or I'll be

giving you flippers and matching pool floaties for Christmas.'
She then slapped her hat on her head and gathered her hair
into a thick loose braid. 'In the meantime, I'll order the wood
from the hardware store. You can pick that up when you
collect Mia's paint, and those new guardian dogs from the
vets.'

'They're gorgeous, big white fluffy bears.' Harper just
swooned. 'I want one.'

'They're not pets,' Cap said. 'Dex is still complaining
about you turning the ex-police dogs into house pets.'

'I don't care what Dex says.' Harper raised her chin. 'I
love spoiling Ruby and Scout, and Sarge from a cordial
distance because he's a boss dog.'

'Alpha,' corrected Cap.

'Yeah, that. And Dex had better not complain to Mia
about Willow, either.' Harper pointed to the kelpie leaning
against Willow's legs, while all the other dogs lay under the
shade of the demountable.

'Willow's not my dog.'

'Are you sure about that?' Bree again playfully tickled the
little boy sitting on Cap's shoulders and said, 'And you,
Mason, can tell your father and his brothers that they're
needed for a working bee on Saturday afternoon. Your Uncle
Cap can put on a barbecue.'

'Unnncle Cap.' Mason's little cowboy boots swung over
Cap's broad shoulders, as he tapped down on Cap's hat like a
drum.

'Easy, Mason, that's my head.' Cap scooped the boy off
his shoulders and held him to his chest as if he'd been doing
it all his life.

The scene only tore at Mia's heartstrings.

'I don't have a barbecue, just that little gas burner for my
kettle.' Cap pointed at his comfy camping chair.

'You can pick one up from the hardware store when you
collect the wood. Keep the receipts to give to the bank.' Bree
waved as she walked off.

'So, it looks like you're moving in,' Harper said to Mia.

She looked at Cap. 'Really?'

'Do you think Mia should move in, Mason?' Cap asked the little boy, who nodded. 'Well, the manager agrees. Do you?'

Hell, yeah, she wanted in. Then she paused with eyes widening. 'Does that mean I have to meet your brothers?'

Eleven

'Everyone, this is Mia Dixon.' Cap swallowed hard as he stood on the edge of the farmhouse verandah in the late afternoon, with Mia beside him. He'd never been so nervous for his brothers to meet a girl before. Which was dumb when they weren't even dating.

Some grown-up man he was, for fate's sake. Cap wasn't like his younger brother, Ash, who used to go through women like flipping the pages of a magazine, easily setting them aside for the latest release that walked on by. Until he met Harper, that is. Nor was Cap anything like Dex, who was so mean to women, he'd toss them aside like some sweat rags he'd used after a fight—and yet the women flocked to him over it. Why? He had no idea.

It was just another reminder of how clueless he was when it came to women.

Still, he was here for a reason, all to do with a certain female. 'Mia, that's Ryder at the head of the table.'

Ryder nodded. His cold dark eyes narrowed at Mia while remaining expressionless as always. Ryder hadn't trusted Harper when she'd first arrived at the station, and he'd been proven right. Sort of.

'That's Dex.' Cap glowered at Dex in warning as he spoke through clenched teeth. 'No betting, Dex. I mean that.' The protectiveness he had over Mia was strong.

'I lost the last bet. Bree fleeced me for a couple hundred already.' Dex tilted his head, wearing that evil smirk. It was either a smirk or a scowl, rarely anything else in between when it came to Dex. 'Mia.' Dex gave a curt nod.

'Hi.' Mia jammed her hands into the pockets of her baggy overalls, that she looked comfy in. The bruising was fading to a yellow. Her hair was a wavy mess, but it beautifully framed her delicate features. With the touch of dirt on her cheek blending with her smattering of freckles, she looked like a very pretty farmer, he hadn't been able to stop watching while working with her these past two days.

'Hey, I'm Ash.' Still wearing the baby carrier, he wore on the days he had Mason with him on horseback, Ash carried five beers from around the corner and offered one to Mia. Like the rest of his brothers, Ash's deep tan blended with the layer of dirt they all wore from working in the yards all day.

'Here, give me this.' Cap took Mia's beer bottle and popped the cap using the edge of the table, then held it out to Mia.

'Thanks.'

'While you're there, brother.' Dex nodded at his unopened beer resting on the table.

Cap rolled his eyes and opened Dex's, Ash's and his own beer, tossing the caps into the large coffee tin on the table.

Mia pointed her beer at Ash. 'Are you Harper's partner?'

'That I am.' Ash gave a goofy lovesick grin, as he unclipped the baby carrier, before flipping his chair around to sit on it like a saddle at their outdoor table.

'I met your son, Mason, earlier. He's adorable.'

'He doesn't look so adorable now, covered in dirt. But he's happy, messing up the house.' Ash sat taller to peer inside the open windows.

'Hey, Mason called me Uncle Cap this morning.' Cap pulled out a chair, even dusting it for Mia to sit at the table beside him.

'Little mongrel calls me Dick,' complained Dex, tilting back to balance on the back legs of his chair.

Cap chuckled with Ash, because Dex could be a prize dick.

'Is that your latest rescue?' Ryder pointed at the kelpie

sitting at Mia's feet. Willow kept close to Mia, while the rest of Cap's dogs lazed on the lawn. He'd trained the muster dogs to avoid the farmhouse verandah, which belonged to Sarge, the big shepherd, who kept guard at the far corner of the house facing the driveway. While inside the house were the other two ex-police dogs Ruby and Scout, lapping up life as house pets.

'She's a stunning pure bred.' Cap patted Willow, who'd surprisingly taken no time to trust him, like most dogs.

'Are you going to use her for mustering?'

'She'll need to build up some stamina for that first. But I'm keen to try her out in the drafting yards. Mia has agreed to help. She used to help her dad with his sheep.' Cap was grateful at how eagerly Mia got involved with the work, considering what she'd been through.

'Kelpies are a good breed.' Ryder gave a brief nod as he twisted off the beer cap from his bottle and tossed it into the tin on the table, where the bottle cap clinked among the others.

'Has anyone asked Charlie or Bree about the branding iron?' asked Ash. 'We could also use their help.'

'Charlie's in, said so yesterday,' replied Ryder, before taking a deep pull of his beer.

'What about Bree?'

'I asked her this morning,' said Cap.

The lines in the middle of Ryder's brow deepened, as did his voice. 'When?'

'While we were looking over the demountable.'

'*We*, huh?' Dex smirked behind his beer, while rocking on his chair's back legs.

Cap frowned at his brother. 'Harper was there too, with Bree.'

'What the flip?' Dex grimaced as if tasting something horrible in the air. 'Did you have some all-female intervention this morning?'

'I wanted their opinion on the place.' Cap was so glad he had asked for Bree's opinion. He could picture the new deck, the new rooms, the roof, the outdoor kitchen, the Mexican heater, everything. It was as if Bree knew exactly what he needed.

'It's brilliant what Bree suggested.' Mia wriggled on her seat beside him, the grin growing with the excitement he could feel himself.

He'd never bothered with a house before, but he was keen to start by getting Mia settled first.

'You've seen the place?' Dex pointed his beer towards the kennels. 'I've heard Bree call it the dogbox.'

'At least I'm not squatting in a tent.' Cap glared at his snarky brother.

'So. I've been busy.'

'Me too. And well, bro, I'm hoping you'll do some grading for me. Bree warned me that the area has a major run-off problem in the wet.'

'Bree said Charlie called it Kennel River.' Mia's hands were so small around the beer stubby she timidly sipped from.

'How bad?' Ryder's deep voice was loaded with concern, shutting up Dex's smart-ass responses, which was normal for those two. Ryder was the only one to take Dex head-on and beat him, because of some sneaky military moves.

'The water looks like it runs right under my place and through the kennels. Dex, I'll pay you a carton to create a channel towards a new reticulation pond.'

Dex shrugged. 'I don't mind playing with the grader.'

He grinned, glad his brother was on board.

'I heard those dingoes again last night.' Dex lowered his forehead, as a sign of trouble, which was dangerous coming from Dex, who wasn't scared to fight or load his rifle to deter wild dogs. 'How long before we get those guardian dogs?'

'They're at the vets, getting checked over. Hey, do we own the tractor? Or does Bree?'

'What tractor?' asked Ash.

'Big sucker. Bree used it as a forklift to drop off some steel girders and dig holes for the framework of my new deck.'

'Hold up.' The front legs of Dex's chair landed with a thud, as he leaned closer to point his beer at Cap. 'Are you saying that you've talked Bree into building a deck? For you?'

'I think she's doing it more for Mia. Bree is suggesting we have a working bee on Saturday to do the floorboards for the deck.'

'We have the drafting to do first. And without Bree—'

'Who's agreed to help with the mustering, and she can get us a stock agent, too. And no, Bree didn't laugh in my face.'

'Bree laughs in my face all the time,' mumbled Dex behind his beer. 'I'd really like that woman if she didn't scare me so much.'

'I thought Bree didn't want to get involved in our business,' said Ash.

Cap shrugged. 'I practically begged her to help with the mustering. But I don't know how we'll get her to do the drafting; I don't think she likes that job.'

'We'll talk to Charlie. He's the one who suggested we enlist Bree's help in the first place,' said Ryder.

'Or you can ask her, Ryder. Oh, wait, she'll tell you to rack off, too.' Dex chuckled behind his beer.

'Me three.' Ash raised his beer the same way Harper held her hand in the air when asking a question.

'Bree's done so much for me,' said Mia. 'I have no way to repay her. I mean, today, Bree found me a single bed. The mattress was brand new, still in its plastic, and everything. Bree said she never had time to use it. It came with these cute little boy's sheets.'

The brothers looked at her sullenly.

'What did I say?' Mia gave a meek shrug.

'That would've been for Liam,' Cap explained quietly, as Ryder and Dex's frowns deepened.

'Who?'

'Bree's son.'

'Excuse me.' Ash dragged himself off his chair. The screen door to the farmhouse creaked open, as he slid off his boots by the front door mat. 'Mason? Where you at, son?' The door clanged shut behind him.

'Bree has a son?' Mia whispered to Cap.

'She lost him to leukaemia.' It was so freaking sad.

'Oh no…' Mia clutched her throat. 'I didn't know. I feel terrible. I was laughing at the kids' sheets with sheep on them. Bree said nothing.'

'She doesn't. And she won't.' Ryder's sturdy Adam's apple bobbed up and down as he sculled back the rest of his beer. He wiped his mouth with the back of his hand, dumping the empty bottle on the table. 'I've got some paperwork to do. Make sure you keep your receipts on the materials for the renovations, Cap. Call me when dinner is ready. It's not my turn to cook.'

'I cooked last night. It's someone else's turn.' Dex's chair scraped across the deck as he stood. 'I'll go take a look at the grading you want done at the kennels.' Dex jumped off the verandah.

So much for his brothers being hospitable, and all that worry over them meeting Mia had been for nothing. Or were they going to give Mia the cold shoulder like they did when Harper had first arrived? They'd better not!

Twelve

'I really stuffed that up, didn't I?' Mia watched the Riggs brothers scatter from the table. They were all big men, all blessed with good looks, but the older brothers seemed harder. 'I've never cleared a room so fast.' So much for making a good impression.

'Not your fault. You weren't to know.' Cap sighed, scrubbing at his face.

'I'm sorry.'

'Why?' The denim of his jeans tightened around his impressive thighs as he leaned back in his chair.

'Your brothers must think I'm an idiot.' She gulped down her beer, the fizzy buzz affecting her brain already. 'Technically they—you—will be my boss.'

'Stop. Please.' His large hand was so tender on her shoulder. 'I prefer partner in the work we're doing. I train the pack to be part of a team, and I'm like that with my brothers, and what we do at this station is a team effort. The good news is, we have Dex looking at the grading, which is a great start.'

'You never mentioned the nursery to your brothers.' He'd only mentioned the kennels.

'I, um…' He gazed up at the corrugated roof with its exposed beams, as if to articulate his thoughts, giving her a clear profile of his masculine face.

He then dropped his head, his eyes dark and clear and so intense, they landed on hers as if to hold them for ransom. She couldn't look away. Not when his voice dropped an octave. 'I hadn't been able to work out the details until you came along.'

Dayummm.

This was a guy who'd already said he wanted her for her brains, her skills, and somehow he knew how to fuel her passion for her work, allowing her free rein to build a native plant nursery her way. But he was also unearthing another inner passion she'd thought she'd long buried.

When most people watched you, they rarely gave you their undivided attention. Normally she'd slide under their radar like an unseen garden gnome. But this was something entirely different.

She tugged at the collar of her shirt, clearing her tight throat. 'Do you think we can talk Bree into welding up those planting tables in the nursery?' Her voice was way too high.

'I can do it, once we've finished repairing the drafting yards.' He sat back in his chair, stretching his muscular legs out before him to cross them at the ankles, with his arms crossing over his powerful chest and his wide-brimmed stockman's hat shading his eyes. He was a gloriously handsome man beneath all that denim and dust.

Mia sat forward, plucking at the label of her beer bottle to keep her eyes off him. She shouldn't find anyone attractive, not after what she'd been through. It had to be the beer amplifying her thoughts.

Yet, Cap had inspired such trust in her so quickly. And the more time she spent with him, especially one on one, like they'd done these past few days, the more attached she got. If she was smart, she would be protecting herself before these feelings got any stronger.

Besides, Cap only looked at her like some wounded animal that was helpless and beyond repair. Which, for some parts of her, was true. 'But Bree—'

'Doesn't work for us. So, having Bree help us with the mustering is rare. I won't take advantage of her generosity.' He stood and stretched towards the roof.

From her seated position she watched as his shirt came

untucked from his jeans, exposing his belly, which rippled with muscle upon muscle. He had veiny forearms to hint at the muscles, but nothing like what she'd seen of those smooth ridges and deep shading of his abs. Just that one small peek had her mouth watering.

This was not happening!

Cap pulled down a large cylinder that was tucked into the exposed beams of the verandah's roof. He opened the end of the cylinder and produced a roll of large photographic images. 'I wanted to show you these.'

'How did you get satellite images?' She helped him unroll them across the table, using the tin filled with beer caps, empty beer bottles, and coffee cups to hold them in place.

'Harper got them to help our case against this new mining site trying to claim our water.'

'Really?'

Cap nodded with a scowl. It didn't last long as his focus returned to the large satellite images. 'These give us a picture of the station's history for the last fifteen years. You can see where the water gathers in the wet season, and where pockets have eroded away, including the stock patterns.' He pointed to areas of the map, and the ages showing the changes over one-and-a-half decades.

'This is brilliant stuff. You have lots of natural waterways, billabongs... This is all yours?'

Cap nodded, the smile barely curved on his lips, but the pride shone in his eyes. 'You should see it from Ryder's chopper, or the videos Ash has from his drone.'

'You said you're collecting the data.'

'Ash is learning to take water samples, too. He's creating some tech for the water troughs to give daily readings of rainfall and water quality, all at the touch of a button. Hopefully reducing the need to clean troughs all the time, so no wasting water or using fuel and manpower to check on them. At the moment we're using Charlie's idea for algae control—dropping a copper penny in each trough. It's simple, works a treat, while still keeping us on the organic list for livestock.'

'I can help with that.'

His lips curved, crinkling the sides of his mouth, but again that smile shone in his eyes. It was a struggle to ignore her foolish feelings for this guy when he looked at her like she was the answer to all his prayers. 'You can?'

'I'd take daily water and soil samples as part of my job in the mines.' Call her crazy, but she wanted to help Cap realise his dream. The guy had been her hero, bringing her out here, but also giving her a job she loved. And she was great at her job—if she focused! 'Can you get a water and soil sampling kit from the hardware store?'

'Any preferences?'

She reached for Post-it notes sitting beside the coffeemaker, and a pen that sat among assorted office supplies resting beneath a whiteboard listing out jobs for the station.

She scribbled down the water testing kit details. 'I know they have this brand in town. It'll be perfect for you guys, easy to read, but it'll show you the minerals while also detecting any contaminants in the soil and water to keep your livestock safe.'

'Brilliant.' He took the paper, their fingers barely brushing, but it was enough to send a spark up to her elbow.

Come on, focus on the job, not on the boss wearing that sexy smile. 'Where is Ash putting his data?'

He read the note, then pinned it to the whiteboard under a magnet. With a marker he wrote: *Harper, can you please collect from the hardware store?* Then he drew an arrow, and a circle around the Post-it note. 'On a spreadsheet, I think.'

'Well, if you were to lend me your laptop, I'll give you a copy of the template I used for my mine samples.'

'You don't have a laptop?'

She dropped her head, the foolishness of her situation prickling heat along the back of her neck. 'I did.' Now, all she had was a phone she couldn't use, as they were out of range, and her purse stashed in her workbag. What happened to her independence? Her wardrobe? 'I'm in the market for a new one.'

'Use mine. I don't like computers.'

Which made sense when he drove a vintage truck. 'Can you use a computer?'

'A bit. I only use it for research.'

'Not to watch any movies or social media?'

He shook his head.

'Do you do anything for fun?'

'Training my dogs is fun.'

The muster dogs were spread out across the strip of grey lawn, always keeping Cap in their line of sight, ready to eagerly follow him with their wagging tails and wide doggy smiles.

'Aren't your dogs meant for work?'

'No. I mean, yeah...' Again, he reached for the roof beams, this time to stretch his spine, exposing his stomach muscles fully. His biceps stretched the material of his shirt to its limit; they were big enough to suit some Hollywood heart-throb.

Hot. Dayum.

Cap wasn't doing it to show off. He didn't seem to realise how magnificently beautiful he was to look at with that raw silent masculine energy underneath. Bree was right, his silence was a strength, a lot more than she realised.

'My work doesn't feel like work.' His deep brown eyes had tiny flecks of amber that reflected the yard's sunshine as he watched his dogs. His smile flickered, so slight, but it only softened as did his stance where he hooked his thumbs through the belt loops of his jeans. 'You should see their smiles when the muster dogs are working. To them it's playtime, and that's enough for me that they get to live and enjoy another day doing what they love.'

Her heart flipped and literally rolled over like a dog in play at the obvious joy he got from rescuing those animals.

'So there's nothing else you're, um, passionate about?' She licked her dry lips, his eyes tracking her tongue's movement.

'Or are you all about work?'

He again turned his attention back to the dogs. 'I get passionate about new projects, like doing the dog trials and getting your native nursery off the ground. What about you? Don't tell me it's just gardening.'

'No, I have a hobby.'

'Is it quilt making?'

She screwed her nose up. 'No.'

'My mother knits and one of my sisters is into scrapbooking. Her birthday cards are like works of art. Some are so good she'll ask me to send them back to her.' He laughed. The sound was glorious, rich, rolling and full. 'You said your mother does show dogs as her hobby. So, what's yours.'

She shared a half shrug. 'It's weird.'

'The way I live and talk to my dogs more than humans, people would call me weird.' He leaned in so close they were sharing the same air. 'I know I'm weird, especially to women.'

'No, you're not.'

He shook his head as if unconvinced, and started clearing the empty beer bottles off the table.

'I think it's incredible what you do, not weird.' Cap was amazing, and her feelings for him were starting to get far too complicated to control. 'I make mosaics from bottle caps.'

'You what?' Cap arched an eyebrow at her as the glass beer bottles clinked inside the empty beer box.

Mia reached for the large coffee tin that sat in the middle of the table, filled with beer bottle caps. 'I'm always collecting discarded bottle caps on mining sites, clearing up the rubbish. Whenever I'd see one, I'd tuck it into my pocket to toss into the bin later. Except I'd forget, and I'd empty my pockets out when I did my laundry and find them.' She grabbed a handful of bottle caps and let them fall like water from her fingers to tinkle like coins spilling inside a treasure chest. 'I had so many of them collecting in this old tin bucket by the washing machine, that I began making things with them. I did this cool owl for Mum for Mother's Day. And I was working on a…'

'On?'

Plonking back into her chair at the table, she turned a single beer cap in her fingers like a coin. 'I was working on these sunflowers made from broken pallets. They would've suited Bree's garden beds as planting stakes.'

'Are you sure you don't want us to collect your gear?'

'No.' She rolled the crimped edged metal cap across her palm, it reminded her of the circular rowel found on the end of the cattle spurs Charlie wore on his boots. 'I'm sure there's nothing left to collect. Gavin would've burnt it or dumped it by now. He doesn't like to keep junk.'

'It's not junk, if you turned it into art.' Cap wore a serious expression, as if processing her or the situation she was in. But he didn't make fun of her, more like he was trying to understand her, with that deep patience to wait for her to react to him.

Sweet sassy malassy her body reacted to him alright. In unexpected ways, it was burying her sanity along with her common sense. She forced her attention elsewhere.

'I could make something for Bree, to thank her.' She looked up to meet his eyes that were so soft, so clear, where the sun-kissed crinkles born from a life in the sun softened across his face. He was the most handsome man she'd ever met, a man who didn't hide his soft side to animals, children, and to her. He truly was a rare male unicorn.

Her breath stalled as he held her gaze. It was deeper and longer, as if he could truly see beyond her cuts and bruises, beyond her messy hair and dirty nails, through to her soul. No one had ever looked at her like that, where the air felt positively charged around them.

When Sarge let out an enormous bark, she jumped in fright.

'Sarge? What do you hear?' Cap jumped to his feet as the large shepherd, bristling with muscles, stood in the fiercest stance she'd ever seen, barking at the driveway.

'Stay.' Cap commanded to the cattle dogs spread out over the nearby patch of dried lawn. Without hesitation, they sat obediently, but alert, with their eyes on Cap.

Ash came to the front door, stepping over the baby gate. 'It's probably Harper, coming back from work.'

'Not with that bark.' Ryder came from around the corner, tapping on his tablet in hand. Mia could feel his sturdy boot steps through the floorboards. 'The security camera shows it's someone else.'

'It'd be handy if there was somewhere we could all see the security screens,' suggested Cap as he leaned over to Ryder's tablet.

'I've ordered more screens to come with the extra cameras, to extend Ash's intranet idea. Once it's up we'll be able to tap into our security system with our phones.' Ryder turned the tablet around. 'In the meantime, does anyone know this vehicle?'

Mia gasped, her eyes widening at the large black ute on the screen, that was slowly coming around the bend on the dirt track, recognising it. 'It's Leo's ute.' Her voice was shrill as she stood quickly, knocking over her chair. With legs trembling, she struggled to stand when all she wanted to do was run for her life!

Thirteen

'Who did you say that was?' Ryder's frown was fierce, only spiking Mia's fear as she watched the black ute get closer, driving down their long driveway.

'That's Leo Travers.' She stepped away from the driveway, with Willow whimpering beside her. 'He's from—'

'Blackwell Mining.' This time it was Ash who scowled, not at her, but at the shiny vehicle on the tablet's screen, then at the black ute cruising closer to the house. 'How do you know Leo?'

Her throat hurt to speak as she squeaked the words loaded with fear as she recognised the driver, parking his vehicle in the yard, looking straight at them. Straight at her. *Leo. Knows. Gavin.*

'Aw, crap.' Cap ripped off his hat to rake fingers through his hair.

Mia bolted for the far side of the house with Willow running alongside her.

'Mia?'

She heard the footsteps behind her, but she didn't expect Cap to be so fast as he gripped her arm, pulling her to a stop as she rounded the corner.

'Hey, it's okay.'

'Leo knows Gavin. He'll tell Gavin I'm here.' She struggled to breathe, fighting against the terror gripping her lungs. Tears and sweat streamed down her cheeks as she searched for somewhere to hide.

Cap gently gripped both of her arms, stepping in so close all she saw was Cap. 'Hey, it's okay, Mia. I promised I'd keep you safe.'

'Then why is Leo here?'

'I don't know.' He shrugged candidly.

It was enough to pause her panic for a moment, reminding her this wasn't her house, and it wasn't her business who visited. She'd just embarrassed herself over someone else's visitor.

The savage licks of shame flared across her cheeks, she had to be glowing. Yet the tight terror that gripped her lungs relentlessly refused to let go.

'Take a deep breath, Mia.' Cap rubbed large smooth circles across her back.

She tried to inhale deeply while shaking the tremors free from her hands, but her whole body was trembling. 'I'm sorry.'

'Don't be sorry.'

'It's none of my business who comes here. I shouldn't even be here.' What was she thinking, getting these people involved like this?

'Stop, Mia, just focus on breathing, honey. Come on, take another deep breath.'

Honestly, she tried, but her lungs were tight, with her mind dancing along that scary edge between fright and flight, because she had no skills to fight.

'Leo is trying to buy this place for his mine,' explained Cap. 'Did you know that he's buying up other cattle stations?'

'Only through Gavin. Leo was going to hire Gavin for the new mine that…' Then it clicked and she looked up at Cap, her fear easing, pushing back on that tight terror band around her chest, even if it still lingered, and her heart hammered as if she'd run some marathon. 'You guys stopped the new lithium mine from happening. How? No one stops mining giants from getting what they want.'

'Harper looked into the Federal Government's zoning.

Technically their Northern Territory–issued mining lease wasn't valid. We're not sure how long that'll stop them, so Harper has started a petition to block any changes to the zoning and to protect farmers' water rights.'

'I'd heard talk between the farmers in the pub.' It all made sense now, thinking hard to push past her body's overreaction. 'They hated us miners drinking in their bar, telling us we were stealing their water.' The same day she'd ended up out here. Almost a week, and she was still full of fear. It wasn't right.

'Leo's mine was trying to take our water, daring to fine us for fixing our own dam. Which is why I'm trying so hard to make sure we're ecologically sound. If they changed the laws—'

'They'd need an environmental impact study.' Finally, she could breathe properly again, as her brain engaged past the panic. 'That new mining site never did an environmental impact study. I know they didn't, because my team and I were talking about it because we're the contractors who consult on those reports for this region. No one asked us.' And she was damned good at her job.

Oh, wait, Leo did talk to her about it, but that had been a while ago and it had only been a casual conversation, before she'd left Gavin at their house to go to work.

The mere thought of Gavin made her heart quicken and that inner terror once again began to tighten its grip around her lungs. She gripped Cap's arm like he was an anchor and forced herself to hitch in a breath.

'You've got this, Mia, breathe.' Cap seemed to understand, gently patting her hand.

Again, she hitched in more air, a little deeper this time. 'Please… Talk… Anything.' To get her mind off her ex.

'Okay, sure, um… The reason why Ash and I are collecting data on this place is that if they ever tried to take our water, we could easily prove the impact it would have on this station. I know a lot of the locals are watching to see what we do, hoping they can do the same to save their cattle stations from losing their water rights.'

'I get it.' Again, she calmed down, squashing that fear deep inside her belly, and finally let go of his arm. It left her palm tingly as if missing his touch. 'So, Leo is…'

'The enemy.'

'So, you really do need me for my brains.'

He gave her a coy grin. 'And your planting skills, and nursery know-how.'

'I've always wanted to build a native nursery.'

'I know. Bree told me.'

She could just hug Bree, and the man with caring eyes.

Willow pushed her nose against her leg.

'It's okay, Willow, I just panicked for a bit.' Now she was back to feeling like a proper idiot. 'I'm sorry.'

'Hey, listen, you have nothing to be sorry for. You've been through something I'd never wish on anyone, and having a panic attack is understandable. Just know it will take time to get past this.'

Her eyes widened as she stepped back. Since when did she suffer from panic attacks?

'I won't push you with the work if you need space.'

'But I want to do it.' She needed it to help keep her grounded, to occupy her mind with the good and not the bad. Mia also wanted to pay everyone back for their generosity, especially Cap for his kindness.

'Do you want me to walk you back to Bree's?'

'I'm okay.' She had to get back to a time when she wasn't afraid of the dark. But she hadn't realised how deeply Gavin's action had impacted on her. 'Come on, Willow.' At least she had the dog.

'I'll see you at sunrise for the drafting?'

'Yeah.' She turned back and unexpectedly kissed his cheek. Shocking herself for being so brazen, the blush burned her face as she dropped her head and mumbled, 'Thank you for everything, Cap.' And rushed for the cottage, taking the long way around the house to avoid being spotted by Leo.

With Leo—their neighbour—showing up like this, it proved that Elsie Creek Station really wasn't safe for her at all. It meant Gavin could be working right next door.

Fourteen

Cap watched Mia disappear around the back sheds with her head down and Willow trotting after her.

He held his hand to his cheek, stunned she'd kissed him. Even grinning that maybe, just maybe, she did like him.

Unexpectedly it made something change inside him.

Hope swiftly heightened his level of protectiveness, which then spun into a fury, that anything dared to threaten Mia's safety when he'd promised to keep her safe!

His hands clenched into fists, and he stormed to the front of the house where this Leo was talking to Ryder, while Ash held back Sarge by the dog harness, with Dex coming over from the kennels.

'What do you want?' Cap wanted the idiot who'd dared to scare Mia gone. And now.

A little older than Ryder, but just as tall, with jet-black hair, Leo looked like any other cattleman, complete with jeans, shirt, and black hat and a three-day growth peppered across his strong jawline. So, how was he part of the mine?

Leo held out his hand. 'Hello, we haven't officially met. I'm Leo.'

'I know who you are.' Cap crossed his arms over his chest. Normally he was the peacemaker who'd greet people and hear them out. But not this time.

'Well then, straight to business, I see. I'm here with another offer on the property.' The man even smiled with his dark eyes all shiny as if amused.

'Not interested.' Cap glared at the man as Dex, the professional street fighter, came up behind him. It only gave him courage.

'As my brother said, we're not interested.' Ryder held out an envelope to Leo. It was the same type of envelope Harper had delivered, containing the mine's first offer to buy the place. Even then, it was less than what they'd paid for the place that was now their home. Was Leo playing them for fools?

'Just look at the offer and call me and I'll come out and transfer my funds to pay in full today. Hey, I'm right next door.' Leo pointed east, while his grin was dark, almost menacing even.

'No.' Cap shook his head. He did not want the neighbour anywhere near this place. 'If you want to talk to us, it'll be at the pub or somewhere else in town. Not here.' He wanted Mia safe. 'Never come back here unannounced again, or I'll have you arrested for trespassing.'

A growl, deep and loaded with warning, cut through the air. It came from Sarge.

Ash let go of the dog's harness, stepping away from the fiercely protective ex-riot dog that stood beside Cap.

But there was more than one growl. Cap's entire dog pack had stealthily snuck up behind them, with their hackles raised.

'Easy...' Cap wasn't telling them off, when it was in their nature to protect their pack.

'I'd back away slowly, if I were you, *mate*.' Dex gave his signature smirk, as he rocked on his heels. 'And you might think twice about coming back, now that the dogs have their eye on you.'

'Hey, I'm just a businessman. We can be neighbourly, can't we?' Leo held out his open palms; they were callus free and on one wrist was an expensive watch.

Then he pointed to the house, where Mason was peeking through the childproof gate with his nanny dog, Ruby, at his side. 'Is that child safe with these dogs?'

'Oi.' Ash frowned, pointing at Leo. 'It was you who dropped that anonymous tip-off to the cops about me abusing my kid.'

Leo gave a lopsided grin. 'I don't know what you're talking about. But is Bree around? I'd like to—'

'Leave. *Now*.' Ryder stood right in Leo's face. 'And never come back.' And when someone like Ryder gave anyone *the death look*, you knew instinctively that he was a man who had the lethal power to back up his words.

But Leo only narrowed his dark eyes at Ryder for a long beat while remaining spookily calm and collected as if sizing him up. 'Hmph. I see we've skipped the civilities to slide straight into the stage where we'll just let our lawyers do the talking. See you later, gentlemen, or do you prefer the term cow*boys*.'

The insult was made worse by Leo tipping the brim of his hat as he climbed back into his vehicle, even grinning at them as he drove away.

'That's not a miner's vehicle. It's got none of their ID numbers or safety lights on it.' Cap pointed to the dust stirred by Leo's ute tearing down the track towards the front gate. 'Leo's not a miner. Is he a cattleman?' He had callus-free hands unstained by the dirt and dust that was usually a sign of a man who worked on the land.

'Maybe Leo's more of a mining manager, dressing up to play cowboy,' suggested Dex.

'Harper said Leo's mining company was buying up cattle country,' said Ash. 'Wouldn't you want a cattleman to manage your properties, or know what to look for—'

'Leo is *not* a cattleman.' Ryder's deep voice echoed like a death whisper in the air, silencing everyone. As an astute businessman, Ryder could read people to cut through the bull. 'Leo is not what he says he is, and that makes him dangerous in my book.'

'Whatever he is, I don't want him here for Mia's sake.'

'Is Mia okay? Did she have a panic attack or something?' Ash asked, concerned.

'Yeah,' Cap clenched his fists, barely containing that rage. 'If I ever see that bloke who hurt Mia, I doubt I'll be able to control myself.' Which was unheard of. Cap never got mad, unless for family. Since when did he consider Mia like family?

'Where is Mia?' Ash asked. While Ryder arched an eyebrow at Cap, then side-glanced Dex who had also cocked his head at Cap.

'Hiding at Bree's.' He turned for the cottage, should he go see her?

'Don't worry, Bree will protect her, brother.' Dex patted Cap's shoulder. 'That redhead even scares me when she gets into mother-bear mode.'

'But *I* want to protect Mia.' Cap dropped his head as his words rang in his ears and in the surrounding air. Sighing heavily, he patted Sarge, the loyal friend indeed.

'Why was Mia panicking over Leo?' Dex asked with a shrug.

'Leo knows her ex, Gavin.' *The scumbag.* 'Leo was going to hire Gavin as the mechanic or something, to work on that lithium mine site.' Which was right next door. Even though there were hundreds of acres between them, it had to be spinning Mia out to realise her ex might be that close. 'We should go back to keeping the gate locked.'

'We can't,' said Ryder. 'Charlie and Bree run their branding business, or whatever it is that Bree does, and the caretakers do get visitors. Charlie said they only lock the front gate when no one is at the homestead. Which is rare. But that's not the issue, here.' Ryder shook his head. 'CEOs do not bother doing job interviews with ground crews like mechanics.' Ryder's eyes narrowed as he spoke. 'You know, the whole lithium mining deal of Leo's wasn't right from the get-go. He must have paid someone off to ignore the land zone regulation to get that mining permit issued in the first place.'

'You're probably right,' said Cap. 'Mia said Leo's mine never did an environmental impact study on the place, either.

And that's part of the application process.'

Ryder cocked his head slightly. 'How does Mia know this?'

'Mia does those reports for the mines and the government.'

'So she's qualified to do our pastures?' Ash asked.

'Over-qualified.' Cap and his brothers had no fancy education or degrees, but a lot of calluses they'd earned from the never-ending life lessons of living in the outback. 'Can you see now why I want Mia's help?'

His brothers nodded, except for Ryder.

Cap ripped off his hat and raked fingers through his hair. 'Yesterday Mia helped me work out the set-up for the wildlife corridors that'll be windbreaks to stop any future dust storms. It won't cost us very much money, except for Mia's wages, plus she's got some great ideas to improve pastures that feed our stock.'

Finally, he had Ryder's attention.

'Mia may be here due to an ugly situation, and if I ever see that Gavin, I'll—'

'Oi? You never get violent.' Ash's brow creased with concern.

'I believe our family's peacemaker here,' said Dex, tossing his thumb at Cap, 'was going to throttle Leo if he didn't leave.'

'I saw that.' Ryder's heavy hand landed on Cap's shoulder as he lowered his head to meet Cap's eyes. 'Mate, I'm going to ask, just this once and once only. So don't tear my head off when I say this.'

'Go on.' Cap raised his chin, preparing for the worst, especially when Ryder spoke cold hard truths.

'Don't you think you're getting a little too involved with a woman who's running from her ex? I saw how Mia was when Leo showed up, she was terrified.' Ryder pointed back to the house.

'I saw that, too.' Ash gave a slow nod.

'How bad?' Dex asked, he'd been at the kennels while all

this went down.

'It wasn't good.'

'Yeah, I know.' Cap sighed heavily, shoving his hands into the pockets of his jeans.

'What makes you think she'll stay and not run the first chance she gets?'

Cap glared at Ryder and his wise words.

'You've always had a soft heart, always the first to help strays.' Ryder nodded at Sarge, a rescued police dog. 'Mia isn't—'

'I know she's not part of the pack. I'm not stupid.'

'Bro, you care for her. We all see that.' Ash scratched the bristles on his chin, his brow ruffling as if a thought had just emerged. 'Do you know what a rebound is?'

Cap scoffed. 'What are you on about now?'

'It's when a woman uses a guy to help her get over a relationship. And rebound relationships never last. Trust me on that,' said the ladies' man who'd had the reputation of never dating a woman longer than two weeks. 'Before I met Harper, I loved being the rebound guy, because I knew a woman wasn't looking for anything long term.'

Dex scowled, crossing his beefy arms over his chest. 'Women aren't worth the hassle in my book. Don't trust them.'

But Mia was worth it in Cap's eyes. He didn't know how he knew that—or when, or why he'd come to that conclusion—he just did.

'After what Mia's been through, bro, you might want to be careful about getting too attached to her,' said Ash.

'Too late, the softie already is. Just look at him.'

'Lay off.' Cap wanted to wipe that smirk off Dex's face.

'Look, none of us want to see her break your heart when she leaves,' said the normally heartless man Ryder.

'Mia's not going anywhere.' Not if Cap could help it.

'That's if Mia isn't already packing after Leo's little visit.' Dex was such a dick!

'She won't. She isn't. I'm not—' *Arseholes*. Cap spun

around and walked away. He hated how his brothers saw straight through him.

What irked him more was they were right.

If given the opportunity, Mia would leave the first chance she got, especially with Leo's visit reminding her why she was hiding out here in the first place. Mia had every reason to run.

Fifteen

The dingo's howl was so close and so clear, Mia woke with a start to Willow's cold nose pressing against her cheek where she slept on the couch in the caretaker's cottage.

'*Bree*?' Yellow light spilled from Charlie's bedroom door as it opened. It highlighted the kitchen. 'Did you hear them?'

'I did, Pop.' On the other side of the room, Bree came out of her bedroom fully dressed in jeans and riding boots, braiding her red hair into a thick rope-like plait.

She scooped up a long, heavy coat from the hat rack, sliding it on as she unlocked a metal cupboard filled with assorted guns. 'Get dressed, Pop. I want you to take the Razorback and wake Ryder. It's their herd. You can reach me on the radio.'

'Where are you going?' Mia quickly slid into her overalls.

'To ride out and protect the herd. We don't need a midnight stampede happening.' Bree shoved a box of bullets into her coat pocket, snatched up a bottle of water from the fridge, slapped on her wide-brimmed hat, grabbed one of the stockwhips and was out the door.

'You up for a bit of adventure, girlie?' Charlie sat on the kitchen chair and slid on his boots.

'To do what?'

'You would've done some spotlighting on your family farm, eh?'

'I did. My brother hunted rabbits.'

'Good. I'll get you to operate the spotlight.' Charlie

handed her a rifle and a few boxes of bullets before closing their ammunition cupboard. 'Put your boots on and do a toilet run before we skedaddle. I'll go first.' He closed the bathroom door, while Mia slipped on her boots.

'HEE-YAH!' Bree's shout was soon followed by a fierce gallop of horse hooves.

Mia couldn't get dressed quick enough as Charlie grabbed torches and water bottles.

Another haunting howl echoed in the air. It made Mia's skin crawl.

'The buggers are close.' Charlie narrowed his eyes at the open back door that only showed a deep blackness. 'Leave your dog here, girlie. We don't want Willow tangling with them wild ones. It's why Cap keeps his dogs in kennels at night—to protect them.' Charlie slipped on his jacket, before sliding on his sweat-stained Akubra with its distinctive crocodile leather band.

'Want a jacket?' He pointed to the rack filled with assorted coats, hats, leather aprons, stockwhips, and spurs. Underneath stood a row of assorted boots.

'I have a jumper.' Mia grabbed her water bottle, holding her jumper with her teeth, she slung the rifle's strap over her shoulder while shoving boxes of bullets down the front pocket of her overalls, as she raced after Charlie.

By the back door, Charlie nodded at Willow. 'Tell the dog to stay or she'll break out and follow.'

'Stay, Willow. Please, stay. I'll be back soon, I promise.' Mia patted the dog, securely closing the wooden door behind her.

The excitement and the sense of urgency had her scrambling as the cool outback air nipped at her skin. She scurried after Charlie, who'd quickly headed for the dark sheds, only guided by torchlight.

At one o'clock in the morning the world was draped in a deep galaxy of stars that allowed the cool heavy dew to fall like an ice blanket. Mia wished she had borrowed one of Charlie's coats.

Inside the shed, the corrugated walls amplified the sound of a deep-throated engine roaring to life, so loud it hurt her ears.

It belonged to a fierce-looking vehicle you'd expect to find in a Mad Max movie. It was a four-wheel drive, with its top half cleanly cut free, leaving only two front seats and a steering wheel, with a large bionic arm and a serious steel bull bar across the front. It had no front windshield or doors or anything for safety like airbags or seatbelts. In the back, it held steel bench seats that ran down the sides like a troop carrier. The odd thing that stood out most was the baby seat in the middle of the two front seats.

'I'm guessing the baby seat is for Mason?' Mia helped Charlie load up the vehicle, before taking the passenger seat.

'That boy loves this thing. I reckon he'll be driving it the second his toes hit the floor pedals, just like Bree did.' Thick diesel smoke spewed out of the twin exhaust stacks like you'd expect to find on the sides of a huge semi-truck.

'What is this thing?'

'This here is the Razorback.' Charlie's wide grin deepened his many weatherworn wrinkles, as he flicked on a bank of spotlights that lit up the world in hot white light.

'A what?'

'The Razorback is a bull catcher, and a bloody good one at that.' He crunched the gears, and the rumbling beast roared with its lethal V8 engine, as Charlie steered towards the farmhouse where he hammered on a foghorn you'd expect to find on a ship!

Mia flinched in the passenger seat, while holding her ears. 'Sweet sassy malassy that's loud.' It was enough to wake the dead.

'Gotta get their attention somehow.' Charlie chuckled as he pushed the horn again.

Hoooonk.

The shepherd they called Sarge, howled with the horn from the front verandah.

The porch lights flickered on as Ryder pushed open the

screen door. Slipping on a shirt, Ryder was a wall of muscle. But his scowl was super scary. 'You'd better have a bloody good reason to play with that horn, Charlie.'

'Dingoes are makin' a helluva racket up near the herd.'

BOOM!

Running over to meet them, Dex and Cap flinched like Mia did in the passenger seat as the sound of a shotgun blast rang in the air. But Ryder and Charlie remained calm.

'Don't tell me that's Bree out there.' Ryder pulled on his boots and jacket.

'Bree's on horseback,' said Charlie. 'You can reach her on the radio.'

Ash rushed outside wearing only boxer shorts. Another brother with nothing but a torso of muscle. Was it a Riggs family trait? Whatever it was, Harper was a lucky lady.

'Did I hear a gunshot?' Ash asked.

'It's those damned dingoes.' Dex dashed past him, heading into the farmhouse.

Ryder slid on his hat while trotting down the front steps to the Razorback. 'Move over, Charlie, I'm driving.'

'Oi.'

'Don't argue with me. I'm not leaving Bree out there alone another second. And I drive a helluva lot quicker than you, old man.'

BOOM!

'Damn that woman.' Ryder mumbled an explosive set of expletives under his breath. 'Ash, stay with your family. Car is full.'

'No worries. You lot be safe,' said Ash. 'I'll put the coffee on.'

More lights flicked on inside the farmhouse to the sound of Mason crying.

Dex rushed back out with his arms full of weapons. A hessian bag swung off his shoulder. 'Let's go.'

'Take my seat, Charlie.' Mia scrambled into the back. Ryder slid into the driver's seat as Charlie scooted over, and Dex and Cap jumped in the back. The sturdy vehicle dropped from the weight of all the men and their weaponry.

'Are you up for this, Mia?' asked Cap, doing up the buttons on his shirt hiding another toned torso—it stopped her ability to speak.

'I told Mia she could man the spotlight while you boys play with the guns,' said Charlie from the front passenger seat. 'I might not have the eye for shooting like I used to, but I can help you mob load up.'

'Done.' Shoving a handful of bullets into his pockets, Dex passed the heavy hessian bag to Charlie who handed out headlamps and handheld radios, while Dex started loading up the assorted guns, he'd laid across the floor.

Ryder gunned the deep rumbling engine as Ash waved from the well-lit verandah, and they were on their way.

In between working his way through the gears, Ryder flicked on the CB radio embedded in the dashboard of the Razorback. On the front by the bull bar, its long thick radio antenna flexed against the wind. 'Bree? Ryder, here.'

'Didn't you take your sweet time to join the party, cupcake.' Bree's voice had the same teasing tone as always, but she was out there on her own.

'Where are you?' Ryder steered them past the sheds where nothing but dark open country lay before them.

'Wrong question, cupcake. You'll want to know where the—'

'Where. Are. YOU. People come first.' Ryder was adamant.

Bree huffed over the radio. 'I'm by the herd. They're safe.'

'See, Bree's in mother-bear mode. Of course, the herd is safe.' Dex chuckled from his seat, only for Ryder to turn around and glare.

'Look, if you're coming from the back of the sheds,' Bree said over the CB radio's speakers, 'I'd suggest you change course. Sorry, but they got one of your heifers. I've sent the pack running, so you might want to go after them.'

As if barely containing the anger at the loss of their livestock, Ryder gripped the CB radio's microphone in one hand, while steering the Razorback with the other. 'How big is the dingo pack?'

'Listen, Ryder...' All traces of humour as well as the nickname disappeared as Bree said, 'They weren't dingoes. It's a pack of six wild dogs. Big bastards, too. I've scared them off towards the drafting yards.'

'Dammit.' Ryder cursed again, planting his foot heavily on the accelerator and the Razorback tore to the right at breakneck speed down the bumpy dirt track, sending a plume of dust high into the night skies.

'Aw, crap.' Cap shut his eyes, shaking his lowered head.

'Why is that different to dingoes? They're a wild dog, too. Right?' Mia asked Cap.

'Traditionally, dingoes are solitary hunters that prey on smaller forms of wildlife, like wallabies and possums. Unless they're training their pups before they leave to become solitary hunters, then they'll hunt in loose packs and will take our calves,' explained Cap.

'These aren't dingos, brother. You heard, Bree.' Dex held the butt of the shotgun to his leg and fed large plastic casings down the magazine tube.

The Razorback hit a pothole forcing it to drop, making Mia's bum lift off the seat. She lost her grip and had nothing to cling onto. 'Oh, no.' She latched onto Cap's chest, gripping his shirt in her fists.

'Gotcha.' Cap wrapped his arm around her as if cocooning her in his aroma of outdoors and sultry male. 'Why don't you sit in front of me while Ryder's racing to catch the pack. Hold onto Charlie's seat.' His large hands were warm on her back as he effortlessly picked her up and put her down beside him. 'There.'

Again, his large hands swamped hers, ensuring she got a grip on the rail that ran along the back of the front seats. 'Good?'

She barely nodded, while trying to hide her disappointment when he sat back beside Dex and continued loading his gun.

Ryder drove them deeper into the night where the spotlights caught the tops of fluffy leafed eucalyptus trees. They soon fell back to open country where the wind whipped around them as they bumped along the track under a massive sea of stars. With the moon rising on the distant escarpment, it would have been magnificent—if not for the breakneck speed and bumpy track.

She needed to focus on something else, so of course she focused on Cap. 'What were you going to say about the wild dogs?'

'They—'

'Hunt in bloodthirsty packs.' Dex scowled as he slid the loaded rifles securely into the gun racks that ran behind the front seats, like fishing rod holders. He then handed Ryder the shotgun.

Ryder jammed it into the gun holder close to the steering wheel, with his eyes on the dirt road bathed in hot white light where wallabies fled from the sides. 'Wild dogs are coordinated, vicious creatures that can have an enormous impact on our herd.'

Dex lifted his seat like the lid of a deep box, to drag out some thick poles. 'The problem with a wild dog pack is once they've got the taste for blood, they'll massacre the herd.' He then dropped a brotherly hand on Cap's shoulder. 'I'm sorry, brother, it has to happen.'

Cap's head hung low, with his eyes squeezed shut. 'I know. I know.'

With one hand still gripping the rail, Mia slid back closer to Cap and gave his hand a squeeze, wishing she hadn't climbed on board. This was a big ask for a man who rescued canines.

Dex slammed the poles together to construct a sturdy tripod. 'Where's that spotlight?'

'Here. Mia's gonna man it.' Charlie rummaged under the raised passenger seat, to pass back a massive globe to Dex, who slid it into place on the sturdy tripod.

'Up you get.' Dex beckoned to Mia with a crooked finger.

The thick steel poles were cold under her fingers, as her hair whipped around her face, now facing the full brunt of the wind as Ryder continued to drive as if in some high-speed police chase, except they were hurtling through the outback.

She had no clue where they were going as there were no signs, no streetlights, not even a road. It only made her grip the poles tighter.

'You'll want to make slow sweeping arcs,' explained Dex, helping her to stand behind the tripod as they bounced over the rubble. 'If you see anything, you hold the light on them and blind them. Ryder will steer towards what you find, and I'll take care of the rest.' Dex pulled back the rifle's hammer, and leaned over the steel bar, armed and ready for anything.

Mia held the large light, the size of a human head, the weight heavy in her hands as she made slow sweeps over a sleeping land. 'Am I doing this right?'

'You're doing fine. Here…' Cap stood right behind her, his arms on either side of her, correcting her stance. 'Hold it here.' Again, his large hands swamped hers to show her the small, raised lip that made for handles. 'Got it?'

'I do.' It kept her steady, or he did, with her back pressed to his chest, and her heart flying. But so was her hair, fluttering in her face. She spat at the ends, wiping at her windswept mop.

'Hold on, I've got something for that.' Cap leaned forward to the front and grabbed something wrapped around the gearstick. 'Will this help?' He held out an elastic hair band.

'Yours?' She even grinned.

His smile was glorious. 'It's Harper's or Bree's? I think. May I?'

'Please. I'm scared to let go.'

'We can't have that.' From behind, he gently gathered back her hair, to then slip it into a ponytail. 'There. Not too tight?'

'It's fine. Thank you.'

'This will help more.' He removed his own cap, adjusted the back and slipped it on her head, backwards. 'How's that.'

'Perfect.' Her hair wasn't bothering her now. Thank the heavens he was there. 'Thank you.'

'Are you okay to do this?' His eyes displayed a clear worry for her and what was ahead. So of course, she began to worry for him.

'I understand you're protecting the herd. My father did the same. But are you okay?'

Cap gave a resigned shrug as he picked up his rifle. 'I hate it, but they are dangerous when they're locked into that wild-pack mentality. I don't want them near the house, they could attack our dogs, and Mason's there, too.' Cap cocked back the hammer of his rifle, resting it over the bar, like Dex, who looked ready to kill anything.

'We're here,' called out Ryder and he started to slow down.

'You're on, Mia.' Cap gave her an encouraging nod.

The massive sweeping beam of bright-hot white light was like a camera flash, highlighting everything from the dew glistening on the blades of grass, to the red eyes of a possum wedged in the trunk's fork of a large gum tree.

When something caught her attention, she steered the heavy light.

'THERE!' The spotlight shone on a pack of massive dogs, much bigger than wolves, their pelts covered in blood. A few of them growled as if ready to attack.

A volley of gunshots rang in her ears as Ryder steered the Razorback closer.

'*Keep that spotlight on them, Mia.*' Dex passed his rifle to Charlie, who was reloading them in the front seat.

'*Two more.* THERE!'

Again, another volley of shots shattered the night. The stench of gunpowder was strong against her sinuses, as her sweaty grip struggled to hold the spotlight, now hot in her hands. It was the most fearsome thing she'd ever done.

Hold on. No, it wasn't.

She'd run from a man who'd hit her.

And here she was in a car with no seatbelts, no roof, no helmets, hooning along the dirt with no road, under a rising moon, in a race across the outback. She'd never felt more alive.

'We got 'em, kid.' Charlie spoke over the radio to Bree.

'All six?' Bree's voice was clear over the speakers now they'd stopped.

'They sure did,' Charlie replied as Ryder dragged out a tarp from under his seat, while Dex and Cap jumped out to check on their targets, hidden in the dry grass.

With the light kept on the men to do their work, Mia turned away, flexing her stiff hands from keeping a tight grip on the spotlight. The globe shed so much heat, she was tempted to remove her jumper.

'Here, Charlie. Let me talk to her.' Ryder took the radio's handheld microphone as he climbed back into the driver's seat as Dex and Cap carried the heavy tarp roll between them. 'Bree? How long are you staying out there?'

'Until dawn. I'll play nightwatchman and sing lullabies to the herd until someone brings me a coffee and some snacks.'

'Out there on her own?' Mia flared her eyes at Charlie, fearing for her friend who'd done so much for her.

'That kid's done it plenty of times before, girlie. Don't you worry none, Bree's fearless.'

Mia wanted to be fearless like Bree, too. Hanging out with Charlie and the Riggs brothers on this midnight adventure was the perfect medicine she didn't know she needed.

She craned her neck up at the sky filled with an astounding depth of stars and smiled to herself, feeling that inner strength re-emerge inside her. It was like she'd found her courage again, to no longer be afraid of the dark.

Charlie snatched the radio's microphone back from Ryder. 'You want my company, kid?'

'I'm good, Pop. You get your rest, especially if you're spending a day in the drafting yards. And before you complain, old man, I want you to keep the Razorback away for a bit. After that bit of gunplay, the herd's spooked enough as it is. We don't want a midnight stampede happening.'

There was a large thud, as Cap and Dex dropped the heavy tarp over the bonnet. 'Bree is right,' Cap said, tossing the rope to Dex so they could tie it in place. 'We can't have the herd running in the dark in a panic, they'll hurt themselves.'

Dex wiped his hands on a cloth before climbing on board. 'You can drop me and Cap off at the back of the sheds. We'll dig a pit there to burn the carcasses.'

'Why?' It seemed a bit extreme to Mia.

Cap cleaned his hands with water from a bottle. 'Wild dogs are usually infested with either worms, ticks, or parvo. And those dogs are a lot lighter than they should be for their build. I don't want them infecting our dogs.'

'Hey, you don't think it's a coincidence that we've had this dog issue tonight, when we had Leo show up earlier?' Dex drank thirstily from his water bottle.

Ryder scowled as he slammed the Razorback into gear. 'I'll be getting out at the stables on the way through.' He steered towards the homestead in a much more sedate fashion than earlier.

'Are you going to help Bree?' Charlie asked.

Ryder nodded. 'The rest of you get some sleep and meet us out there at daybreak. If I know Bree, and if the cattle are that jumpy, she'll start mustering under moonlight, which will put us ahead of our plans to start the drafting.' He pointed to the large moon that hung like a massive light globe in the sky.

'How can they see the cattle to move them in the dark? Mia asked Cap.

'The brahman's white coats will be easy enough to see in the moonlight.'

'I taught my granddaughter well, that herd will follow her.' Charlie gave a proud nod. 'I'll pinch some of the coffee Ash was making for the thermos to take to Bree. I'll lend you one, too. And some smoko.'

Ryder nodded, keeping his eyes on the road, steering them back to the homestead.

Charlie spun around in his seat. 'How are you at making sandwiches, girlie?'

'I'm okay. Nothing flash.' Mia shrugged, once again holding the spotlight. 'Why?'

'If Bree's gonna be out mustering she won't have time to make lunches like she'd planned. She's already made roast whatnots, cupcakes, and everything else. All we need to do is whack 'em together. We'll make a few for Ryder to take with him to meet Bree.'

'Now I'm hungry,' said Dex.

Mia nodded, suddenly famished as well.

'You did good, Mia, well done.' Dex patted her shoulder like a mate. 'You can sit down now.'

Her inner pride had her smiling, more at the realisation that Gavin hadn't beaten her, not after this little adventure.

She sat beside Cap as Dex stripped the spotlight's tripod apart. 'Are you okay?'

Cap nodded. 'I should ask you that.'

Now away from the spotlight's heat, the wind blasted her with icy cold air. She huddled closer, using Cap as a windbreak as her grin grew on its own. 'The *rush*. I know I'm supposed to be all about the environment, but...' Her teeth chattered, unsure if it was the cold air or the adrenaline passing.

'I get it.' He winked at her. 'Want my jacket?'

'No, you'll need it. Just block the wind.'

'We can share.' He slung an arm around her shoulders, bringing her close to his side. The fresh outback air blended beautifully with his earthy aroma of mixed spicy sandalwood, making her inhale deeper. She was deliciously warm here, sliding her arm around his waist, dropping her cheek against his strong shoulder as they swayed to the bumps and dips of the rocky road. And when his arm tightened around her it became the safest place on the planet. Her ex was exactly that—her ex, gone and buried in the outback's dusty dark behind her. Now looking forward to tomorrow's muster.

Sixteen

Red dust stained the sun, to fall like fire from the sky. It was in her hair, layered on her skin like sandpaper, and rubbed inside her clothes, but Mia couldn't wipe the smile off her dust-covered face as she steered the quad bike alongside Charlie, with Harper driving the Razorback where little Mason waved from his baby's seat.

Before dawn, they'd left the sheds in their small convoy of vehicles. It hadn't taken long to spot the dust cloud's long trail of red smoke you'd expect from a bushfire that signified the herd was on the move.

As the sky shifted from a mushroom pink, to slithers of soft blue, with the escarpment behind them, the large herd of cattle walked behind Bree on horseback.

Bree, with her thick red braid running down her back, resembled a fierce warrior on her mighty black stallion, with two shotguns in her saddle, effortlessly commanding an entire herd of over a thousand head of moving boulders of beef with sharp wide horns. And the Brahman were massive.

Mia was grateful to be placed at the rear of the slow-moving herd, with Charlie giving her pointers as they rode on either side of the Razorback. Even covered in dust, it was the best view of how they mustered the herd.

Cap was stunning to watch as he effortlessly rode his horse as if born in the saddle. From there, he whistled and gave curt commands to the dozen cattle dogs that circled the herd, keeping them contained.

The muster dogs moved as a team, each taking a post, backing each other up as they barked at a cheeky bull to move along, or they'd just circle the slow-moving, dust-stirring herd without a sound, to keep the cattle calm and moving.

It was pure poetry to watch the muster dogs in action, and how effortlessly Cap controlled them all. It only made her admiration for the man deepen.

Commanding the air, Ryder piloted the helicopter. It swooped in an impressive aerial display that had Mia spellbound. Over the radio, Ryder coordinated the ground crews while using the swift moving chopper to channel the strays towards either Ash on a motorbike, or Dex on his fast horse, to bring the stray cattle in to join the main herd.

That's where the muster dogs took over to keep them contained, while Bree led them closer to the fencing channel that grew narrower like a funnel collects liquids to fill a bottle.

By then they'd become one big line of vehicles, bikes, dogs, and horses, with the helicopter shadowing above, to form an impenetrable wall, giving the herd a final push past the hessian wings and through the wide-open gates.

As the last of the herd passed through, Bree shut the gate with a clang, and the herd was contained.

A cool breeze blew the red dust away like a veil being lifted to expose an enormous cornflower blue sky and a large, roofed structure, with lots of yards made of thick rails taller than Mia.

It was the drafting yards.

Bree removed her hat, lowering her scarf she had covering her nose and mouth, and wiped the dirt and sweat from her brow. 'And my job is done.' She slapped her hat on her head and trotted away on her towering black horse. 'I have a hot shower owed to me.'

'Aw, come on, Bree, we could really do with your help to man the gates,' said Dex, circling her with his horse.

'Hey, hold up, kid. Job's not done yet.' Charlie scrambled

off his bike to grab her horse's reins.

Nearby, Ryder landed his helicopter in the open field as Harper parked the Razorback alongside Ash's bike. That's where Mia parked the quad, wiping at the thick dust covering her face and staining her clothes.

'We can start training Harper to do the sticks,' said Charlie, still holding Bree's horse in place.

'I can't wait to learn,' said Harper.

'See, kid. I'll need help with the training.'

'Pop, my care factor has hit the *I-don't-give-a-damn* level.' Sitting high in the saddle, Bree didn't look impressed at all.

'There's only three of them in the pit, until Cap gets Mia confident enough with Willow at the back. Please do it for me, kid. We'll just do the sortin' today. That's all.' Charlie patted Bree's denim thigh in a fatherly manner. 'With you on board, we can knock over that part of the draft in no time, to let them lads finish the rest, and do Cap's deck on Saturday, just like you planned. Then Mia can move into her new room and start working, which you said would be good for the girl.'

'But—' Mia went to say something, but Dex—the bully— blocked her view using his horse to get in the way, while shaking his head at Mia to shut up.

Mia glared at Dex. She hated being used as a tool to manipulate Bree.

'How many more days in the drafting yards have we got left, kid?' Charlie was good.

'Oh, man.' Bree slapped her hat back on her head and climbed off her saddle. 'You owe me big time, old man.' Bree led her horse away to the shaded trough where she began unsaddling the horse with Dex beside her.

Harper passed Mia a bottle of icy cold water, fresh from the large esky that sat on the back of the Razorback. 'I'm starting to think that this might not be fun.' She pointed at Bree, who didn't look happy at all.

'Nah.' Charlie hitched up his trousers as he headed for the gates. 'The kid's been up all night. It's not easy mustering under moonlight, takes a lot out of you, but she'll be right, you'll see. But you two, c'mere. First lesson about the yards.' He pointed to the tall, thick-railed gates. 'Never, ever, under any circumstances, do you ever put your hands, fingers, tongues, or toes anywhere near these gate panels. Especially when you've got a bull charging at you. They'll hit the fence with a full tonne of their weight, and if your hand's caught you'll lose digits.'

'Now, that sounds scary.' Harper gulped, looking at Ash by the Razorback.

Ash scooped his son out of the baby seat and slung one arm around Harper's shoulders. 'It's all good, babe. If you and Mason stay up there on the high boards with Charlie, you'll have the best time.' He passed Harper the baby carrier.

'Mason's growing out of this.' Harper clipped it over her shoulders, then around her waist.

'I can see that. Did you bring that box out?'

'I tucked it under the passenger seat. Next to the spotlight.'

'Cool.' Ash rummaged under the seat, while holding Mason, who was eagerly pointing at the cattle and babbling.

'Can you?' Harper turned her back to Mia. 'I can't reach the back clip.'

'Oh, sure.' Mia clipped it into place; it was the first time she'd done that, when she'd done her best to avoid all things that involved babies and small children.

'Where are you going to be, Ash?' asked Harper.

'We'll be in the pit. Charlie can explain what our jobs are.' Ash helped Harper slide the toddler into the pouch, then kissed Harper's cheek, sharing a tender smile that openly showed his love for her.

Ash then ruffled the boy's hair, kissing his son's forehead, before slinging on his hat and tucking the box under his arm. 'Look after them, Charlie.' Ash warned, as he ducked under some of the rails.

'Pfft, they'll be fine.' Charlie's voice was like gravel. 'Harper, you can follow me. Mia, you go with Cap. That dog of yours is keen to get in on the action.'

'Willow is not my dog.' Willow sat by Mia's leg, whimpering with excitement, her body quivering as if being held back by an invisible string. 'I don't want her to get hurt.' The cattle were so big, they were nothing like sheep who had wool to soften the impact.

'That dog is smart. And by the look of her, she's been here before. Don't worry, Cap will help you, he's a pro at this.' Charlie hobbled up a metal staircase to the thick planked walkway with Harper following while holding Mason to her chest.

'We'll be watching.' Harper encouraged little Mason to wave at her.

Wearing his tiny cowboy hat, the toddler Mason was as dirty as the rest of them, but just as excited. 'Wiwow?'

'Wil-low,' corrected Harper.

The boy moved his mouth as if mumbling the word to himself. 'Wil-low?'

'That's it, good boy.'

'Willow.' Mason's eyes were as wide as his smile as he waved at Mia and Willow. '*Willow.*'

'That's right, Mason, we'll be *Team Willow.*' Harper gave Mia a double thumbs up, with the small boy copying her.

It only filled Mia with such a rush of feel-good warmth, she had to be smiling brighter than the sun.

All morning she'd felt part of a team mustering the mob. With everyone willingly helping her, Mia felt like she belonged. Sure, she may be a farm girl, but this was different because cattle were ten times bigger than sheep and they came with pointed horns.

Used to shearing sheds, the drafting yards were bigger than she'd expected. They contained a complex maze of railed yards she had to jump or duck under to catch up with Cap, who was with his brothers in a round yard where a fire was blazing in an old fire pit.

'Good, you're here.' Cap gave her arm a squeeze before crouching down to Willow. 'Are you ready to stretch those legs, girl?' The dog loved Cap, her tongue lolling to the side as she got a hearty pat from the man.

'I'd take that as a good sign.' Dex strapped on some thick leather chaps over his denim jeans and then some thick gloves like Bree wore in the blacksmith's shed. He then removed a long rod that had been sitting amongst the hot coals of a roaring fire. 'Behold, brothers, it's *the brand.*'

He held up the metal rod like a sword under the sun, its red glowing tip a complex series of bent metal.

Dex pushed the end of the rod against an old log as smoke curled like wisps of fog around the metal edges, leaving behind a mark in the wood: *E. C. S.*

Elsie Creek Station.

Like the Riggs brothers, Mia leaned in for a closer look and raised her eyebrows in surprise. 'Oh, wow. It's so pretty and so unusual.' The letters intertwined in an intricate pattern, like old-fashioned lace, but made of steel.

'It's an original legacy brand made back in 1902.' Dex's eyes shone as if holding the holy grail. 'Charlie's grandfather made this. The patterning is flawless.'

'I see now why they call Charlie's family master brand makers.' Ash nodded with admiration while shifting the small box to his hip.

'Do they still fire-brand cattle?' Mia asked. Dumb question when they had the fire pit and the brand. 'Dad painted the sheep or branded certain ram's horns, or used tags.'

'If we don't and they wander, anyone can lay claim to them,' explained Cap. 'In the city dogs, cats, even horses get tattooed and microchipped to make them identifiable to their owners. Branding is the same for cattle, pigs, goats, even alpacas. And in the Northern Territory it's compulsory for cattle to be branded from eight months of age.'

'It's a tradition that's been around for centuries, girlie,' hollered Charlie, high on the stands. 'But you'll find no finer branding iron than that one. It's art.'

'Nothing wrong with his hearing, is there?' Ash chuckled.

'Bree? Got that salve, kid?' Charlie whistled.

'Yeah, I'm coming.' Bree climbed under the rails, dragging a heavy bucket and a large garbage bag.

'For you.' Dumping the garbage bag, Bree peeled back the bucket's lid and gave the thick goo inside a stir with a long-handled flat spoon. She then wrapped the end of the spoon with a thick cloth that soaked up the goo. 'In the garbage bag, you'll find spare rags to change these cloths when needed. I designed this flat spoon to wrap these rags around the end with a quick release, so you don't get the muck on your hands.' Bree was known for making all sorts of gadgets to make life easier, like her homemade shower. 'I'd recommend you do a change every ten brands. Toss the rags into the fire, it's not toxic, but it really arcs the flames to give you a good coal to reheat the branding iron in half the time.'

'What is it?' Dex sniffed at the goo that smelled of eucalyptus, screwing his nose at it. 'Not another one of your witchy potions, is it? Should I buy you a broomstick?'

'Listen, stormcloud, I don't mind being the villain in your story, just know that you're the clown in mine. I'll get you a costume, complete with green hair and a red nose, and I'll wear a cape. I've always wanted a cape.' Bree's green eyes sparkled with the hint of a grin, thankfully her bad mood shifting.

'What is it?' Ryder's deep voice cut through their bantering and Ash's chuckling.

'It's a herbal salve my grandmother created specifically for branding.' Bree stirred the concoction, then used the ladle like tongs to toss the rag into the flame, where it arced and hissed, turning green. Then she slid the branding iron straight into the green glowing coals. 'Don't panic, precious, it's not toxic.' Bree even winked at Mia. 'In fact, you'll be happy to hear that this salve effectively takes the sting out of the branding process, so you're not causing any harm to the beast.'

'That's a relief to hear.'

Charlie hollered from the stands. 'I use it when I get burnt on the pizza oven. Takes that sting out straight away.'

'Oh, is that the stuff you gave me, Bree?' Mia showed her arm. 'When I got burnt doing the jars when we preserved your tomatoes.'

The men looked at her face, not her arm. *Aww, come on.* She'd forgotten about the bruising on her face, because it didn't hurt anymore.

Bree gave her a soft smile. 'The same, precious.' She stirred the bucket again, putting the lid back on securely. 'The other benefit of this salve is that it helps the beasts heal quicker, like an antiseptic tattooist cream, giving you an extremely clean outline of the Elsie Creek Brand on their coats, making it harder to tamper with. It's one of the tricks of being a brand master, along with how to stoke a good coal fire to ensure the rod is hot enough. But if you want my secret recipe, you'll have to make a blood oath under a blue moon. Dex can bring his broomstick.' Bree grinned as she removed the branding iron from the fire; it was now scalding white. It was hotter than an oven. 'Want me to show you how effective it is on your rump, Dex?'

'Oi.' Dex backed away from the redhead with his hand on his butt. 'Told you I'm not your toy for anger management. I am not the bigger person my mother wanted me to be. I will hit you if you get too close with that branding iron.'

'Watch yourself.' Cap thumped Dex's shoulder while angling his head at Mia.

'Sorry, Mia. Bree and I were just mucking around.' Dex wiped a hand over his face, the remorse was so unexpectedly raw and real. 'Our mother raised us to never hurt a woman, and we've got sisters. But give me five seconds with any bloke who'd dare to raise their fists to a woman, and I'd soon sort them out.'

Coming from the professional street fighter, she believed him.

'It's fine. I know you were just sharing a joke.' Mia wished they'd stop treating her like some fragile egg, ready to fall to pieces at any second. She was made of tougher stuff than that. But the constant reminder was wearing her down.

But then she did have her first panic attack yesterday, when running from Leo. It only made her more determined to prove her mental toughness moving forward, giving them an encouraging smile.

'As long as that ointment works, we'll use it,' said Ryder. 'We appreciate it, Bree.'

'I'll add it to the bill.' Bree slid the branding iron into the large water drum with a hiss, unleashing wisps of curling steam. 'See you on the other side.'

'Where are you going?'

'Because of my grandfather's manipulation, I'll be helping Charlie with the culling calls in the pound, sorting your stock out like a croupier at a casino.'

'Oi, what's that about my calls?' Charlie barked from the balcony. 'I know what I'm doing.'

'I know, Pop. But don't get cranky when I spot something from the ground.' Bree then turned to the men; her seriousness shone in her eyes. 'And don't think that taints any of Charlie's calls. He's got half a century of experience on him.'

'I know,' said Cap. 'We're lucky to have both of you on board.'

'I don't work for you mob, remember that. Take care of Mia, Cap. And Mia? Trust what Cap has to say. Oh, and don't get jealous if I want to play with your dog in the pound.'

'Willow is not my dog.'

'Denial is not a good look on you, precious.' Bree gave the dog a pat. 'See you in there, girl.' She then adjusted her hat, tightened her gloves, and climbed a set of rails like a ladder to pick up a set of long white poles that rested on a boarded walkway. 'Let's get going. I'd like to be home before sunset, boys. I'm overdue an ice bath and a decent liver kick of gin.'

Seventeen

Ryder began strapping on a thick set of leather chaps over his jeans. To Mia they looked like the ones western cowboys wore. 'Ash, you ready?'

'I am.' Ash smiled and waved at Harper and Mason standing on the gangway at the drafting yards.

Ryder tapped the back of his hand sharply against Ash's chest. 'Oi, no show ponying stuff because your kid is watching. I want this to be an injury-free day in the yards.'

'Okay, okay. Relax, Ryder.' Ash opened the box he'd been carrying. 'I've got a hundred of these new ear tags I want to trial before producing more in the future.' He handed out a few plastic tags that looked similar to luggage tags.

'Are these the trackers you've been designing?' Cap asked, passing one to Mia, who inspected the hard plastic with numbers on one side.

'Can't you use the ear tags for identification instead of branding?' Mia brushed her thumb over the cool plastic.

'Sure, we could. But they're easy to swap out, which is why we use the brand as well.' Dex held up the tag towards the sun as if to see through it. 'What do these do, brother?'

'They've got a built-in GPS tracker to keep count of each member of the herd to never miss one in a muster,' explained Ash. 'We'll know where the pregnant cows are. Who sired what. Everything.'

'All from this.' Dex pushed his hat back as he flipped over the tag. 'Is that a solar panel?'

Ash nodded.

'What makes them different from the other tags on the market now?' Ryder asked.

'I've added an built-in alert system. If a beast stops moving, or if one of them breaches the set boundary, like if a fence is down, it'll send an alert.'

'That'll be handy.' Cap nodded with his other brothers.

'Mia?'

She looked up from the gadget at Ash.

'Cap was telling me you have a template for collecting water and soil samples.'

'I do.'

'Can you and Harper work out a way to collate the raw data from these plugs that all of us can read? Especially Cap who hates all things computers.' Ash cheekily winked at his brother.

'Sure, I'd love to.' Finally, a job not from pity, but for her skills. 'Are you saying you'll get some sort of report about your cattle, using these ear tags?'

'Absolutely. I've designed an app, so you don't need any fancy gadgets, just a smartphone that can scan the numbers if close enough, or just key the numbers into the phone. Ryder can use his satphone, until we get our intranet set up completed.' Ash gave Ryder a hopeful look.

'I'll add it to the list,' mumbled Ryder as they gathered around Ash's phone screen.

'The app will allow us to get an instant snapshot of the beast's number, vaccination history, age, frame size, how many calves they've had and what their sex was, with room to add comments like deformed horn, crooked nose, cranky ass.' Ash aimed his phone at the plug and the app displayed a screen he scrolled over to show the information they had access too.

With a stick from the nearby wood pile, Ash drew a diagram in the dirt. 'I've got cameras set at these peak points in my paddock here… Here… And here. To give me a clear overview. Harper hooked me up to some cloud to record the information, and if we keep using the satellite images for comparison, we'll be able to use all that data to estimate how much feed we'll need for the herd, the nutrients they'll receive in the pasture grasses that Mia's helping Cap grow, through to the water quality in the troughs. With the bonus of me training the cattle to get used to the drones to muster them from sections I'll cut off from Cap and Mia's plan for crop rotations. I'll be able to automate the entire process all from the comfort of my gaming chair, saving us a tonne in fossil fuels and labour.'

'Wow, that is brilliant.' Mia was as excited as Ash. She'd never realised her in-depth conversations with Cap had been shared already to make something like this possible. 'My dad and brother would kill for this type of tech.'

'So all those hours playing video games are paying off?' Dex playfully mussed up Ash's hat like he was a boy.

'Good work, Ash.' Ryder patted his younger brother on the shoulder. 'Have you patented these tags yet?'

'Huh?' Ash screwed his nose up, giving a shrug.

'That's a good idea.' Cap nodded. 'Our little brother might be sitting on a goldmine.'

Mia nodded, even if it was none of her business.

'Remind me when we get home to talk about patents for your tech gadgets, Ash.' Ryder tossed the tag back into the box. 'Do you want to do a random test from the cattle going to your paddock and the bush paddock?'

Ash nodded, hope filling his eyes. 'I'd love that. I just didn't think you guys would want to use them with the herd.'

Ryder rested his hands on his hips. 'Does anyone object to Ash's cattle tags being used as a test on our beef?'

'Oi, I'm all in,' said Cap, giving Mia a sly wink. 'I saw the potential of Ash's plans a while back. It'll be good to see it finally happen.'

'Thanks, Cap.' Ash dropped his head to hide under the brim of his hat.

'No way, the lad's gone all humble. That's rare.' Dex playfully punched his brother's shoulder. 'Well done, brother. I'm keen to see it in action.'

That left Ryder, who gave a nod. 'Let's do this.'

Ash scooped up the box. 'So, I'll be tagging them?'

Again, Ryder nodded as he assisted Dex with a stack of tools and a metal looking cradle. 'Cap, you know what to do. Mia, you would've helped your father with the sheep?'

'Before you delegate Mia to work, I want her to help me with Willow.' Cap tugged on her sleeve. 'This way, Mia.'

'Let me see if I've got this right...' She faltered as he half-stepped, half-turned towards her, and bumped into him. 'Sorry.'

Cap's warm hands held her arms, to send a scurry of tingles to rush beneath her skin. 'I think you should stop saying sorry when you have nothing to be sorry about.'

'Sss—' She lifted her shoulders to her earlobes. 'It's a habit.'

'I noticed. Like the way you twist your fingers when nervous.' He stared at her for a beat, then those delicious malt-whisky eyes roamed over her face before turning away. 'What were you saying?' Cap adjusted his long-legged gait to match hers. He did that a lot, stopping to let her catch up, even lowering his head to match her height, always asking her opinion.

But he was also her boss, and after what she'd been through, could she really trust her feelings?

She cleared her throat, getting head back in the game as they walked through the yards. 'If it's like sheep, we'd herd them into the yard, pushing them down the chutes where we'd vaccinate them, shear them. Is this similar?'

'Close. We want to maintain a decent herd, and with Charlie's incredible experience, he'll help us cull our stock. We don't want any beasts with defects or bad temperaments. We're looking for clean coats, no scaling on their necks, and decent body frames.'

'How do you cull them?' All she saw was a shifting sea of white coats.

'Where Bree is, that's what we call the pound.' He pointed

to the smaller round pen under the shade of the tall, corrugated roof, where Charlie stood high on the boardwalk, with Bree on the other side.

'It looks like a small show jumping arena.'

'Each beast will enter the pound to be inspected. Bree will manage the network of gates, like a sorting yard, where Charlie will call out to Bree which gate to send the beast through. Half of these will go into Ash's paddock. Hopefully, it'll be our paddock in the next muster.'

She stopped still, as the heat washed through her chest as her smile grew. *Ours?*

But it shouldn't be like this when they'd only just met.

Cap kept walking towards the back pen, only to stop and wait for her, again. 'There's also a poddy gate for the little guys that have lost their mothers or those smaller weaners that need a little extra help. They'll score a truck ride back to the homestead's yards, which Dex has finished repairing. They'll live there for a few months under the care of the guardian dogs.'

Again, they walked in unison, side by side, his gait easy with the smooth confidence of someone who knew and loved this land. She'd never known anyone to have such a sexy stride.

'When are you collecting the guardian dogs?' She liked hearing him speak, even more when his eyes locked onto hers, where the hint of a smile showed she'd asked the right questions on topics he cared about.

'The vet has organised someone to bring them out.'

'And *our* job?' It slipped out, but it felt right saying it.

'We'll be the backyarders, pushing the cattle through the chutes.' Cap bent under a metal rail, his hand out to help her. She'd noticed that was a habit of his: opening doors for her, pulling out a chair, always offering her the first choice of food or drinks, treating her like a lady—she'd never been so spoiled.

'Our job is to guide the herd through, while keeping watch over Bree, who'll need to have eyes in the back of her head to watch what's coming down the race. There's nothing more terrifying than a beast snorting just behind your ear.' Cap physically shivered. 'We need to keep the pace slow and gentle on the animals, so no rushing them. We only want Willow to push them through one at a time.'

'Do you think she can do it?'

'Like I said, I've got Atlas and Fern to show her how, and from what I've seen, Willow is an experienced working dog. Her natural instincts will kick in, and our job is to harness what she loves to do.' Cap gave a different whistle she hadn't heard before, and the two cattle dogs trotted over as the rest of the pack rested in the shade by the water troughs. 'It's time to bring the masters into the game. This way we'll get a tonne of practice in for the local campdraft.'

'Where you take your show dogs—sorry, I mean the dogs you want to show.'

'Eh?' He arched an eyebrow at her.

'My dad was always telling me off if I said show dogs, he said it sounded like they were going to sing show tunes and do high kicks in some conga line.'

Never had a laugh sounded sexier on a man. 'Are you ready to see what Willow can do?'

Eighteen

'*B*ush. *Bush. Pit. Bush. Bush. Heifer. BLOCK UP—fat cow!*' Charlie's voice was loud from his place high above the rails, where he carried Mason in the baby carrier strapped across his chest, as he looked over the condition of each beast that entered the pound.

'*Bush. Heifer. Pit. Bush.*'

'No. Look at him, Pop. His hindquarters are crooked.' Bree and her grandfather would haggle over the condition of certain animals before she let them through the correct gates. 'He's a fat that's due his day at the markets.'

'I taught you well.' Charlie tipped his hat to Bree, who was using the levers on the far side shutting the gate from the high boards. Charlie turned his pencil to erase his tick on the clipboard. 'Keep 'em coming, Harper.'

Harper waved the long sticks to urge the cattle to move along the narrow chutes and the drafting process continued.

'So let me get this straight,' Mia asked Cap. 'They're sorting cattle into separate holding pens, the paddock, or into the pit where Ash, Dex, and Ryder are busy branding and tagging.'

'What my brothers are doing will take weeks to finish. Bree and Charlie are sorting this herd into groups.'

'They move so quickly.'

'That's what we call the coachers. They've been here before and know what to do. That's the group we used the dogs to hold them back because they're keen to get back into the paddock.'

'Oh, that's the first group?'

Cap nodded. 'You'll notice,' he said, pointing to the nearby paddock, 'they've got ear tags, and are already branded.'

They were also very calm as they walked through the railed corridors to end up in one of the nearby paddocks that had a few large bales of hay waiting for them.

'What happens to them?'

'They'll get walked back to another paddock in a week or two.' Cap gave a satisfied nod. 'The others will need a little more hands-on animal husbandry and they'll be set aside for the vet's visit.'

'For what?'

'Castration, spaying, pregnant testing. It's a process that prevents unwanted breeding traits in livestock, and to control some unruly bulls. We're after quality in our herds.'

'It really is a process, isn't it.'

'It is. But the bonus is, Bree and Charlie are super quick in their calling. Come on, I'd hate to keep them waiting.' Again, Cap whistled for the dogs, the cattle flowed down the railed chute, the gates clanged and the drafting calls continued.

'Heifer. Heifer. Fat cow. Pit. Bush. Bush...'

'BULL COMING.' Cap's voice was loud. It made everyone take pause as they watched the massive beast barely fit through the narrow chutes. Even Dex, Ryder and Ash paused to lean over the fence as the proud beast entered the main arena.

'Hello there, big fella.' Charlie poked up the brim of his hat, leaning his boot on the rail, holding Mason to his chest in the baby carrier. 'Are you ready to retire yet, mate?'

'Should we?' Dex asked his brothers.

'He's a good-looking animal.' Even Ryder removed his sunglasses to look at the proud beast.

Bree fearlessly jumped down into the pen and held out something in her hand.

'Bree!' Ryder and Dex both started to climb the rails.

Mia gasped, grabbing the nearest thing—Cap's arm,

which was all muscle.

'Settle, cupcake. This fender bender and I are old friends. Hello, Freckles.' With a dusting around his nose that looked like freckles, the bull sniffed at Bree's hand, then his tongue flickered out to eat the treat she'd offered.

'I remember when Bree brought Freckles home from school one day. He was a sickly-looking poddy calf she had to bottle-feed,' explained Charlie. 'Flamin' weakling he was.'

'Not so small now.' With arms leaning over the rails, Ash pointed at the bull. 'How did you manage to keep him around, when those contractors came through the place?'

'You can thank Bree for that.'

'Pop, you don't need to tell all our secrets.'

'It's true. Bree refused to let that big boofhead get taken by the contracting mob that was stripping the place bare. It's what gave me the idea of selecting this mob and taking them out to Wombat Flats. We could only do a few at a time so they didn't notice.' Charlie sheepishly shrugged from the high boards, to adjust Mason on his chest.

'Bull,' said the boy.

'That's right, mate,' said Charlie. 'An old bull.'

'No, he's not.' Bree tickled the bull's chin while she looked over his stance; he arched his neck and groaned as if she'd hit some secret spot. 'He's got a few more seasons yet before he retires. Sorry boys, I'm making an executive decision on this one… Straight back to the bush paddock you go, Freckles.' Bree swung open the wide gate and patted the beast's massive rump. 'You go play nice with the ladies, ya hear.'

The bull snorted, and with his wide horns he casually ambled through the open gates to head for the large bale of hay waiting on the other side. And the drafting process began again.

'Bush. Bush. Heifer. Pit. Fat cow…'

'We'll pick that one. It's had long enough to polish the rails.' Cap pointed to the massive beast. 'But it's your turn to start telling Willow what to do.' Cap gave her an encouraging nod. '*Rest up, dogs. Willow, stay.*' He handed Mia the long and light poles to help her guide the dog and beasts. 'I don't think you'll need these poles for long.'

The confidence he showed in not only Willow, but Mia, made her heart bloom for the man. It was an intoxicating emotion she could easily get addicted to.

But she needed to focus. Mia gripped the thin rods, not expecting any miracles, not when she feared for the dog's safety.

Yet Willow was eagerly looking up at her, then at the cattle, then up at her, obediently waiting for the command as her sweeping tail created a small dust cloud.

'*Away,*' Mia said to Willow.

The dog bolted, lightning fast.

'*Take time…*'

And she lowered her lithe body as if stalking the beast.

The other cattle shifted aside, and it wasn't long before Willow had the beast singled out.

Mia hesitated. 'What now?'

'Point to where you want the dog to push the beast.' Cap's breath was so warm in her ear, his hand ever so lightly rested on her waist, that even though he wasn't touching skin, it felt like it.

'In the beginning, muster dogs will follow seventy per cent of your hand signals and the rest by voice. Just use the simple commands I taught you. It'd be good if you can whistle.'

'Nope. Never could.' Not like Cap, who could control a dozen cattle dogs at once like magic.

'All yours.' He stepped back, giving her room.

She swallowed hard, as a nervous bead of sweat trickled from her forehead, and her stomach swirled with the fear of doing something new. What if she stuffed up? What if Willow got hurt? What if—

'You've got this, Mia.' The simple pat on her shoulder gave her the courage to try.

'*Come round.*' She pointed towards the open chute where

the beast hesitated to go through.

Earlier, when the holding pen had been full, the beasts pushed through so willingly. But now the herd was thinning, the ones left were more cunning, they were what Cap called *the ferals*, the cattle who hadn't seen a human before.

Mia was learning quickly about the process and knew to react fast whenever Cap would shout *Run!* And she'd run for the nearest fence to climb. The first few times, Cap gripped her rump to hoist her fast over the rails, where they'd land in the dirt with a thud, laughing at each other, while the beast stood on the other side of the fence, snorting at them.

'Come on, my little dirt bunny,' he'd say to her, holding his hand out to help her to her feet, where they'd dust themselves off, adjust their hats and climb back inside to do it all over again.

The adrenaline rush was intoxicating, and through Cap, she'd learned to love the game. He'd given her the confidence, yet treated her like an equal, even though he was teaching her the process of using the muster dogs.

Willow ran in semicircles back and forth, yapping and nipping at the beast's heels, then it dropped its head and huge horns at the edge of the open chute, dragging its front hoof as if to charge.

'Oh, no.' She wanted to scream at Willow to run.

Cap dropped his hand on her shoulder and gave it a squeeze. 'Willow's got this. Tell her.'

'*Steady…*' Mia tried to keep her voice steady as she swallowed hard, the fear creeping up her spine.

But Willow held her ground.

'*Put 'em in.*'

Willow dashed around those large hooves, barking at the beast, and eventually it moved through the chute as if to escape the pesky canine.

'She did it.' Mia clapped, all jittery with joy, and patted Willow.

'Good job, Willow. Now, let's do the rest.' Cap pointed at the rest of the herd. 'You've got this; both of you have.' He even took away her poles.

Mia adjusted her hat, feeling the responsibility of the job, but also the fun, and the pure joy of Willow responding to her commands as they worked as a team in a whole new way. *'Willow, look back.'* Mia pointed to the herd that was still there. *'Go round and bring them in… Steady.'*

Willow's little paws and sleek body ducked, weaved, rounded and danced among the hooves of the heavy beasts. Her eyes kept an intense focus, but the doggy smile was undeniable. Willow was a natural at this, even with a few muck-ups from Mia's commands. *'Go back. Wait…'* She'd look at Cap as the dog looked at Mia with confusion, after she'd split the herd into two groups.

'Where do you want the dog to go?' Cap gently coached her, standing behind her, offering loads of encouragement, while letting Mia have control. 'Start small, go for that one.'

Cap pointed at a beast, and Mia sent in Willow to single it out, and escort it to the chute. From there Cap had her commanding Willow to do groups of two, then three, even five.

'Dammit! Gate's jammed.' Bree's voice rose over the dust. *'Cap, I need to borrow a dog to hold them back.'*

'No worries. Call for Willow. She's ready to try, like you said.' He grabbed Mia's arm. 'Hold on the commands, let Bree run her for a bit.'

'What's going on?'

'Bree will use Willow to help keep the cattle back in the chute while she works on the gate,' explained Cap. 'Bree has to watch her back especially while the beasts are nearby.'

'Willow, come.' Bree whistled like Cap did for the dog. 'Harper, use your pole to stop the flow in that chute.'

'I'm trying,' cried out Harper from the rails.

'Want me to help, babe?' It was Ash, ripping off his gloves.

'Harper can do it,' said Bree, giving Harper an encouraging nod.

'Hello, girl. Ready to earn your dog biscuits.' Bree patted

the kelpie, then pointed. '*Willow. Block.*'

The dog got low, barking as it approached the chute.

'*Low, Willow. Hold.*'

Willow followed the simple commands and kept the cattle still.

'Keep an eye on them, Pop.'

'I will, kid. You fix that gate.'

'Ash, I could do with a bit of muscle.' Together Bree and Ash worked on the gate, as Cap and Mia held back the cattle from entering the chute, while Harper managed the cattle inside the chutes to a standstill where their assorted lowing were raised in complaint.

Finally, the gate swung free.

'We didn't fix it right,' said Ash, giving it another swing.

'Listen, snowflake, we've almost done three-quarters of the herd. It's been a dream run until that jam.' She playfully tapped Ash's hat brim. 'It'll hold for today, but you can add it to that whiteboard you boys have up at the farmhouse, to fix later.'

'We will.' Ryder gave a firm nod, watching on with Dex by the fire pit.

Mia noticed they were all ready to jump in. Just like Harper had said: the brothers would drop everything to help.

'Are we ready?' called out Charlie from the high boards.

Bree dropped to one knee to give the dog of hug. 'Good job, Willow. Go back to Mia. Let's do this…' Bree adjusted her hat, and climbed back up the rails, as Willow zipped under the rails with her tongue lolling to the side, eager for more.

'Well done, Willow.' Mia had never been so proud of a dog. She now understood why her dad loved the kelpie breed so much.

But she also had respect for Cap's cattle dogs, too. The heelers were a barbed-wire-tough type of dog breed. They were fearless enough to tackle anything, especially when Willow shied away, and Cap would send in Atlas and Fern, where the trio of dogs worked as a team.

As the sun trekked its path across the sky, the dust rose, and time flew until Charlie gave the last command, *'Bush. Bush. And that's beer o'clock everyone.'* Charlie waved his hat in the air as the final clang of the gate sent the last beasts to join the rest of the bush herd, who were happily grazing.

'Take a swim, dogs.' Cap gave the command and Atlas, Fern, with Willow following. The dogs eagerly jumped into a nearby cattle trough to splash in the water.

It was the best place to be at the end of a long day under an outback sun. Mia now understood why Bree had her own trough to slip into at the end of the day at the back of the caretaker's cottage to watch the sunset.

'Well done, you mob. Bloody good job, all of you.' Charlie clambered down the steps with Mason still strapped to his chest to pat the kelpie. 'Oi, that Willow is something special, for sure, Cap. You've gotta good one there.'

'I agree. Except Willow's Mia's dog.' Cap winked at her. 'Stop denying it. Willow listened to you.'

'And Bree. Especially in the pound. I was so worried they'd both get hurt.' A few times Bree threw herself over the fence, only to scowl, then jump straight back in. Her long rod sang like a whip and her commands were fierce and sharp. *'Get in there or you'll be lunch meat.'*

'I know that feeling,' said Harper, joining them. 'There's no way I could jump the rails like Bree did.'

'And that will be the last time I do it, too.' Bree flipped herself over the rails and tore off her gloves. 'I'm too old for the pound, Pop.'

'No, you're not, kid.'

'I'm in my dirty thirties. It's a young mug's game to jump in the pound and hike those fences. I ache all over, my shins are bruised, I've got a whopping big lump on my thigh, I'm covered in cattle slobber, and I'm sick of wiping yard dust off my teeth. For what? It's not our cattle, Pop. We don't get a share in the profits, remember that.' She then turned to Cap. 'Next time you lot can train a jackeroo in the pound. I'm done. I'm officially retiring from the drafting yards. Here, now and forever.'

'Aw, come on, kid.'

'Stop, Pop.' Bree glared at her grandfather, wiping hard at the dust and dirt from her cheek. 'My social battery needs a decent recharge, and all my empathy pills have well and truly left my bloodstream, which leaves me in a bad mood that needs some serious cooling off. I'm. Done.' Her boots kicked up the dust as she headed for her horse and quickly set about resaddling it.

Ash sauntered over. 'Where's Bree going?'

'Kid needs to blow off some steam,' replied Charlie.

'But we were going to have a few beers and a barbecue to thank you guys for your help. Harper made salads.'

'We're always having a barbecue. What's the difference?' asked Harper.

'Only until you can use an oven and not burn the house down, babe.' He kissed her cheek.

'Ugh, you reek.' Harper screwed up her nose, pushing Ash away.

'We all do. And look at little Miss Snooty, all dirty as well.' He went to hug Harper. When she squealed and ran off he gave chase, their laughter making Mia smile.

'Where's Bree going?' Ryder pointed to Bree climbing onto her horse.

'Home.' Charlie narrowed his eyes at her. 'Best we steer clear of her for a bit. Bree's tired and cranky. But she did a good job. You all did. Over a thousand head got sorted today it'd almost be a record.' Charlie adjusted his hat, with the toddler still strapped to his chest. 'You've got a good-lookin' herd, with a few fats this time round.'

'To sell, right?' Cap asked his brothers.

Ryder nodded as he spoke to Charlie. 'Cap mentioned you might know of a stock agent.'

'Bree's got somethin' sorted for you mob. I reckon they'll either be here tonight or tomorrow.'

'I hope tomorrow.' Dex dragged off his hat and wiped at his brow with his sleeve. 'I'm beat. You must be too, Ryder.

You and Bree have been up all night.'

Ryder began unclipping the straps of his chaps, his eyes narrowing in on Bree riding away. 'Charlie, please tell Bree thanks for us. And when she won't snap my head off, I'll go see what she wants for her time and effort. That woman worked her arse off for us, fellas, and she's not even on our payroll.' He shook his head, annoyance showing in his frown. 'Come find me when the stock agent shows up.' He tossed the chaps over his shoulders and sauntered off to the waiting helicopter.

The helicopter's engine started with a whir, the blades began spinning, the dust stirring, and with a lazy salute, Ryder steered the helicopter for the homestead.

'Come on, Mia, we're nearly done, then you can have a nice hot shower.' Cap tugged on her shirtsleeve, and they set about packing up for the day.

In a small convoy of vehicles, they left the drafting yards with Ash leading the way on his ag bike. Charlie, Harper and Mason were in the Razorback carrying the bulk of the muster dogs on the back. Mia had Willow with her on the quad, riding beside Cap who had Atlas and Fern with him. And bringing up the rear was Dex in the truck carting the stockhorses and calves that they all helped deliver to the new paddock, before returning to the homestead.

Ash pointed while riding his ag bike. '*Visitors*.'

It was the police paddy wagon, parked out front of the caretaker's cottage.

Mia slowed her quad down. She wanted to hide in the shed, where Charlie parked the Razorback alongside Ash's bike, and Dex's truck.

Cap rode over to her side. 'Look, it's Porter. He's bringing out the guardian dogs for me. Come on.' His grin was wide as he rode the quad to the cottage, parking near the front fence that contained the flower garden. Ryder and Bree were out the front talking to the policeman.

'*Willow*,' the cop called out.

The dog gave a bright yip. With tail wagging, she raced

over and jumped straight into Porter's arms.

'Look at you, girl.' Porter gave the dog a hug, as she eagerly licked at his face, then did circles of joy at his boots. 'How has she been, Cap?'

'Brilliant. Willow was incredible in the drafting yards today. It proved she's had some training or came from a farm. Any ideas over who owned her?'

'No. She wasn't microchipped or anything when I found her. We put up notices around town, but no one claimed her. That's when Ryan microchipped her for me, and I've brought the paperwork to sign her over.' Porter looked so sad handing the file to Cap.

'You can give that to Mia. It's her dog. You'll be happy to know that Willow chose Mia, and they make a great team together.' Cap grinned, his teeth so white against the dirt and dust from a very long day.

'What the hell!' Porter ripped off his sunglasses and peered at Mia. 'Are you okay, miss?'

'You'd better tell him your story,' said Dex, leaning against the paddy wagon with Ryder beside him. 'Or Porter's gonna think we're the animals who did that to you.'

'No, they didn't.' Mia tried to hide the bruises on her face with her hand. She'd been having such a great day that was now ruined.

'Pull up, Porter, stop being a policeman for a sec and listen,' said Bree, leaning over the fence of the cottage garden. 'Mia has been staying on my couch and before you lecture me for not calling you —'

'It's mandatory to report any form of domestic violence in the Northern Territory. You and Charlie know this, Bree.' Porter glared at Charlie.

'*Of course I do!*' Bree shoved open the gate, wagging her finger at the cop with her eyes dark and dangerous. 'None of us were witnesses to the event, because Mia showed up like that. And before you say anything, Porter, I asked Mia many times to call you to report the sociopath who dared to treat her like that. Believe me when I say I want you to lock the prick up, but only *after* I've performed my special brand of dental work on that prick's teeth!' Her angry words echoed over the compound.

'Easy, Bree…' Ryder's deep voice may have been low, but somehow it got through to the angry redhead.

Bree took a deep, calming breath and stepped back. 'Mia declined to report the incident. It's her body, it's her choice. And now that you've met Mia, who is taking good care of Willow, you should give her one of your fancy police cards in case she changes her mind.'

'Cranky much.' Porter removed a notebook as he approached Mia. 'Hi, I'm Senior Constable Porter, but everyone calls me Porter. And you're Mia who?'

'Mia Dixon.'

'Don't tell him that. The copper will do a name search now,' muttered Dex.

'Mia is *not* a criminal.' Cap thumped Dex's shoulder.

'I'm okay, Constable. Really, I'm fine.' Mia hoped the policeman understood. 'Everyone at Elsie Creek Station has been amazing towards me.'

'I know they're good people.' Porter's brown eyes were filled with a genuine concern as he looked over the bruises Mia wished she could hide. 'Here's my card if you ever change your mind. I'm here to help people. I can help you, if you let me.'

'Save yourself the paperwork, I'm sure my ex is long gone by now.' There was nothing keeping Gavin here, not now the new lithium mine's plans had been scuttled. As an experienced diesel fitter for the mines, Gavin could get work anywhere.

She also realised this was the first time she'd thought of Gavin and not shudder in terror. She was not going to let her ex ruin a perfectly good day. 'I'm fine, I swear it.'

'If Mia says she's fine, it's enough for me.' Cap gave her one of his sly winks that always made her smile. 'So, did you bring the dogs out?'

'I did.' Porter juggled his keys and unlocked the back

cage.

'Listen, everyone,' called out Cap, holding the cage door. 'No offence, but I'd rather there weren't too many people around for this. How would you feel having all these strangers gawking at you.'

'Point taken,' said Porter. 'Charlie, while I'm here, I was hoping you'd show me the car you found in the Stoneys.'

'Did you learn something about my brother?' Charlie's grey eyes filled with hope.

'No. But I have paperwork you can fill out to claim the money he left in the bank.'

'I'm not after the money. I just want to know where Harry is.'

'Pop, think about it,' warned Bree. 'Harry ran away for a reason. Do you really want your older brother to face murder charges and the possibility of spending his last days in prison?'

Mia's eyes widened with surprise at the reminder that Charlie's brother was a murderer on the run. Did she dare ask the details?

Charlie hesitated, dragging his hat off his head as if it weighed a tonne. 'I didn't think about that.'

'Charlie, I'm only working on a missing person's report, like you asked me to.' Porter gently patted the old man's shoulder. 'And I'd like to check out the car for clues as part of my preliminary enquiries. That's it.'

'Well, okay then, Harry's car is this way. You can tell me what you think of the work these boys did in restoring it. And Cap can settle in his new dogs.'

'Want me to come with you, Pop?'

'Nah, I'm good. You take a shower, kid, and get your jug of gin. You deserve it. This way, Porter.' Charlie patted the police officer's back as he led him off, his bandy-legged walk seemed weary.

'Psst, Dex? Do me a favour and go play babysitter for me until I get my jug of gin and play catch-up?' Bree angled her head at Charlie and Porter.

'No worries. Don't forget to bring me a glass.' Dex trotted after them.

'Bree, before you go?' Ryder held open the gate. 'Thank you for today.'

'I didn't do it for you.'

'I know. But I'd like to give you a bonus for your work.'

'I don't work for you. You don't own me, and you can't buy me. I'm here for Charlie. What I did today was for Charlie. But that was the last time I'll do the pound again for anyone. And you can forget putting me near the pit, I'm no one's dogsbody in the drafting yards.'

'But your skills in cattle selection were spot on. I heard you correcting Charlie.'

'Because I was on the ground, wiping the yard dust off my teeth. Charlie is and will always be the king of the drafting yards to me. I may correct him, but the man taught me.'

'Just know we appreciate—'

'Stop sucking up to me, cupcake, when it's Charlie you need to thank.' She turned away, closing the cottage door with a bang.

'The cranky, irritating, pig-headed, redhead! I wasn't sucking up.' Ryder scowled at the closed door.

Cap gave a low chuckle from the back of the paddy wagon. 'Mia? Now that the crowd has thinned out, can you put Willow inside the cottage yard with Atlas and Fern while Ryder and I get these dogs out?'

'Sure.' Mia hustled the three dogs into the front yard filled with assorted flowers, closing the chest-high gate she peered over to watch.

Ryder opened the heavy cage door at the back of the police paddy wagon and out jumped two massive, white and woolly dogs.

'Now I know why Harper kept calling them bears.'

'They're big enough to scare off a dingo, I hope,' said Ryder, inspecting the dogs. 'At least they're bigger than those wild dogs we saw.' He frowned, standing tall to face the farmhouse. 'Which reminds me to check on those cameras.'

'Do you think there's any truth to what Dex said about those wild dogs being deliberately brought out here?' Cap asked.

'Last night, Bree told me they've never had wild dogs before, just a few dingoes that never bothered them because they kept the poddy calves close.' He leaned down and patted the big dog. 'How soon before you can put these dogs to work with the calves we've brought in?'

'I'll start training them tomorrow. You can help me, if you want, Mia.'

'Really?' She loved how Cap included her in his adventures.

Cap looked like a kid with some shiny new toys. 'What do you think? They'll make an excellent addition to the pack.'

'They're gorgeous cuddly bears. They're coats match the colour of the calves, they'd blend in well.'

'That's the plan.'

'Won't the heat bother them?' Considering how thick those coats looked she couldn't tell if they were male or female. But she itched to hug them to see how thick that fur was.

'No. It's a self-insulation. They're from the Top End and are used to our climate.'

'Are they soft like a bear?' She reached out to touch the pelt, but Willow nudged her leg. 'Don't get jealous, girl.' She patted the kelpie instead.

'I'll get these two settled and come back for Atlas and Fern.' Cap walked the dogs towards the kennels.

Ryder leaned his elbow over the gate, watching his brother. 'How long are you planning on staying, Mia?'

'Um…' She swallowed. 'I don't know. But I can help. Seriously, I can.' Now she was the one doing the sucking up. 'I understand what Ash wants for the data. I'll train Cap and Ash to do the soil and water samples, and—'

'We do have plenty of work for you, and you will be fairly compensated for your skill set.'

'I'm not here for the money.'

'No, you're using this station as a place to hide.' Ryder's brutal words were cutting. Yet, he was right. Cold, but right.

Ryder removed his sunglasses to give her a steady glare. 'Just don't break my brother's heart. And don't abuse Charlie and Bree's generosity, either. They've been through enough.'

He left Mia stunned, holding the card of a police officer, alone with three dogs, standing in the yard of a stranger who had given her a couch to crash on, feeding her and even clothing her.

Hold the phone—did Cap like her enough for his big brother to warn her off?

Was it too soon for her to face the fear of falling for someone new, when the marks across her skin had yet to fully heal?

Nineteen

The front door of the cottage swung open, and Bree swaggered out, tossing her thick red plait over her shoulder, her face still dirty and her eyes blazing green. She was carrying a big jug full of a lemon-coloured liquid, with cut limes, and a handful of glasses.

'Here, Mia. Try this.' She poured Mia a glass.

'I thought you were having a shower?'

'I'll get there. Gin first. It's a new bottle. Don't worry, I'm breaking you in gently. Come on.' With her hip, she pushed open the gate, allowing the dogs free.

'But I'm supposed to look after the dogs.'

'Cap will have those new dogs in their kennels by now, or they'll follow you.' Bree held open the gate. 'Come check out the car we found.'

Trying not to spill her glass, Mia and the three dogs trotted after Bree. 'Can I ask you something?'

'Sure. Just don't ask about being a bother, again. You're not.'

'Um, well…' She was.

Bree stopped. She was so much taller, and stronger that her shadow engulfed Mia's. 'Fine, I'll say it again. You're more than welcome to stay as long as you like. Don't worry about me, I just get cranky sometimes. It happens and I won't apologise for it, especially when I live here.' She held out her jug to Mia and clinked it against her glass. 'You know how family put up with each other's faults?'

'Yeah, of course. That's family.'

'Do I need to explain what my faults are? Because we'll be here a month before we even get halfway through my list.' Her grin was wide, her eyes sparkly, full of mischief.

'Does that mean we're family? Charlie told me you'd be an instant best friend.'

Bree's laugh filled the air as she nudged one of Mia's shoulders. 'That. Or you can just call us your found family. But you should also call your family.'

'I don't know what to say.'

'How about telling them where you are, for starters? Was that what you wanted to ask me about?'

'Um… no.' She stopped and stared at the dirt. 'It's silly.' Her fingers fidgeted with the cool glass. 'Is it wrong to be attracted to someone when I'm…' She pointed at her face.

Bree tilted her head and didn't speak for the longest time. 'You and Cap, huh?'

'I just copped the *don't hurt my brother* speech from Ryder.'

'Really?' Bree spun around on her boots to face the farmhouse wearing a cheesy grin. 'Maybe there is a heart beating under that cupcake's ice façade, after all.'

'You don't think it's wrong? Or too soon?'

'No one can tell you what's right or wrong. Only you can know that. My grandmother always said a girl has to trust her intuition. For some it's that feeling in their heart, or that shifting in the gut, or that tingly feeling on the back of your neck. But it's there for a reason, if you listen. And I bet its saying nice things about Cap.'

Mia shrugged. What was there not to like about the guy who filled her with hope and warmth. Yet, she did feel a deep gratitude for him every time he asked her a question about the job she loved, that he'd hired her to do. But it was much more than that. Especially when those malt-whisky eyes locked on hers to give her a curt nod when she did something right, she wanted to smile at the sun.

He'd been so gentle teaching her to work with the muster dogs. Those moments when he'd stand right behind her, keeping his tone low and smooth as if nothing would ruffle him, and how his voice slid across her skin like silk to wrap itself around her, unleashing a shiver to skate down her spine.

'You like Cap. He likes you. What's the problem?' Bree shrugged.

'I'm supposed to be heartbroken over Gavin.'

'Oh, right? Because who said so?'

'I don't know.' She tugged at her hair in frustration, feeling the dirt and dust embedded in it.

'Okay, how long were you with Gavin?'

'A few months. It was pretty serious. He wanted me to look at the farm, said it could be ours.'

'So he knew what you wanted to keep you happy?'

Mia nodded. 'Gavin accepted my faults.'

Bree arched an eyebrow.

'I—I—' She swallowed hard. 'I can't have children.'

Bree didn't move, didn't flinch, didn't react at all. 'And this bothers you because…'

'When I was younger, I grew to accept it. As I got older and with my first few relationships, I didn't say anything. But when they found out, the good guys left me.'

'No, sweetie, good guys don't do that. You're not a heifer, you're a human being.'

'But Cap is a good man, and he's amazing with his nephew. He'd make a wonderful father.'

'Sure. He'd be brilliant at it.'

Mia dropped her head, feeling Bree watching her. 'I've never had difficulty falling in love. It's the staying in love I can't seem to figure out. I know this makes me sound pessimistic , but when a woman can't have children, I learned that only a certain type of guy will accept that idea. And Gavin he was…' She didn't want to say it, but Bree patiently waited. So with a deep breath, and on a whisper she finally admitted the truth, 'Gavin wasn't the best. He wasn't a good guy.'

She lifted her head expecting to be judged for her poor

judgement. 'I think I knew that already, but...' Again, another long pause, she couldn't help but give a pleading face to Bree to fill that awkward silence.

'Let me guess, I'd say he's *not the forever* type of guy, but the chemistry is just too damn intense to ignore, especially when his touch sets you on fire and his kisses make you crave more. Oh, and don't forget how he draws you in with his charm to not only break the rules, but your heart, and sometimes your bones, before you learn that everything about him is wrong. Yet you can't stay away, while he cleverly pushes all your friends and family away leaving you to think that all you have is him.'

Mia's eyes widened and she stepped back from the redhead who had somehow cracked her open to peer deep into the well of secrets that Mia had hidden from herself.

'Maybe the reason you can't stay in love is because you're picking the wrong kind of guys because you don't think you deserve better. When you deserve the best kind of guy. A good romantic partner makes everything in life easier and they will add value to your life,' Bree said. 'A bad romantic partner makes everything more difficult. You learn to walk on eggshells, watching for the signs, the secret codes, the unwritten rules that bend and twist the way light flows through a prism, waiting, wondering when he's going to snap. Most of all, you learn to not feel, because they've pushed you so much that if you don't feel, you have nothing to fear because they can't hurt you then.'

Mia felt the tears stinging her eyes, never feeling more exposed. 'How do you know?'

Bree remained eerily calm. 'I know. Believe me, I know. I also know the power of learning to fight for yourself, for what is right for you. You need to be true and fierce in your beliefs. And all that can be summed up in one word: *Fearless.*' She then pointed at Mia's chest. 'You have that inside. I saw it today in the yards. Pop saw it in you, last night while spotlighting. You are far stronger than you realise, Mia.'

Bree then sighed, her voice and stance softening. 'You

shouldn't see the fact that you can't have children as a fault. It's just a part of who you are, like me, with my red hair. I know I'm simplifying it, but you said you'd accepted it already, which shows how strong you are. And if a person can't accept you for you, and decide to use your infertility — that you see as a flaw — against you as a form of control, they don't deserve to even share the same air you breathe. You, my friend are imperfectly perfect.'

Mia wanted to hug the woman, standing there sipping gin, while covered in dust and dirt.

Bree once again nudged Mia's shoulder. 'If you feel Cap is right for you, go for it. Forget what the world is telling you, when it's you who has to live with your decisions. And if I had a vote, I'd say fate brought you here for a reason.'

Hope filled her chest as she looked up at Bree. 'Cap believes in fate.'

'I know he does.' Bree gave a schemer's wink. 'Come on, let's go hassle these boys, before Pop spills too many secrets to the police.'

The men's voices greeted them as they walked into the shed. 'Anyone care for a thirst quencher?'

The shed was like a garage with a wide workbench, filled with assorted tools, that ran the length of one wall. On one side was a deep pit with stairs to allow them to work under the cars, the other bay held a hoist.

'Not another witch's brew?' Dex mumbled by the workbench.

'My best one for the day. It's full of goodies to help us replace the salt and sugars we all used up today, or we'll all be suffering with night cramps.' Bree poured Dex a glass, then one for Charlie. 'Porter?'

'How potent is that mix?'

'Mild. You can breath-test yourself later, and then you can charge yourself for DUI. But you can't have the couch. Mia's got it until we paint her room.'

'Yeah, alright, small glass. I don't mind your mixes. When are you guys having another pizza night?'

'Not this week.' Bree passed Porter a glass.

Mia took a sip from the glass she'd been carrying. The cool lemon drink wasn't too fizzy or overly sweet, but smooth and refreshing. 'Mmm, this is good.' She held up the glass. 'I can't taste the gin, though.'

'That's the problem,' said Porter, also taking a sip. 'Bree's gin goes down so smooth you'll drink half a jug before you know it and start wearing wobbly boots.'

Charlie laughed, clapping Porter's shoulder. 'Talking like a man who's been there before.'

'I can see why.' Dex drained his glass and held it out for more. 'It's a thirst quencher. And as you are my favourite friend, Bree, let's have another, eh?'

'Please, don't give yourself false hope that we're friends, Dex. I'll still pretend I don't know you in public.' But Bree poured him another glass. 'What do you think of Pop's car, Porter?'

'I gotta hand it to the Riggs brothers, they did a great job helping me restore it.'

'It's in great condition.' Porter stepped back from the pale green antique car. It was so big and shiny, like a gangster car, but a retro green.

'It's gorgeous. I love the colour.' Mia peered inside. The leather work was immaculate. 'How long have you had it, Charlie?'

'We found it hiding in the Stoneys a few months back. It belonged to my brother. I was there when he bought it spanking new in Melbourne. We took turns driving it home when the Stuart Highway was just an old wallaby track, when roadhouses never shut their doors or their pub, making it one long pub crawl to get here. We blew our savings that trip, making it back with only spare change in our pockets and half a tank of gas, just in time for the musters.' Charlie pulled out some papers from the glove box and passed them to Porter. 'This is Harry's rego papers, the service book and everything.'

'What are you going to do with this car?' Mia asked

Charlie. 'It looks like it should be in a museum.'

'I've gotta hand it to the lads, Dex and his brothers did a helluva job restoring it. But we'll keep it in the family. Bree drives me to the pub on Fridays on account I've got no licence for the road. Why pay, I say—'

'Pop.' Bree hissed at Charlie. 'Stop.'

'What?' Charlie shrugged.

'This car's registration ran out in 1962.' The policeman held up the paperwork.

'Now you've done it, old man.' Dex chuckled, leaning back against the workbench covered in tools.

Charlie pulled up his breeches. 'Now hang on a second. Why should I pay for some smancy registration when we drive it just to blow the dust off, on dirt roads, where there is no traffic. I'm not paying—'

'I can get you a specialised registration,' cut in Porter. 'This car is over sixty years old, so it'd qualify for a historic car classification, and you'll pay a reduced rate. But it does mean there are restrictions on where and how often you can drive it.'

'I agree with Porter.' Bree took a sip from her jug like it was a big beer stein.

'That'd be a first.'

'It needs to be registered if we're going to insure it, Pop.'

'If you want, I can do a vehicle inspection on it now to start the registration process?' Porter shrugged. 'Got the MVR book in the car.'

'Can you do that here?' Charlie asked.

'Unless you want to tow it to the pits all the way in the city, where I hear it's a five hour wait these days.'

'Take the inspection, Charlie.' Dex pushed off the bench and started moving tools and equipment aside. 'I'll put it over the pit for Porter to inspect. I'll even bet a carton that it'll pass muster, no sweat.'

'Well, alright then. Obviously, there's a reason you came out, then.' Charlie patted Porter's shoulder. 'I'll give Dex a hand.' He climbed in behind the wheel of the car. The six cylinder wasn't nearly as loud as the Razorback, as he backed it out of the shed, to do a slow wide circle in the red dust.

'It's a nice car.' Porter's head tilted as he watched it shine under the sun. 'I've always liked the 1957 FJ Holden. They make good hot rods.'

'I didn't know you were a car fanatic,' Bree commented.

'I used to race. Started with the fender benders in Speedway, as a kid with my dad.'

'Did you keep racing?' Dex asked, moving a large toolbox aside.

'I got Street Stock Champion just before I moved out here. Now I just use the buggy for bush bashing on my day off, going hunting with my mate, Luke.'

Dex patted the policeman's shoulder. 'Remind me to never get into a car chase with you. But if you ever need a passenger or want someone to race on the street, give us a hoy.'

Mia peeked past the truck and farming machinery. Nearby, sat the silent Razorback that commanded attention, parked beside their horse truck and assorted motorbikes. Beyond them the shed stretched out to hold other vehicles.

'Whose cars are those?' Mia pointed to the many utes. 'I know the mustard Tojo is Cap's. I'm guessing the beat-up Hilux belongs to Dex?'

Porter chuckled. 'No. That's Ash's. The sleek black, V8 ute in the corner is Dex's ute.'

It looked like a mean street-racing machine. Now she understood why Dex would take on Porter in a road race. 'Is the black pick-up truck Ryder's, then?' It was huge.

Bree nodded.

'And the sleek Audi?'

'Harper's.'

'What do you drive, Bree?'

'A bright yellow combi van. I've always wondered if it glowed in the dark.' Porter grinned.

'How come it's not here with all of these other cars?'

'I park in the caretaker's sheds. This is the boys' property and this shed is a better equipped area for mechanical repairs, like the pit and the hoist. It's where Pop's been spending all his time, ever since they dragged that thing out of the Stoneys, Pops has been obsessed with it like a Pandora's box.'

'How so?' Porter's brow creased with concern.

'Charlie wouldn't sleep. He was out here at all hours, going over every inch of this vehicle, repairing it. I was hoping he'd go back to normal when it was done.'

'If Charlie lodged a missing person's report with me, I guess he didn't?'

Bree shook her head. 'Charlie has dragged out photo albums, and all sorts of stuff from the storage shed, which dug up lots of the past, too.' She stood squarely in front of Porter. 'Before Charlie found this car—that should be named *Pandora*—he was happy. Charlie hadn't forgotten about his brother, but he'd accepted it. Now, I don't want him to have all this false hope come crashing down and fill him with disappointment.'

'Charlie wants answers.'

'I get that. But do you really think Harry wants to be found?' She tapped Porter's chest. 'The truth. Just between you, me, and Mia, who won't say anything.'

Porter took a long time to answer. 'If Harry went to ground, then he's hidden himself well. There's been no movement in his bank account since the last deposit he made on the twelfth of November 1962.'

'No withdrawals?'

'Nothing.'

'So, you've looked into it?'

'Not any further than that. If Charlie asks me to, I will dig deeper.'

'That's what I'm worried about.'

Mia was dying to ask about the murder, but it wasn't her place.

'Don't you want to find your uncle?' asked Porter.

'No. The man deserted his family sixty years ago. What

worries me more is the stress this whole situation is putting on Charlie's health.' Bree watched her grandfather talking to Dex as they lifted the car's bonnet.

'Charlie seems healthy enough. He didn't stop all day in the drafting yards,' said Mia.

'Charlie sees every day as an adventure, because he knows he's running out of time. As much as he wants to keep up with everyone, he is exhausted.' For the first time Bree showed a deep worry that was reflected in her voice. 'I can see it. And that's putting pressure on his bad heart.'

'You know the doc in town was some big city heart surgeon,' said Porter.

'You don't think I know that? I've already dragged the old sod in there by the scruff of his neck for tests. The doctor recommended surgery, but Charlie refuses to let them operate. Said he's done his time in hospitals already.'

'It is true Charlie got pretty banged up from a rodeo?'

'Bull got him. Big time. He was in hospital for ages and then my grandmother nursed him back to health. It was a year before Pop got back into the saddle, but he never did a rodeo again.'

By the green antique Holden, Charlie pushed back his hat, revealing his white hair, and the deep crevices around his eyes of a man who'd been on this earth a long time.

'I hate to admit this,' said Mia quietly, 'but I forget Charlie's old when he acts as young as the brothers.'

'Bless him, he tries so hard to keep up with them,' said Bree. 'And all I can do is monitor his health, feed him the good stuff and do what I can to minimise the stress factors—such as digging up old murder cases.' Bree's frown darkened as she glowered at the car. 'I just wish they'd never found that damned car.'

Twenty

'**W**ell, hello there. Who might you be?' The blond, wavy-haired cowboy stood at the kitchen table pushing back the brim of his big white cowboy hat. His bright blue eyes highlighted his deep tan that went with the smile, making him the most handsomest cowboy Mia had ever seen. *Dayum. Dayum. Dayummmm.*

Lying on the couch, she held her bedsheets up to her chin. 'Who are you?'

'Craig. Do you like pastries?' He held up a white cardboard bakery box full of baked goods. She could smell them. 'They were fresh out of the oven when I collected them.' The microwave beeped, and he pulled out a tray of takeaway coffee cups, making himself right at home.

'Who? How? Where?' She looked around for Willow.

The back door opened, and Charlie stepped inside. 'Morning, Mia. Have you met Craig?'

'I, um…' Hiding under the blankets, she slid into her overalls, and tried to tidy up her hair. She was in desperate need of a toothbrush, face wash, or a shower.

Craig didn't seem real—he was way too handsome, with a set of strong straight shoulders and a waist that trimmed down into a dusty pair of jeans that rolled over his strong thighs, and an astonishingly beautiful butt. He even wore a rodeo-style belt buckle, just like the many Charlie had crowding his bookshelf.

Mia rubbed the sleep from her eyes, anything to stop watching the blond cowboy who should be on the cover of some cowboy calendar—and of all the days for this guy to show up, it had to be when she looked like a dog's dinner gone bad!

'Here, I got you a decaf, old man.' Craig held out a takeaway coffee cup. 'Freshly heated from the microwave.'

Charlie frowned as he sniffed at his cup. 'You could've said it was normal and I wouldn't have known.'

'Bree's orders. You've got a tricky ticker to look after. And I'm guessing the extra cup Bree ordered is for you, Mia.' Craig put the cup on the table.

'Where is Bree?'

'Coming. She's just finishin' a job.' Charlie reached for a pastry and sniffed at it. 'And before you ask, girlie, Willow's outside. She needed to do her business.'

Mia looked at the grandfather clock. It was nearly nine. 'I slept in.'

'Me too. Been a busy couple of days.' Charlie dragged out a chair at the table. 'Come have some mornin' smoko, girlie. Just don't touch the cupcakes, they're Bree's favourite. Lord knows that girl could do with a sweet treat. Swear she was gonna rip off that Policeman Porter's head at one stage.'

'Why were the cops out here?' Craig removed his hat and dropped it on the spare chair, on its crown, to then brush fingers through his soft curls. Without the hat, but with that deep tan and blond curls, Craig looked like a stunningly hot surfer.

Charlie shrugged. 'It was just Porter. He did a vehicle inspection for me. Brought out some big guardian dogs for Cap, to watch over the calves. I've never seen it on beef cattle, you know.'

'I'd heard of that being done in the north-west. You'll have to let me know how it goes. I know a few cattlemen who'd be keen to try it on their stations to protect their calves.'

'Mia can mention that to Cap. Come on, girlie, take a seat. Craig don't bite.'

Mia gingerly sat and sipped on her coffee. The caffeine flavour was rich and creamy, coating her tongue. 'This is excellent coffee.' She hadn't had a coffee all week, as Bree didn't keep coffee in the house because of Charlie.

'The Station Hand's daughter makes a fine coffee.'

'Who?'

'Lucy. She runs the food van at the train station in town that she's branded it as *The Station Hand's Daughter*.' Craig pushed the box of pastries towards her, then he stopped to lean closer and wince. Sitting back, his brow ruffled. 'Are you okay?' He glanced at Charlie.

'I'm okay.' Brushing her hair to hide the bruising on her face, Mia turned away from the stunning male specimen.

'Mia's doing good, aren't you, girlie?'

Mia nodded.

'Take a pastry, go on. Bree calls it comfort food. Don't worry, girlie, we burn off plenty of calories out here from the hard yakka, you don't need to worry about the weight.'

'Thanks.' She gave a meek smile and plucked up a croissant.

'Before you ask, Craig, Cap and I found Mia stowed away in the back of Cap's old Tojo with all his dogs. And they liked Mia. So does Cap. So, no flirtin' with the girl or you'll have Cap on your case.' Charlie wagged his thick finger at the younger cowboy. 'About time Cap found himself a nice lady.'

Mia nearly choked on her coffee.

'Which one is Cap?'

'Haven't you met them?' Charlie asked. 'Aren't you mates with the younger one, Jonathan?'

'Sure. I know Dex and Ash. I know *of* Cap through my mate Ryan, the town vet. But not Ryder, the oldest. He'd been gone ten years.'

'Well, Ryder's the one runnin' the show. They call him the bank. But they're good lads, all of them. Elsie Creek Station is in good hands.'

Charlie chuckled, as he pointed to the wall where three metal branding irons hung like swords over a mantelpiece. 'But they're ticked at me for taking back the Station's brand after the drafting.'

'How was the drafting?' Craig asked.

'Good. The brothers are going all high tech with drones, and data whatnot with their fancy cattle tags, apps, and now the dogs. Anyhoodle, what do I owe you for bringing this lot out?'

'Nothing. Bree asked me to come.'

'That I did.' Bree slipped off her welder's boots at the back door, sliding off her skullcap and gloves to leave them on the side shelf as a beagle trotted inside with Willow.

'Morning, Willow.' Mia eagerly patted her furry friend with her wagging tail.

'There's my favourite redhead.' Craig gave Bree a hug and a kiss on the cheek. 'What's with the dogs? That's a nice-looking kelpie. Don't see many this far north.'

'I was going to ask if you knew of anyone who uses kelpies on their stations.'

Craig shook his head. 'Just heelers, the odd border collie or two, some bull Arabs as pig dogs, and the usual Territory Special camp dogs. What are you doing with a beagle? I've never seen one out here.' It sniffed all around Craig's boots, then the hat, nose down, tail wagging.

'That's Scout. She was one of Caps dogs, a retired police dog, but now she's Harper's pampered house dog. Aren't you, girl.' Bree tickled the beagle's ears as it plonked itself down, lapping up the attention.

'Why is Scout here?' Charlie asked. 'Are we running a doggy day care or something, kid?'

'I thought Scout could come along for a drive when we check the boundary fence.'

'Besides getting me out here for my good looks and charm, is this your way of asking me to help you do some fencing?' Craig slid on his hat, standing tall, to tuck his shirt into his thigh-hugging jeans. If Mia had been standing, she would have fainted in a female swoon!

Dayum!

'Don't worry, my friend, I have a job for you, too. Ooh, cupcakes. I love a good cupcake.' Bree plucked a tiny cupcake with cream frosting and inhaled deeply, as if savouring its aroma. 'Dearly beloved, we are gathered here today to join these mixed groups of sugars in the holy art of cupcake heaven. May our cholesterol and blood pressure remain steady for another day.' Bree bit into her frosty cupcake, her eyes rolling with pleasure. The men chuckled as she ate her cupcake, then arched an eyebrow at them. 'Well, what are we waiting for? I'm hoping we'll be done early enough to enjoy a long liquid lunch.'

'Want me to come with, kid?'

'Always, Pop.'

'Quick, let's go get the Razorback before the granddaughter changes her mind.' Charlie shuffled out the back door with the cowboy following. Mia couldn't take her eyes off that denim-clad butt.

Bree cleared her throat, wearing a cheesy grin.

Busted! The heat rushed to Mia's face.

'Do you want to come with us, Mia?'

'I don't know. My bum was sore from those metal seats the other night.'

'Because Pop didn't put in the cushions I had made. Come on, I could use your professional opinion today, too.'

'Really?' Didn't that make her liven up. A job.

Bree nodded. 'Did you just wake up?'

'I did.'

'Well hurry up, get ready.' Bree grabbed a small cooler from the wide shelf that held their boots and assorted hats by the back door.

Mia scooted over to the couch and folded up the sheets and blanket. 'Should we tell the brothers what we're doing? It is their station.'

'We're just doing a boundary run.'

Mia dashed to the bathroom, took care of business and then loaded up her toothbrush. Glancing up at the mirror she grimaced at her reflection. The bruising was now a garish greeny-yellow with tinges of brown. At least the swelling was gone, and her lips were back to normal.

At the main hat rack, she slid on her oversized shirt to protect her from the sun, that hung with her hat. This almost felt normal, getting dressed to go to work. 'I think I heard Ryder say something about security cameras, wouldn't that stop the need to take long drives?' She knew Cap and Ash were keen on cutting down on fossil fuels.

'I forgot they had those.' Bree juggled her keys, unlocked the tall cupboard and removed her shotgun that rested among many others. 'But it's a long fence line to check. Who knows how many hours of footage Ryder has to troll through? If we find something, we can fix it and let them know. So, in a way, we're helping.'

Mia paused buttoning up her shirt, to grin at the determined redhead. 'I thought you weren't helping them.'

Bree shrugged. 'We're just doing a boundary run. It's just another job on a cattle station, checking the fences and the firebreak. It is the dry season and we're wary of bushfires this time of the year.'

Mia attacked her woolly hair with the brush. 'You're going fencing with shotguns?'

'Don't worry, it's just a precaution. I'd hate to come across a sick beast and not help put the poor thing out of their misery.' Her shotguns clicked loudly as she checked the load.

'Oh…'

'Sadly, it's the ugly side of the job.' Bree slid into her riding boots, slapping on the large Akubra she wore when on a horse. Bree had many hats, some with hatbands wound in various materials, like twine, leather and wire. Some had playing cards and matches or some shiny charms in them. But she also had a large collection of colourful skullcaps. Today, it was the wide-brimmed Akubra, grey and weatherworn with lots of twine and strips of leather and lace to make up the unusual hatband.

'Don't worry, I'll radio Ryder to meet us at the drafting yards later,' Bree said, handing Mia her soft brown hat. 'By then, they would have finished walking the bush mob out to Ash's paddock. What are you doing later? You're welcome to join us, to hear Charlie and Craig swap rodeo stories.'

'I was going to help Cap with the new guardian dogs tonight.' She was looking forward to seeing the big bears in action.

Bree grinned widely. 'Well, well, well…'

Mia winced. 'It's not like that. It's work.'

'Riiiight.' Bree giggled to herself. 'At least Craig can have the couch. Take my swag and have a night under the stars.'

Mia felt like a loose end. 'You know, I can't wait to get into a routine again, and know what I'm supposed to do. I feel like I'm on holiday, sleeping in while everyone else is working.'

'You needed the rest, Mia. And that couch has a habit of putting people to sleep.'

'But I can't live on the couch forever.' She needed to get her independence back. 'Do you want me to help you with Cap's house?'

'I finished putting in the struts for Cap's new deck, earlier. I'm just waiting on the concrete to set before I can do any more. I even reinforced the braces on Cap's kennels. He'd need it with those big dogs.'

'Did you look at the nursery? The nursery tables need repair.'

'Nice try, Mia.' Bree gave her a sly grin. 'I don't work for the boys, especially when they can do that themselves.'

'Oh, yeah, sorry.'

'But good news. Harper is bringing out the paint today after work. We can do an undercoat of your room, before I drink too much gin.'

'Really?'

'It's what you want, a room and a routine to help you get over…' Bree gently brushed the hair from Mia's face like a sister. 'I know that once you have a room, and the nursery started, you'll be so busy doing what you love, that this will all be a long distant memory to forget.'

Why couldn't that be yesterday so that everyone looked at her normally today. 'I really want to help the brothers.'

'We can all see that.'

'Why are you helping Cap with his house?'

'Because Cap gives up a lot for his dogs. In the time he's been here I've seen how he cares for them. Cap is the type of guy who'd rather feed his dog pack first and let himself go hungry, and he has done so for their vet fees. I know Cap has saved countless working dogs. He's found good homes for those dogs, or he'd kept them, like Scout there who struggled being around people in suburbia after what happened to her.' Bree pointed at the beagle sniffing around the room.

'What happened to her?' The beagle looked so happy and healthy.

'A druggie hit her nose after she'd busted him at an airport. Scout won't do crowds anymore. So, on behalf of the many dogs Cap has saved, this is me paying it forward for those canines who can't. Do you understand what I'm saying?'

'I do. Do the brothers know this?'

'I don't care what they think. I'm doing it for the puppies. Come on, Scout, let's put that nose of yours to work.'

Twenty-one

'What the flip?' Dex pointed at the Razorback cutting through the outback, as Ash started to curse under his breath.

'What's the matter?' Cap stood beside Ryder, high on the viewing platform, giving them a grand view over the drafting yards.

'It's time to lock up the ladies,' said Ash, 'because Cowboy *freaking* Craig, is here at Elsie Creek Station.'

'What have you been drinking?' Ryder asked Ash.

'Sounds like he's been into Dex's stash.' Cap chuckled.

'He'd better not have.' Dex crossed his arms, his eyes shaded beneath his hat's wide brim. 'You know, that's the first time I've seen Bree driving the Razorback.'

The dust plume was high as the Razorback skimmed over the red soils like a boat flying on air. Charlie sat in the passenger seat and in the back stood Craig and Mia, holding onto the rail, with Willow beside her. The wind blew back Mia's hair, exposing her wide smile. She was obviously having the time of her life.

'They've got Scout with them.' Cap pointed to the beagle sitting on Charlie's lap with her long ears flapping like wings.

Ryder positively growled deep in his chest. 'What is that woman up to now? She's got her shotgun with her, too.'

Bree parked the Razorback near the stairs. Craig held his hand out to help Mia climb off the back like a lady in a carriage.

Cap frowned.

'Careful, Cap. Cowboy Craig loves the single ladies, or they love him,' teased Dex.

'Mia is her own woman.' He didn't dare expect anything with Mia, not after what she'd been through.

Yet, the heated pangs of jealousy created an unexpected rage that crept up his shoulders to skim across the back of his neck. He removed his hat and used his shirt's sleeve to savagely wipe the sweat from his brow. He'd never been jealous of anyone.

Somewhere along the way he'd begun to care about Mia, so much so that she'd become his first and final thought of the day. She'd become his number one priority so quickly and so easily, it worried him. Tangling with the emotions of a woman who was in Mia's situation was not right. She needed to heal and not have some tool like him in her space.

Yet, he couldn't help but worry about her—it was maddening.

It was also madness that he was experiencing a whole new range of emotions he only felt when he was around Mia. Like jealousy and a territorial protectiveness that easily turned into rage. He'd never been like this with anyone. It wasn't right.

He shifted in his boots, crossed and uncrossed his arms to at least pretend he didn't care, while slyly sneaking glances at Mia to check she was okay. She had been through enough, she needed time to heal. By then she wouldn't even give someone like Cap a second glance.

'Hey, fellas. Have you met Craig?' Charlie slowly clambered up the steps with his bandy-legged swagger, while the taller cowboy effortlessly took two steps at a time.

The show-off.

'Congrats on the boy, Ash,' said Craig. 'Mason is a good-looking lad, and so is your clever little lady, Harper.'

'Thanks, Craig.' Ash shook hands with Craig.

'Craig reckons he knows you two,' said Charlie.

'Craig came out home with Jonathan one Christmas,' replied Ash.

'And it was Dex here who knocked me out cold in the boxing ring. Rum and boxing do not go together.'

'Especially when you'd started with our grandfather at breakfast.' Dex chuckled, shaking hands and patting Craig on the back like old friends. 'This is Ryder. And have you met Cap?'

'I've heard plenty, but we've never officially met. Ryan, the local vet, is a good mate of mine. He speaks highly of what you do with the muster dogs, Cap.'

Cap shook Craig's solid working hand, noticing the shiny belt buckle. 'Rodeo?'

'Bronc champion.' Old Charlie lifted his chin with pride, as if Craig was his son. 'I trained Craig on the bulls, I did.'

Craig peered over the rails to check out the cattle in the yards. 'I prefer the broncs these days, they don't come with horns.'

'Bree?' Ryder's deep voice cut through the chitchat. 'Care to explain why you have Scout with you, and why you were coming in from the east boundary?'

'It's a nice day for a drive.' Bree walked up the stairs, carrying a clipboard, the same one Charlie used for the drafting.

Dex started humming Darth Vader's imperial march from *Star Wars*.

Bree sneered at Dex like he was an insect. 'Well hello, stormcloud. Shoot, punch, or maim anyone today?'

'Shouldn't I be asking you that?'

'Charlie, what's going on?' Ryder's voice was deep, and even though his eyes were hidden behind his dark sunglasses, he managed to glare at Bree and Dex.

'I thought you were getting us a stock agent, not another stockman,' said Dex. 'No offence, Craig.'

'None taken.' Craig shrugged.

'Listen, stormcloud, do you want me to steal some of baby Mason's crayons and draw you some stick figures for the presentation? Or can you put your big cowboy pants on and let me explain?'

'Bree, play nice. They look like they want to hoist me into the pen,' said Craig.

'Why are you here, Craig?' Ryder was blunt.

'Because Bree told me about the hidden herd kept out at Wombat Flats that were never noted on the land sale as assets.'

'But—' Charlie's eyes widened as he gaped up at Bree, then at Ryder as if only now realising the legalities of their actions.

'It's true,' said Ryder. 'I was able to negotiate the price down a substantial amount because we were all under the impression there was no cattle on the station.'

'Listen, Pop, technically, we did squirrel away their best stock. Craig, what is the average sawdust price for a grey Brahman?'

'About twelve k for a scrubber.'

'They're not scrubbers.' Charlie's frown was ferocious, as he pointed to the cattle milling around in the pens below them. 'Bree's bull, Freckles, has gotta be worth twenty times that amount, more.'

Bree lifted the clipboard to read out loud, 'We escorted one thousand, three hundred and forty-five head from a hidden valley. And at sawdust sale price—'

'*What the flip!* That's sixteen million, one hundred and forty thousand dollars' worth of beef at below basement price.' Dex, the family's maths genius, had calculated the sum in the blink of an eye.

Ash let out a low whistle, pushing back the brim of his hat, as they all looked at the herd milling around in the yards below them.

'So, we screwed up, kid? Is that what you're saying?' Charlie's brow ruffled with worry.

'No, you did good, Pop. That's a healthy bounty, in that mob.'

'I had to do something. They were going to rape this property and leave the new owners with nothin'.' Charlie rubbed at his forehead. 'All that hard work me, Darcie did, and you too, kid, stolen like that. I couldn't let 'em do that.'

Bree stroked her grandfather's shoulder. 'I know, Pop. That's why I agreed to help you hide that herd in Wombat Flats.'

'I wish you'd told me. I would've helped,' said Craig.

Bree grinned. 'You're here now, to save us from being busted for cattle rustling.'

'Are you for real?' Mia stood behind them, with wide eyes. '*Cattle rustling*, is that really a thing?'

'You bet your sweet chilli sauce cattle thieving is a problem, girlie. Flamin' bloody mongrel duffers they are,' mumbled Charlie, pushing back his hat to expose his scowl.

'Listen, Pop, we might be able to argue that those mustering contractors missed these cattle. It's why I brought Craig out—to cover our arses. But, Pop, you have to stop telling people that we hid them in Wombat Flats.'

'I only told these boys, as the owners.'

'And the Station Hand. And—'

'I swear we won't say anything to anyone.' Cap had to help them. 'We wouldn't even have a herd if it weren't for you two.'

'Cap is right. The stock you took gives us a great head start,' said Dex.

'Technically, we didn't take them,' said Bree. 'We just moved them.'

Ryder crossed his arms over his chest. 'What happens on the station, stays on the station.'

'Aw, cupcake, now you're speaking my language.' Bree even tapped his arm. 'Look, guys, Craig is a stock inspector, who can sign off on your herd's Waybills to stop any questions being asked. It'll be like glossing over the details on the paperwork that other stock inspectors would be asking. And I don't trust them, like I trust Craig with our business.'

'It'll just be for the first sale, that's all,' explained Craig.

'Thank you.' Charlie sighed with relief, patting Craig's back.

'It's the least I can do for you and Bree. You're family.'

'Not to interfere with your business, guys,' spoke Bree, 'but as the new owners of Elsie Creek Station lots of eyes will be on you, *especially* when you take your first lot of fats to the Elsie Creek train station. Everyone in town will wonder where they've been. Especially when they take one look at your beef and see their age and exceptional condition.'

'So, Craig is here to make it all look legit?' Ryder asked.

Craig nodded at Ryder. 'With the disbandment of the local co-op, I can hook you up with a few stock agents I'd recommend. Not only will they get you a good price for your stock, they won't ask too many questions, because they trust me enough to know I'll only trade a decent beast. But I need to see the stock first, because I'm putting my reputation on the line, too.'

'As a ladies' man.' Dex playfully punched Craig's arm.

'Leave off. Craig's one of the best stock inspectors in the district. He just hates doing paperwork, so we're lucky to have him on board,' said Charlie.

'You taught me, but I'll never have as good an eye for stock as Bree has.'

'But the kid could never track a hoof trail as good as you.'

'I knew it!' Ryder pointed at Bree. 'You went to the east boundary searching for where those wild dogs came onto the property, didn't you?'

'We did. And they came in through the east fence line.' Bree dragged out a map from her back pocket. 'It was two vehicles, heavy tread, big utes. Craig, you agree?'

Craig nodded, pointing at the map. 'They weren't buggies, bikes, or trucks, but utes. One of them had these special all-terrain tyres, the type you'd expect to find on fancy tyre rims used by concrete cowboys. But they came from your neighbour's block. One was extra heavy, like it was weighed down by a steel cage, probably for the dogs.'

'You didn't jump the fence and follow those tracks, did you, Bree?' asked Ryder.

'Bree wanted to, but I made sure she didn't.' Craig tapped on the map. 'We worked out that someone cut your boundary fence here… They then backed up to let the dogs out of the cage, fixed up the fence and the rest you dealt with. We saw your cameras. Those fake ones look fake, mate.'

'Sorry, Ash, the weather got to them.' Bree patted Ash's shoulders.

'It was only a temporary measure while we were out mustering in Wombat Flats.'

'At least we have those poles in place to add the new cameras,' said Dex. 'Are they here?'

'Yep. Box on the porch. I've ordered more for Ash's intranet system, too.' Ryder straightened out the map to extend the area. 'I've already put camera's here and here. Could you tell if that cut fence was in clear sight?'

Bree shook her head as Craig said, 'We think they picked that area purposely because it's a blind spot.'

'Damn.' Ryder wiped over his mouth. 'Can you estimate when it happened?'

'The same night you guys got that visit from those wild dogs. From the condition Bree was telling me they were in, I'd hazard a guess to say that they hadn't been fed in a while and the smell of prey…'

'No way.' Cap's stomach dropped at how people could be so cruel to animals. Only to blink in surprise at Mia's tiny hand on his arm giving him a squeeze to console him.

'I knew it wasn't a coincidence,' muttered Dex, shaking his head. 'We'd only had that mongrel, Leo, visit that same day. He'd been planning this—he's playing us.'

'Bree agreed. It's why she asked me to check it out,' said Craig.

'We've never had wild dogs before,' said Bree. 'Have we, Pop?'

'Nope. Never. Dingoes, sure. Just so you know, Cap, that little Scout is a brilliant tracker. She followed those dogs' tracks right to where Bree cut them off from the herd.'

'What do we do now? Call Porter?' Ash asked.

'We've burnt the carcasses and can't prove anything,' replied Dex. 'And cutting the fence like that, they could claim they were being neighbourly fixing it.'

'All we can hope is that the cameras picked up something. I'll look again.' Ryder rubbed his neck. 'Ash, does your drone do night vision?'

'Not this one. But I've ordered a new one that does. It'll have more range and speed for mustering.'

'Good. In the meantime, Dex, can clear any blind spots along the perimeter, and I'll put in more cameras to replace the fake ones.'

'I'll widen that firebreak big time with the grader, so they'll have nowhere to hide,' said Dex. 'I do like playing with that grader.'

'Good call, the wider the better,' said Craig. 'Charlie said they started a fire that destroyed the crops last dry season.'

'I'm hoping that by putting in wildlife corridors we'll be able to minimise the risks of that happening again,' said Cap.

'Yeah, well, I'm sorry, brother...' Dex dropped his heavy hand on Cap's shoulder. 'I'll be tearing down trees when I expand that firebreak.'

'That's brilliant.' Mia piped in and they all looked at her like she was weird.

'Aren't you meant to be saving trees?' Dex arched his eyebrow at her.

'Cap, it's a good thing. Trust me.' Her tiny hand squeezed his, practically jumping with excitement. 'We can use the best saplings from that area and transfer them to your new wildlife corridor, as an enormous head start. Bree, Charlie, and Craig were helping me collect samples all morning.' Mia jumped down the steps.

From the high boards they watched her rummage around the back of the Razorback filled with heavy hessian sacks, where she scooped out handfuls of seeds. '*Look*. We collected all these viable native seeds to start your native nursery.'

Cap leapt over the rail to land beside her and poked around the bags. There had to be thousands of seeds from countless native varieties.

Mia was so excited, opening one bag, then another as she

tapped his chest. 'It's just like you said. It's all here.' She reached into another bag and pulled out thick clusters of seed pods as if she'd struck oil. 'Bree showed me how the entire eastern firebreak has an amazing number of saplings available and recommended which varieties to use. We can transplant the best ones to get your wildlife settled in long before the rains come, repurposing the trough water from Ash's paddock to water them.'

It was music to his ears, a dream that Mia was making into a reality for him. 'For fate's sake, you're a godsend, you are, Mia. This is brilliant.' He wanted to hug her, but his brothers were watching.

'And you thought we were up to no good, Ryder?' Bree crossed her arms, wearing a smug look.

'Hmph.' Ryder rubbed the tip of his nose. 'Cap, when are you letting the guardian dogs loose?'

'Tonight.' Cap dusted his hands, looking up at his brothers.

'I'll help.' Mia used some string, that curiously matched the twine wrapped around Bree's hatband, to close the hessian sacks. 'We can sort out the seeds and create a nursery plan at the same time.'

'You don't have to.' But he'd love to see all that she'd collected.

'I want to. You've only got three weeks before the campdraft is here to get them ready for sale.'

'What are you selling now?' Dex asked.

For fate's sake! He pursed his lips together and began the climb back up the stairs to finally share his plans with his brothers. 'I was planning on selling the excess of these native seedlings at the campdraft to contribute towards the dog food, and any future vet bills.'

Mia rushed up the stairs behind him and tugged on Cap's shirt, her excited eyes so pretty in the sunlight. 'We'll have stacks to sell. And Craig says he knows people who'd be interested in the guardian dogs, too.'

Dex screwed his nose up. 'You haven't even let those

fluffy bears out of the kennels yet.'

Cap frowned at his brother. 'I will, and they'll work brilliantly. I'd even bet on it.'

'How much?'

'A pineapple?'

'Nah, a grey nurse.'

'You're on.' Dex shook hands with Cap.

'A what?' Mia asked Charlie.

'Pineapple is fifty dollars, and the grey nurse is a hundred.'

'What's a twenty?'

'The redback.'

'Now that's all sorted,' said Bree. 'Can we let Craig get on with his job, so you boys can sell your cattle, Ryder can beef up the security, Dex can start stripping the scrub, and Mia can start playing garden gnome to regenerate the property.'

'And what will you be doing?' Ash asked.

Bree's grin widened, full of mischief. 'Charlie, Craig, and I are planning on a long liquid lunch. Remember, I don't work for you boys.' She then nudged Mia. 'And for you, precious, I'll make you a hamper to share with Cap, because Craig's got the couch tonight. You can collect it when you pick up my swag.'

Eh? Cap raised an eyebrow at Mia. What was Bree up to?

Twenty-two

'**W**hy are we building these new kennels out here in this paddock? When you have those ones near the nursery.' In her overalls and hat, Mia squinted up at him in the most adorable way. It was a look that made Cap grin at her with admiration.

But if he kept staring at her, she'd think of him as a weird stalker or something. It didn't stop him from taking sneaky glances in her direction every chance he got.

The freshly cemented floor was so white, where he cut the bindings from the roll of mesh wire. 'This will be for the Maremmas. I plan to use this as a future training area for all guardian dogs and calves. Can you hold this wire up so I can attach it to the poles?'

'Sure.' Mia rarely said no, always keen to get her hands dirty. And she was such a tiny thing that he could easily secure the mesh to the poles above her head, while enjoying her summery aroma.

'Can you explain the guardian dog process to me?' She tucked her wind-tossed hair behind her ears, revealing more of her face and her delicate neck.

He licked his lips, imagining what her skin tasted like. 'With any of the new guardians, I plan on keeping them inside the kennels to allow both the calves and dogs to get used to each other. Eventually they'll move out with that group of calves to the larger paddocks, where they'll live with the cattle until the next lot of calves arrive. Don't stress, we'll be feeding them at various watering points in the paddocks while they keep doing their job of deterring any dingoes.' He didn't want his brothers suggesting the use of dingo baits, not when he could use these guardian dogs and the wildlife corridors.

'When will these dogs be ready for that?'

'Not long. They've come from a cattle station that's well skilled at bringing out their natural instincts. It's the calves who need to get used to the dogs. But with their coats looking similar in colour, and the calves' age, it should be a quick transition period.' With one side of the kennel secure, they moved around to the rear of the simple shelter.

'You said they came from another station. Didn't the owner want them?' Again, Mia held the mesh to the pole while he worked around her body, securing it in place. It was torture to not touch her, but it was also a pleasure to be this close.

'They're rescue dogs who go to this Western Australian station that works with this type of dog breed, the way I rescue cattle dogs. These guardian dogs came through various animal shelters. People like the fluffy bear look but can't deal with the reality of looking after dogs like this and end up surrendering them.'

'Why would anyone want to surrender these gorgeous, fluffy animals?' Mia reached down to pat the female resting on her chain, while the younger male, still in his juvenile stage, strained on his chain to demand a pat from Mia, who was smiling at the dogs, in a way he'd never tire of.

'Unfortunately, they don't make very good pets, Mia.' Didn't that kill her smile.

'But...' Her brow rumpled with confusion, as she helped him shift the roll of mesh along to the last post.

'Maremmas have a powerful instinct to guard livestock. It's a trait that's been bred into them for centuries. They originate from Italy, where they protected sheep from predators like wolves. It's what makes them perfect for guarding livestock. But not so good with people.' He nodded at the dogs calmly lying in the cool shade of the new kennels while watching the skittish calves in the paddock. 'Unlike cattle dogs or most other dogs, guardian dogs are an independent animal, which is what they're bred for, to not depend on humans, so you can't bribe them with food, or expect them to behave in an apartment when they're bred to live outside.'

'I see. How often does this happen?'

'My friend gets a new Maremma a month from city shelters. Sometimes she'll drive across the country to rescue them. The usual return age is about eight months, when the owners struggle with that cute puppy, that suddenly weighs thirty kilos and is still growing. They eat like horses, and struggle to live in small backyards, and they can easily push over young children they're trying to herd. Imagine having one of these in the house.'

'It'd swallow up Bree's couch.'

He chuckled as he unrolled the mesh across the kennel's frame while in the shade of its simple roof.

'Do they have names?' Mia tenderly stroked the male dog's nose.

'You can pick one.'

Her head swivelled so fast to face him with wide eyes. 'What?'

The attention made his heart slam into his chest. He had to look away from her too-bright, all-seeing gaze, to pluck the wire cutters from the toolbox. But when he raised his eyes, her ready gaze locked onto his, as if waiting for a response. 'I think you should pick a name for the new dogs.'

'Don't they have names already?'

He shrugged. 'Probably. But as they're in their permanent home now, you get to give them a new name.' Hopefully it would give Mia that feeling of being more connected to this place, because he wanted her to stay.

'You didn't give Willow a new name.' Mia pointed to the parked Tojo where the dogs were lying beneath it, keeping their packs separated to give the new guardian dogs space.

'Willow is not my dog.' He winked at Mia, who playfully rolled her pretty eyes. 'So, pick a name.' He finished clasping the mesh to the kennel's outer frame, tested the new doors, checked the water in the troughs they'd share with the calves, and left the door open. He wasn't ready to lock them up, not while the sun was still shining.

'I've never named a dog. What do you do?'

'I usually go through a list of names to see which one they answer to. But I have been known to change their names based on their personality traits later on.'

'So why did you pick Atlas?'

Cap turned to grin at his red cattle dog, the proud alpha flicking his ears at full attention. 'For his endurance.'

'As a cattle dog?'

'And his will to survive. I found him on a track as a young pup. His paws were so worn down he must have been travelling for miles mapping out the territory. Even now, Atlas is a marathon running kind of dog. On a muster, Atlas will outlast the other dogs with his stamina.'

'Was Atlas dumped?'

'I think an eagle took him from his pack. It happens more than people realise when they let the puppies play on their lawns. When I found Atlas he had claw marks across his back. And you've seen how big those carrion birds are.'

'They wouldn't dare go near Atlas now.' She pointed to the large cattle dog, who was not only loyal but fearless.

'No. Atlas chases them away.'

'What about Fern? Did you find her in a group of ferns in a damp woodland?'

'No.' He dumped his tools back into the box and snapped the lid shut. Collecting up the wire roll, he carried it back to the Tojo. Atlas thumped his tail to greet him and he gave him a pat.

'Fern...' She came towards him, and he patted both intelligent dogs.

'What is Fern's story?' Mia followed him, as he refilled their water bottles from the cooler resting on the back of the ute and handed one to Mia.

'Fern came to me via an animal shelter in Queensland. She was part of a working dog's litter of six pups on a small cattle station.' He looked over the landscape that surrounded him. A large newly fenced paddock that contained the future herd on his family's cattle station. It was a dream come true.

'But?'

'Unfortunately, the station fell on hard times—from drought, mounting debts and dwindling resources. The owner had a stroke just before the pups were born, and he was sent to Brisbane for emergency care. He was there for a while, with his wife and daughter with him. Sadly, his daughter had no choice but to sell the property and move her parents into the city where her father could receive medical treatment. Unfortunately, during the move and the sale, some of the pups were abandoned.'

'How could the owner do that?' Her voice was loaded with protectiveness. Willow trotted over to lean against Mia's leg for a soothing pat.

'It wasn't the owner's fault; the poor bloke was stuck in hospital. He knew his dog was pregnant but had no clue how many pups there were in the litter. His wife and daughter did manage to find most of the dogs and give them new homes. But some of the puppies got away from them. It took the animal rescue group a few weeks to trap them. By then Fern was wary of humans.'

'How long was she at the shelter?'

'A month. Fern wouldn't go near anyone. She'd been deserted once. Why would she go through that again?' Even today he still felt honoured whenever Fern allowed him to pat her coat, and the smile she gave him as she sat by his leg, always eager to please. Fern was a highly intelligent dog with a strong work ethic, like Atlas. They were the perfect muster dog team.

'It was you who named her Fern?'

He nodded. 'Ferns symbolise new life and beginnings.' And Fern had that with him, as he patted her sleek coat. Then he faced the one female he adored the most. Mia. 'Now, it's your turn to name the dogs.'

'How?'

'Take the male and walk him around the inner perimeter, let him get used to the boundary. He likes you.' With Mia following him down to the guardian kennels, the dog chain clanked to the ground, as he clipped the young male onto a lead.

'What do I do?'

'Just take him for a walk. I'd like you to do a counterclockwise walk along the boundary fence, keeping the dog on your left so he can sniff out the territory. If he wants to pee, let him. He's marking his turf, which will be a great deterrent for any dingoes. Go on, you've got this.' He gently pushed Mia's shoulder.

With their backs to Cap, it looked like a polar bear was being walked by a child. Chuckling to himself, he dragged out his phone to take a sneaky photo of the odd pair. It was going to be a keepsake that would always make him smile.

'Don't come back until you've given him a name.' Of course, there was no pressure. He'd noticed Mia preferred operating towards a deadline in the conversations they'd shared when they worked together. It never felt like work when he was with Mia.

Leaning his shoulder against the new wall of the kennels, with the female Maremma shifting close enough for him to scratch her behind the ears, he settled in for the show. And Mia was worth the watch.

Twenty-three

The new guardian dog was enormous, and full of fur, like a big off-white sheepdog. Every time he stopped to sniff at the fence, he easily dragged Mia to a stop like a rag doll.

Her boots crunched on dry grasses, gravel and red sand as she followed the fence line, while the dog's paws were practically soundless.

Their shadows were so distinct, Mia with her wide-brimmed hat beside the dog that looked like a grizzly bear stalking across the red soils. Harper was right, these dogs were big bears.

And she had to name one.

No pressure.

'What do you want to be called? Rover. Roger. Dog. Wolf. Wolfdog…' She went through a list of names, looking to the sun for inspiration. It was blinding, but so deliciously warm, she closed her eyes and basked in the glow. It was a glorious dry season day, and here she was walking a dog as if on holidays while the group of twenty plus calves watched them.

Or should she say the dog walked her along the fence line, with his tail wagging, nose down, sniffing at everything, but not responding to any of the names she'd come up with, so far.

'Grizzly. Polar. Bear. Panda. Pepper. Salt. Ginger…'

Again, the dog lurched to a standstill and peed.

How big was this dog's bladder?

Then he trotted along to sniff at the ground, and Mia continued with the names. So far, nothing had stuck.

'Fluffy. Titus. Brutus. Netflix. Sky. Breeze. Spirit. Star…' It was like she was playing the childhood game of I Spy, but for a dog's name.

Again, he lurched forward to something new, tugging the lead tight to sniff at a group of wildflowers.

'Flowers? Wildflowers?' Did she dare start listing out the plants' Latin names?

The dog continued with a staggering swagger, nose to the ground, tail wagging.

She followed.

'Blue? No. I can't use that one. Cap has a dog called Blue. Cap also has a dog called Diesel, and the brothers called Spanner and Wrench. Do you want me to go through the toolbox to find you a masculine name?'

He lurched again.

'You keep lurching like that, and I'll have no arm left.' She rubbed at her shoulder.

The dog stopped and looked at her, finally giving her his attention.

What did she say?

She narrowed her eyes at the dog. 'Lurch?'

He sat down with his ears cocked, head tilting and tail sweeping across the dusty paddock's floor.

Mia crouched down before the dog. 'Do you want to be called Lurch?'

The dog licked at her. She barely ducked away in time. But the big dog nuzzled into her, knocking her onto her back in the dirt, leaving her with no choice but to hug his furry body. 'Hello, Lurch. Nice to meet you.' Her laugh echoed in the surrounding air.

'I'm guessing you found a name?' Cap looked so sexy leaning against that pole, arms crossed, with his stockman's hat shading his eyes. *Dayum.*

'I did.' Covered in dirt, she could barely contain the excitement as she rushed up with the dog. 'His name is Lurch.'

The dog stopped drinking from the trough to wag his tail at Mia.

'Good name.' Cap patted the dog. 'Was that because he was pulling on your arm? Or you have a thing for the Addams Family?'

'You saw, huh?' Dumb question, because every time she'd peered over her shoulder, Cap had been watching her. Or maybe he was just watching the cattle, the way a surf lifesaver watched a public beach to keep everyone safe.

'Here. Remember to keep hydrated.' He passed her the cool water bottle, their fingers brushing, to send a scurry of electricity along her fingers, up her arm, to then tingle over her scalp.

Judging by the way his Adam's apple shifted as he swallowed hard, she wasn't the only one reacting.

His tan throat and dark stubble moved against the collar of his blue work shirt, inspiring another strike of electricity to rush through her body. She found herself wanting those strong hands of his to get handsy with her, but he pulled his fingers away, leaving her holding the bottle.

'Um, thanks.' She drank thirstily from the water bottle to not only fill that awkward void, but to push down her desire to touch his warm skin and hard lines, while hoping that maybe, just maybe, Cap was feeling the same way she was. Or was she reading the signals all wrong?

Cap cleared his throat, his attention on the guardian dog. 'While you were walking Lurch—' It made them mirror their grins at Lurch thumping his tail on the ground. 'I found a name for the female.'

'Please tell me you didn't call her Cousin It, to go with the Addams Family theme?'

'Mamma Bear.' The dog groaned as she happily rolled over to get her tummy tickled by Cap.

Cap gave her the sweetest smile. Small, but genuine. But it lit Mia up from the inside to smile right back at this man.

'Welcome to the family, Lurch and Mamma Bear.' But the way he said that, as he looked at her, it was as if Cap had just welcomed Mia to the family, too.

Twenty-four

'**D**o you know the names of the stars?' Mia asked Cap, as she lay back on her swag stretched across the cage roof of Cap's Tojo. With only the stars for light, they had the best view over the calves getting to know the new guardian dogs in the small paddock below them.

'Only the Southern Cross and the Milky Way.' Cap pointed to the luminous river flowing from horizon to horizon, painting the night sky with a soft, silvery sheen. 'You?'

'No. Maybe I should learn. They're so incredibly clear out here.' So was his masculine outdoorsy aroma that wove around her like a spell.

'You would've seen them on your father's farm.'

'Back then, I didn't appreciate them like I do now. At the mines they have so much industrial light pollution it tainted the skies. But this…' She sighed, admiring the outback's vast landscape enveloped in a deep, inky blackness, where the night had settled a cool stillness over the sunburnt land.

Stars upon stars pierced the darkness, like a million tiny diamonds scattered over a velvet backdrop. In the distance, the escarpment's ruggedly stark silhouette ran like a jagged line that separated the earth from the sky. To the east, a faint glow ran behind the edge of the escarpment, hinting at the moon's arrival.

'It's a great way to end the day.' Should she wish upon a star?

'I agree. Bree's idea of the extended deck will give us the

same effect. But I'll invest in a decent set of outdoor chairs.' He lay back against his swag, his silhouette perfect against the skyline of stars that draped around him as if he were a gift from heaven itself.

'How long are you planning on doing these nightly visits?' Mia asked Cap, who was playing guardian angel to the new maremma sheepdogs, Lurch and Momma Bear, who were playing guardians over the small herd of calves, and this was night three.

'I think by the end of the week they'll have settled in nicely.'

'The same time my new room will be ready. If not sooner. And your deck, too.'

'It's all happening, isn't it?' His smile was delicious, with a rare dimple making an appearance.

She was excited for him. 'Can I ask you something?'

'Sure.' Leaning on his elbow, he stretched out his body, so lean and muscular it made her mind go blank that she could only focus on the sight of Cap. He was so beautiful that it hurt to look at him, like she was staring at a masculine angel with his hair tousled and messy from running his hands through it too many times.

Before she could turn away, he looked up. Their gazes fused, creating a thrill that rushed down her body to suddenly become a taut bundle of fire and electricity.

She forced herself to look away, her eyes landing on the ute, now remembering her question. 'I get the collection of trucker caps you keep across the dashboard of your Tojo. They're like the way you'd collect stickers of places.'

'Most were given to me.'

'So the nickname Cap is for caps?'

'It's not from hats.'

'What then?'

His grin was wide, as if reliving some fond memory, and he sat up, crossing his legs. 'When I was a young kid, I saw this visiting farmer use the side of Dad's workbench to pop the cap off his longneck bottle of home-brewed beer. To me, it was like magic.' His grin was boyish and surprisingly contagious; she grinned back. 'From there, it was an obsession to use everything but a bottle opener to pop the caps off my brothers' sodas, Dad's beers, to opening jars for Mum in the kitchen. I'd use the bottom of cigarette lighters, metal rulers, metal spoons, even the latches in car doors.'

'I've seen your brothers pass you their beers to pop their caps.'

'It's a habit for all of us in the Riggs family. One of my sisters posts me a bottle cap opener every year for my birthday. And the other one would send me a collection of bottle caps she'd find in her travels.'

'Where are those bottle caps now?' She liked making art out of bottle caps. What was the coincidence of that!

'They're in a box somewhere. Dex said we could use them for a home bar, or a special bourbon room for Ryder. Maybe I'll get you to build a display. Some are pretty special.'

She shrugged meekly, unsure about doing another project like that. Was it too soon, after the debacle with Gavin to settle down with someone else. Even though planting the wildlife corridors was a job, committing to a craft display might be getting too comfortable. Yet, when it came to Cap, he made her feel at ease within herself.

'So, what is your name?'

'It's Caleb.'

'Oh…' She sat taller, not expecting that at all. 'Do you like being called Caleb?'

'I'm so used to Cap that when I'm called Caleb, it's for something serious, like bills.'

'I get it.'

'Any more questions?'

She shifted her legs into a cross-legged position to mirror him. 'Why do you have that red dog collar hanging from the Tojo's rear-view mirror? The old leather one that rattles and has that faded tag.'

'Hmmm…' He sighed heavily, peering out to the field.

'I didn't mean to pry.'

'It's okay. No one has asked me that one before.' He sniffed heavily as if to draw strength from the crisp night air. 'The collar belonged to my first muster dog, Dodge. A blue heeler cross. We went through a lot together until old age caught up with him. But I kept the dog collar.'

'Why?'

'So that whenever the Tojo runs over the corrugations, I hear the rattle of Dodge's collar to remind me to keep going, especially through the tough times, to know I'll find paradise on the other side.'

'Was Dodge, um…' She peered down into the Tojo's cage where Willow was sleeping on a blanket Bree had given her, which she shared with Atlas and Fern, while the rest of the muster dogs were tucked up safe in their kennels. '…dumped, like Willow?'

'Worse. I saved him from a bullet. I nearly swallowed that lead myself.'

'Seriously?'

'I was only a young station hand then, when I realised what was happening. I'd sprinted from the sheds, slid across the dust to drop to my knees and put myself directly in front of that shotgun, keeping Dodge to my back, where he'd been chained to a tree.'

She gasped. 'Why?'

'That prick called Dodge a mutt and said he was no good as a muster dog, and wouldn't listen to him.' He scowled at the sky. 'That farmer was so wrong. Dodge taught me so much, he helped me train the other dogs, like Atlas does now.' He sighed and looked at Mia with such sorrow in his eyes. 'Dodge would've loved this place.'

'You're lucky to call this place home.' She nodded at the expansive sleeping landscape that stretched in all directions beyond the hidden horizon. Even with the other dramas unfolding in the background, it was like sitting in paradise.

'It's taken a long time to get here. Without my brothers, Ryder especially, none of this would have been possible. I mean, I never pictured living in a house the way Bree did, but

I can now.' His voice was deep and raspy, prompting images of sultry summer nights, soft sheets and nothing but skin on skin.

It wasn't fair.

No, it was worse, especially when his malt-whisky eyes drank her in like she was sunshine on a rainy day, and he was desperate for the rays.

'The many dreams I thought would've taken decades to achieve, I can actually reach out and touch them now, because of you.'

'The revegetation?'

He nodded. 'Your input has been invaluable.'

And that meant he only saw her as an employee, nothing more. She hugged her knees, desperate to squash her inner emotions playing havoc with her mind—she had a job to do. He was the boss, and she was the contractor.

She looked up to find Cap still staring at her.

He then leaned over and gently brushed the hair from her forehead and tucked it behind one ear as the blood whooshed through her. With the moon rising behind him, it cast an ethereal, magical glow around him. 'Thank you for everything, Mia.'

She sighed at the sound of her name crossing his lips. 'I should thank you.' When she really wanted to kiss him. Wouldn't that be the best way to properly thank the man who'd been her hero from the second he'd helped her out of the back of the Tojo, giving her a place to stay, and her dream job?

But his intense gaze had her pinned as he stared at her for so long that the demons that haunted her vaporised, and all she saw, smelt, heard, and needed to feel was Caleb 'Cap' Riggs.

She leaned in closer to kiss him, but he pulled back, and she gasped. 'I'm sorry.'

'No, I'm sorry.' He sat back higher in his swag as if to get away from her.

'I shouldn't have done that.' She hid her face in her hands

where the heat radiated through her fingers. What was she thinking? Cap wouldn't touch her, not when he'd seen her at her worst.

'Hey…' He tenderly stroked her hair. 'Were you going to kiss me?'

She couldn't look at him, barely nodding. 'I got my wires crossed and read the signals wrong.' Cap was just being kind to her, like he was with all the other strays he rescued. 'I should go.' She went to pack up, but he held her wrist.

'Mia, look at me.'

It took a while to find the courage to meet his eyes. She was expecting to see disgust and disappointment, but what she saw was unexpected.

Cap leaned in so close, his breath warm, his eyes blazing with hunger for her, but it also came with a whole new level of tenderness. With the tip of his finger, he traced along her bottom lip, then her chin, to cup her cheek while his eyes roamed over her face.

'It's the bruises.' She pulled back, hating them.

'You've been through a lot. I don't think you're ready for anything.'

'I'm trying to forget.'

Cap sat up, tenderly taking hold of her hands. 'Mia, I'm quite prepared to wait. I just don't want to be your rebound guy.'

'My what?'

'You barely broke up with—'

'Please don't say his name and ruin the mood.' Too late, it was already ruined. Her bottom lip dropped into a sulk, with the need to hug her pillow and hide under the covers.

Cap dipped his head closer, enough for her to once again admire his earthy fragrance in the outback's crisp night air.

He swallowed hard, his voice like gravel. 'I do want to kiss you, Mia. Very much.'

She blinked at him, a surge of hope and desire flaring through her body. 'I want you to. You have my permission, if that's what you're looking for.'

'I-I don't want this to be something casual. I'm not built like that.'

'Can't we just take it day by day?' She wasn't ready for the full commitment phase either.

But as the air between them grew heavier she couldn't stop herself from closing the distance to melt into his soft lips and his warm chest. And when her arms wrapped around his shoulders there was a groan, as he swept his tongue across her lower lip, begging her to open for him.

With a tiny sigh, she happily complied and slid her tongue against his, while her fingers dived through his hair, to hold him closer in a kiss that felt like pure heaven.

Her body sang out for him on some primal level. Despite what it'd been through, it was hungry. She was alive. And she was desperate to be loved by him.

'We'll take this slow, Mia.' His raspy voice sent a tremble of pure fiery lust to lick down her spine and around to her lower belly.

'What if I don't want you to take it slow?'

Once more he smiled that delicious smile. And she finally got to stroke the dimple that had been teasing her.

'We have all the time in the world.'

'Well, excuse me if I want to be a little greedy.' Her lips crashed into his, dragging him closer as their kiss deepened.

'Are you sure?' He mumbled against her lips, pulling her away.

Oh, great, now she was being all needy. She frowned. 'Don't reject me.' The heat coming out of her heart for him, was unlike anything she'd felt before.

'I wasn't.' He sat back.

'This,' she said, pointing at the gap between them. 'This feels like a rejection to me.'

Cap wiped his hand over his face. 'It's not you, it's me.'

'Huh?' Oh no, not the classic words—*it's not you, it's me*—before you got dumped by someone.

'It's been a long time since I've been with anyone. Are you sure you want to be with me?'

Didn't that make her smile. She didn't hesitate to walk on her knees to straddle his thick thighs and sit on his lap. 'Yes.' She held his face in her two hands. 'And I don't want you to hold back.'

'But—'

'Stop.' She placed her finger over his lips. 'I'm not some fragile princess. I'm a girl who likes to get dirty. So why can't we have some fun?'

Twenty-five

Cap's brain scrambled, scattering all common sense into nothing but dust. There was no logical reasoning, just a primal urge that swept over him. 'In that case…' He hands surrounded Mia's tiny waist to drag her closer onto his lap.

Her fingers sank deeper through his hair before she softened her mouth to settle against his, where he took each of her lips between his, one at a time. 'I'm going to savour this, Mia.'

'Whatever you want.' He felt the hunger in her voice, and the eagerness she displayed made him want to roar. He thumbed her chin to part her rosy lips wider, then when the tip of her tongue touched his, it fractured and heated something inside his chest.

Mia was so sweet, he wanted to be gentle with her. But she responded with a purring sound from her throat, while her fingernails raked down his chest—he wanted skin. And now.

He flipped her over, pressing her back against the cushioning swags, his knees on the roof of the ute gave a muted thud as he tucked her against him. Her hands scraped along his back, to tease the edge of his shirt free from his jeans. Suddenly, there was nothing shy or gentle about this, even if it was going too fast, with his body stiffening as she ground herself against him. *For fate's sake!*

Dragging his lips from hers, he grabbed her wrists to

regain control. Pushing her hands above her head had her back arching, her taught shirt displaying her hard nipples, as her lips parted, and he was swimming in a whole new world of trouble.

'My beautiful Mia.' Her name belonged on his lips.

They stared at each other, as the world crawled to suspend time in a place where wishes did come true. She was his Christmas morning, his sweet summer surprise, the New Year's desire, and his birthday blessings all wrapped into one sweet prize that his fingers slowly unwrapped, button by button down her shirt as his lips traced her slender neck that stretched back to give him access.

His teeth skated across her bottom lip, unleashing a hum of pleasure that made her smile just as his mouth sank hot and light against hers, coaxing it to stay open for him. She tasted like sweet summer desserts, as lashings of heat raced over him to thicken his bloodstream. Her sweet moans made his body stiffen rock hard. Far too soon.

Desperate to control himself, his hand swept up the side of her neck, his fingers curling into her hair as she sighed into him as he kissed her again, only this time slower, deeper, yet somehow rougher and tastier.

When her greedy tongue found his, suddenly they were all groans and hands, exploring, wild and free. No regret, no fears, nothing holding them back except their clothes.

This woman was in control, pushing him to sit back. She followed to hook her legs around his waist, sitting right over his hard length that was tight against his jeans. 'I'm going to make this so good for you, Cap.'

Before he could respond, she stood, the buckles on her baggy overalls rattled before they fell in a whisper of material. She kicked off her boots and ripped off her shirt, exposing all her soft curves under the moonlight.

This wasn't a dream. This was truly happening.

Twenty-six

The way Cap looked at her as he knelt before her, made Mia feel like a queen. The way his hands slid around her waist to the lace edge of her panties had her shivering. His fingers softly ran back and forth along the top edge of the material, and her body broke out in goosebumps.

It only got better as his warm soft lips traced over her skin, as he lowered the lacy material down her legs. Then he ran his hands up her shaking thighs, and her body was so hot and wet in readiness for him that she started to pant in short sharp breaths.

Never had she been naked under the starry sky with a man on his knees for her, attending to her, caring for her with his fingers and tongue to caress free her inner secrets and desires. He had her burning so brightly she could barely stand as her body trembled. It wasn't just stars she saw in the sky but exploding stars behind closed eyelids as her body unleashed a new heaven.

Standing, he ran his hand tenderly down the side of her face and neck, as he stood before her with his eyes blazing with hunger that looked her over inch by inch, then as a whole.

'Why are you still dressed?'

His grin was lopsided, but sweet sassy malassy, it was the sexiest smile she'd ever seen from this man.

She helped Cap rip off his shirt, push his jeans down, and then he was gloriously bare before her. *Dayum* he was thick, strong, and a perfect example of masculine beauty.

'I don't have any condoms.'

'It's okay, you're safe. We're safe. I made my ex wear them.' Which might have been on a subconscious level for some reason. 'But with you, we're safe.' And she felt safe with Cap.

Plus, it was too late to explain everything now. Not while she was in a place with no walls, butt naked to the world, standing high in the sky. Somehow, this man had drugged her with his midnight kisses that came with lots of stolen soft touches, and she needed more.

Stepping towards her, he gently tugged on her hair, pulling her head back, forcing her to look up at him. Her lips parted, eager to kiss him again.

She swallowed without any nerves, but quivered with anticipation as his free hand trailed a finger down her neck, over her racing pulse, opening his palm to cup her aching breasts.

The moan he unleashed inside her was so foreign, she nearly buckled to her knees.

His arm snaked around her back for support, allowing her to arch back, as his hot, hungry mouth worked from one breast to the other. All she could do was hold on to his strong shoulders, as his hard length pressed against her lower body.

When he suddenly lifted her to gently lower her to their bedding, the weightlessness surprised her.

Then he was above her, where once again the stars surrounded him like the fallen angel he was, and she willingly opened herself for him.

One of his hands pressed on the linen beside her head, as his other hand clamped onto her leg. His wide finger span covered her thigh, while wearing a look of pure admiration in his eyes.

Clearly, Cap liked what he felt, sliding a hungry hand over her round stomach and breast, as he positioned himself between her legs.

He leaned down.

She reached up.

And they paused.

They both sucked in air, then held their breaths as his tip brushed into her.

She forgot to breathe. Forgot how to speak. How to think. Not when her entire world fell into this one perfect moment as he moved so slowly, one glorious inch at a time.

From the back of his throat, he made a noise of triumph. An earthy, grunt. *Dayum*, it had to be the sexiest sound as he pushed all the way into her.

He grabbed the side of her face, pulling her into him, his breath heavy as his lips crashed down onto hers in an all-consuming kiss that wasn't gentle, but it was a kiss that told her how much he wanted her.

A moan escaped her as they moved, slowly at first, her hips lifted to meet his deep rhythmic thrusts as his muscles rippled while he hovered over her, making her entire body vibrate with the weight of him.

He claimed her and he owned her with a fierce intensity that was so gentle it took little for her body to combust into millions of bright lights, as she came apart and clamped down on him.

He growled in her ear.

'Fates…' His face dropped into the crook of her neck, his grip tightened around her body as his muscles contracted into steel and he unleashed a warmth that flowed through her, soothing every jagged edge of life's hardships into something amazing.

As the night air nipped refreshingly against their slick skin, his forehead pressed to hers. Still in a tangle of limbs, his body limp on hers, they stared long and silently at each other, communicating to each other in a way that didn't need words.

The moon rose over the escarpment to bathe them with beams of soft creamy moonlight, and he shared a soft smile as his fingertips stroked her face. 'My beautiful Mia.'

And she'd never felt more beautiful.

Twenty-seven

It was two weeks later, when Cap parked his Tojo at the drafting yards, with Ash in the passenger seat. The sun hung low on the distant horizon, highlighting the haze of red dust that floated in the air.

'Why are we here?' Ash asked.

'Ryder said he wanted a meeting.'

'We have one twice a day at the farmhouse at the outdoor table. We should just call it the boardroom.'

'The table covered in empty beer cans and coffee cups.' They chuckled as they climbed out of the ute. Cap let Atlas and Fern out of the Tojo's back cage. The rest of the muster dogs were already chilling in their kennels after another big day.

Ash bounded up the staircase to the high boards that overlooked the drafting yards that they were now using as a fancy feedlot to fatten their cattle for market.

Up top, they found Dex leaning over the rails with a beer in hand. 'There's beer in the esky, boys.'

'Cheers.' Ash plucked a can from the ice and passed one to Cap.

Cap eagerly guzzled on his beer that was like heaven on the tastebuds to chase away the day's dust. 'Where's Ryder?'

'Down there.' Dex nodded, his dark eyes shaded by the brim of his hat. 'Checking the gummy gate again.'

'Didn't we fix that already?' asked Ash.

'I did, today. As well as the gate that jammed up during

the drafting.'

Ryder's heavy boot tread was felt on the boards as he climbed the stairs. 'Save me any beer?'

'Here.' Ash rummaged through the esky and handed a beer to Ryder. 'So, why are we out here?'

'To talk about this weekend's campdraft.'

'Why out here, and not at the table?'

'This conversation is for partners only.' Ryder might not have said it, but he was talking about Harper and Mia.

'Hey, I don't keep secrets from Harper—'

Ryder raised his hand, cutting off Ash. 'This is a business meeting. Straight and simple.'

No, it wasn't. It showed Ryder didn't approve of the women at all, especially Mia, who'd done so much for Cap.

'I don't think you lot realise what an opportunity this is for us.'

'It's not our first campdraft. Relax, Ryder.'

'That's what I said.' Dex turned and leaned his back against the rails. 'I'm going to drink beer, look at the cars, the occasional cow, and score a buckle bunny. So I'll be getting a ride in with you, Ryder.'

'Ash? What do you plan to do?'

Ash shrugged. 'I'll be checking out the horses, like I normally do, and drinking beer. I'll get Harper to drive.'

'That's not what I meant.' Ryder shook his head. 'Your cattle tags and water tech is now patented, so while you're still running your trials, it's time to see if there is a market out there—which we know there is. And the local campdraft would be a good place to learn how to talk about your products.'

'Do you really think so?' Ash rubbed the back of his neck.

Ryder plonked a heavy hand on their younger brother's shoulder. 'I believe in your products. It's why I'm financially backing them all.'

'I agree,' said Dex.

'Ditto.' Cap held his beer up in a toast.

'What about you, Cap?'

'I've entered Fern and Atlas for the muster dog trials, under the name of Elsie Creek Station.' He'd been practising with them daily, alongside Mia and Willow.

'To do what?' Ryder crossed his arms, waiting.

Cap removed his hat and raked fingers through his hair. 'I want to show how easy it is for new farmers to use a muster dog and their benefits such as cutting down on labour costs. They've saved us stacks.'

'Weren't you looking at doing some puppy school?' Dex smirked behind his can.

Cap narrowed his eyes at Dex being a dick. 'Look, cattle dogs aren't new. But I want to be known as the go-to person for re-training those problem dogs, so that farmers can come to me, and not shoot or discard their dogs. Nearly all of my muster dogs were like that, where now I could sell them back to those farmers if I wanted to.'

'But we know you won't sell them,' said Dex, for once not being a dick as he patted Cap's shoulders. 'They're part of your pack that is an asset to this place, brother.'

'And the Maremma's?' asked Ryder.

'As much as I'd like to show them, I'm not ready yet. Even if those guardian dogs have easily proven themselves to be a success, I'll show them next time.'

'Harper wants one of those dogs for the house,' said Ash.

'Like hell.' Ryder frowned. 'There are enough pampered dogs crowding the farmhouse now as it is. What else, Cap?'

'Um…' He scratched at his neck. 'Mia's nursery is doing well.'

His brothers may have said nothing, yet he knew what they were thinking: Mia wasn't a partner. Harper wasn't either, but she worked for the vet in town, had her own money, and did a day in the office while helping on the station like a trainee stockwoman.

Mia was their only full-time employee.

'What do you want to do, Cap? For this station.' Ryder obviously chose his words carefully to exclude Mia.

Cap wasn't a fool. He knew Ryder was doing this to

protect their assets. 'Mia has become an asset. She's helped recognise and provide plant stock to not only feed the cattle, but to create wildlife corridors that double as windbreaks to stop dust storms. Our plans on soil repair, which reduce and offset carbon emissions, are working much better than expected.' His grin broke out to share the news. 'My paddock is done, brothers.'

'No way?' Dex's beer can froze halfway to his mouth.

'The fencing, the wildlife corridors, and the no-till pasture planting is done.' The thrill of completing a project, his dream, was such a high for him, one he shared with Mia. 'Now we just watch it grow.'

'They're starting on my paddock next.' Ash playfully nudged Cap's ribs.

Ryder tilted his head, his voice low and steady. 'Even then, there's still a lot of stock growing inside that shade house.'

Cap could never hide anything from Ryder. 'Mia's native nursery has created enough seedling stock to supply other farmers, other mine sites, with room to expand big time to make it a full-time gig.'

'A commercial nursery?' Ash asked.

'A small-scale commercial native nursery.' Cap nodded. It was Mia's dream, too. 'Mia knows what other mines want for their revegetation programs. And we're hoping to sell some of that plant stock at the campdraft to pay for dog food and future vet fees. The costs have been minimal and we're repurposing the water from that pond you dug, Dex. We've got solar running the pumps, using the irrigation pipes Bree found out the back of the sheds. Only the seedling trays and pots we've bought new. The rest Mia and I have been able to use what we have.'

'Will it make a profit if you sell those seedlings?' asked Dex.

'Ninety-eight per cent.'

'You forget Mia's wages are a part of that equation, too,' said Ryder, their bank.

'I think it sounds like a good idea,' said Ash.

'You really want to save the world, don't you?' Dex playfully punched Cap's shoulder. 'Sounds good to me, too, brother.'

But Ryder stared, cold and unemotional as always.

'Do you see a problem with us selling those seedlings, Ryder?' Cap only saw benefits.

Ryder took a deep guzzle of his beer. 'I think you should give them away.'

'Say what?' Ash shuffled his boots, as Dex paused mid-drink.

'But aren't we meant to make money?' Cap asked Ryder, who held the purse strings on this station.

'If you give one seedling pot and a brochure as a package deal to advertise your commercial native nursery, it'll sweeten the deal for future customers.'

'I get it,' said Ash. 'Harper says some authors offer their new readers a free book to try out their writing style. It'd be the same concept if Cap gave them a seedling they can't kill, with the brochure the girls designed.'

'They'll need to be update, if we want to put in the native nursery details on them.' Cap nodded eagerly, not expecting that out of Ryder.

'They have time. Which is why I am calling this meeting here today.' Ryder patted Cap's shoulder. 'I think your native nursery is a good idea and it goes with my plans to diversify this station.'

'Huh?' Dex arched his eyebrows. 'Isn't this a cattle station?' He pointed to the small herd in the yards below them.

'We have a cattle station with little cattle. So we need to bring in other forms of income until we've got decent-sized herds again.' Ryder looked at the three brothers. 'We'll have that with Ash and his tags—'

'And my water trough tech?'

'That too. And maybe you can design a drone specifically for mustering. In the meantime, you could teach farmers how to use drones, like Cap with his muster dogs and guardian dogs. Maybe build an arena, just for that dual purpose.'

Cap and Ash nodded like kids being given free rein in a candy store.

'And what do I do, besides look pretty?' Dex scowled as he adjusted his hat over his eyes.

'Volunteer your skills to help them build things, like finishing my house before the wet season hits.'

'Right, so I'm the mug on the tools.' Dex crossed his arms over his chest, showing off all the muscles he had. Any wonder when the guy was training in the mornings, working all day, then he'd train at night for his fights.

'You're mechanically minded, and we all know you like playing with the tools,' said Ryder.

'Dex should have been an engineer,' said Cap.

'He is, just without the fancy tickets.' Ryder was handing out the compliments today—which was rare. 'I'm sure you have ideas, Dex. You still have a paddock to play with, too.'

'Well, I have an idea for a new cradling system to make things quicker in the yards.' Dex pointed at the pit they were all well-acquainted with. 'I want to build it and test it when the vet comes and checks our stock.'

'Good.' Ryder patted Dex's back.

Their normally gruff brother was being so nice. Should Cap ask Ryder if he was okay?

For a moment they drank their beer as they watched the sun grow heavier as it kissed the edge of the horizon, spreading shadows over the drafting yards, when they heard a horse galloping behind them.

'It's Bree.' Ash pointed at Bree riding up on her black stallion.

'Oh look, the queen of chaos is here.' Dex leaned over the rails to smirk at her.

'Isn't daycare shut this time of the day, boys? Why aren't you lot messing up that table at the farmhouse?'

'Why aren't you wallowing in your trough, slugging down a jug of gin?'

'I thought I'd look for some bunyips and drop bears,' she said with a straight face.

'Are you saying you still believe in fairytales?'

'I'm no damsel in distress, and I'm too busy to bother saving any male from themselves. But let me guess,' she said, wiggling her gloved finger at them like a worm. 'Your little crocheting corner is to do with the campdraft?'

Ryder crossed his arms, glaring at her. 'We know what we're doing.'

'But do you realise that this is Elsie Creek's annual campdraft, and you'll be there as the new owners of Elsie Creek Station?'

'Are you worried we'll embarrass you?' Dex asked.

'Do you really want me to answer that, stormcloud?' Bree gave a positively wolfish grin.

It had Ryder lifting an eyebrow. 'Play nice, Bree.'

'I am. I know you've all got your own projects, and before you bite my head off, cupcake, and tell me to butt out, I'm here to tell you I've booked you a tent.'

'For what?'

'To show your cute butts off to whoever walks past like strippers on a Sunday.' She giggled to herself. 'I'd sell tickets for that, and then I'd invest in my favourite charity—being me, and my future holiday to watch padded men play ice hockey.'

'We're not stripping.' Dex scowled at her.

'You strip off your shirt to get all hot and sweaty in front of strangers for your fights. What's the difference?'

'Why did you get us a tent at the campdraft?' Cap asked Bree.

'I usually get one for the family's cattle-brand business. Only this year I booked a bigger one to include you guys, if you want in. No skin off my nose, if you don't.'

'Whereabouts?'

'Main thoroughfare. Best spot to catch everyone who walks past.'

'Why?' Ash asked with a shrug.

'To network.' Ryder responded curtly, while nodding at Bree.

'Good to see someone's got their thinking cap on. But you can skip the tent, Dex, you'll scare the children. The beer tent is your playground to mingle. They'll have the cars there.'

'See, you do love me.' Dex grinned at Bree, as Ryder scowled.

'What else can we expect?' Ash asked.

'You'll get to meet your other neighbours, who could be future customers for the ideas you guys have. If you're going to talk about your cattle tags, Ash, I'd suggest you have Harper create a sheet for customers to leave their names and email addresses for future sales. You can use it for Mia and Cap's commercial native nursery, too. Oh, and for the guardian dogs and the dog school. Plenty of customers will be there.'

Ryder growled as he looked back at his brothers. 'How is it Bree knows all about this before me?'

The three of them shrugged.

Shaking his head, Ryder crossed his arms over his chest and glared down at Bree. 'What's it gonna cost me?'

'Pfft, nothing, cupcake.'

'Everyone has a price for doing favours.'

'Like I said, I get a tent every year.' She barked out at him, her horse shifting beneath her, but she remained steady, matching Ryder's scowl. 'It's no skin off my nose if you don't want it, cupcake. I'll just pretend I don't know you, if you're going to be like that.' She went to ride away.

'*Fine!* We'll take it.'

'I'll scribble out a mud map for you. Charlie can deliver it to the farmhouse later. He'll gladly fill you in on the gossip. Ash, I'd suggest you take the drone to tape Cap at the muster dog trials. Harper can then spin it for a social media campaign.'

'Good idea.' Ash nodded with a grin. Cap widened his eyes; he'd been living so far off-the-grid he had nothing to do with social media.

Meanwhile Ryder's scowl just got deeper.

'See, cupcake, not everything has to have an ulterior motive.' She gave Ryder a filthy look, then rode off, not even glancing back.

'That woman can be so irritating.' Ryder gripped the rail so hard it groaned as if about to crack under the pressure.

Dex patted Ryder's shoulder. 'Easy brother, Bree is only helping us.'

'So why was Bree riding out here when she normally rides in the mornings? What were those saddlebags full of? And how is it that she knows more about this station and your ideas than I do? When that redhead takes great pleasure in constantly telling us she doesn't work for us!' Ryder pointed angrily in her direction, mumbling a set of expletives under his breath, as if to expel the hot air.

Cap side-glanced his brothers. No one ruffled Ryder quite like Bree did.

'That irritating, sassy-mouthed redhead is right, though…' Ryder exhaled heavily, dropping his hands to his hips, and lowering his head. 'The campdraft isn't just a social event for us like it used to be. We're station owners now, which means it's a place of business.' Ryder turned and faced his brothers.

Cap instantly felt the pressure land heavily on his shoulders, noting Ash was the same.

'But I don't want you lot to think of it that way, because we're not just investing in a business, we're investing in a lifestyle and a legacy. So, right here and now, I want you all to speak openly about any ideas you have for the future of this place. Say it now, free from judgement. So I'm not hearing it second-hand from someone who has no investment in this place.' Again, Ryder scowled in Bree's direction. 'Agreed?'

They all nodded, and that afternoon, long after the sun

had set, they discussed many ideas for a long-term future, standing on the high boards of the drafting yards. But they knew the real test was to come at the local campdraft, where they'd hopefully make a name for themselves as the new owners of Elsie Creek Station.

Twenty-eight

Twenty-eight

ormally, Cap wasn't bothered by nerves. But today prickly nerves quickened his bloodstream as dust kicked up from his boots as he entered the shade of Mia's native nursery. Coarse gravel crunched under his boots, and the heavy humidity rose, but the shade was cooling. It's where he found Mia in the centre of the many tables filled with flourishing seedlings that rested across the racks.

The kelpie trotted over to greet him.

'G'day, girl.' He gave the dog a hearty pat. 'Mia?'

'Oh, hey.' Her smile was pure dynamite that made his heart ka-thump in his chest. 'I've got the boxes sorted for the seedlings we'll be taking tomorrow, to load up the Tojo tonight. And I stored all the information pamphlets Harper and I made, in my old room.' She giggled at the words *old room.*

It was their in-house joke because, even though the first stages of the renovations to his demountable had finished weeks ago, Mia had never slept in her room, and Cap had never slept more soundly than he did with Mia's warm body against his, with her silky hair brushing against his chest. It's where he'd tuck her close against him to let her know that she was in a safe space, as his most precious gift.

He'd fallen so hard for her it was terrifying at times.

How could he not be terrified? This was his once-in-a-lifetime kind of love—where you knew instinctively that you'd met your other half, that perfect half of yourself that made you whole. And it was her. All of her.

'Got a sec? I, ah, want to show you something.' He was hoping it would help her understand how big a deal she was to him.

'Sure. Where are we going?' With Willow following close on their heels, Mia tightened her ponytail. These days she kept her hair away from her face, rather than using it to hide, but she was still hiding at this station.

'It's this way.' He headed around the back of the sheds where he kept the empty beer cans and other recyclables that contributed to the cost of caring for the dogs.

'You don't have to like it, or anything.' He unlocked a solid wooden door, twisted its rusty handle, and used his shoulder to force it open. 'I'll oil that later. But I did make sure there's nothing hiding in here.' No snakes or nasty spiders, that's for sure.

Mia wiped the dust off her button nose that only highlighted the smattering of freckles. She was never afraid of getting dirty, and he liked that about her. He especially liked how dirty she got with him after dark in ways that didn't require clothing, with the body she hid beneath those baggy overalls. It was like unwrapping his Christmas present every night of the week, and mornings had never been more glorious.

'What is this place?'

'An old storeroom. Now it's yours.' He hoisted some boxes onto the dusty bench.

She peeked inside: 'Is it for the nursery?'

'No. It's for your hobby.'

'Huh?'

From the box, Cap pulled out a handful of beer bottle caps. 'I've been collecting these ever since we moved onto the station. I had no idea why I was saving them, but I did. And Charlie scored you a box of caps from the local pub and now they're all yours.' They had so much in common that he truly believed that meeting her was fate, as if they were made for each other. How could he not when her favourite hobby involved bottle caps, which was the reason he ended up with his nickname, Cap.

'You said you enjoyed making art with these beer caps.' He laid out the tools he'd scrounged across the old workbench that sat in the centre of the room. 'I got you some hammers. I'm not sure if this glue is any good, but we can get you some next time we're in town.' If she ever left the place. 'And I got you some scrap wood to use as bases.' He pointed to the stack he'd leaned in the corner.

'I also got you this bar fridge and filled it up with your favourite drinks.' He opened the small fridge full of colourful cans and a large plastic container. 'In here, I filled it up with all of your favourite chocolate treats you like but won't let me bring into the house.' He didn't understand that bit. If you liked something, you ate it, right?

Mia remained still, holding a few bottle caps, with her mouth open, wearing an expression he couldn't read.

Had he gone too far?

'All of this space?'

'Is for you.' He uncurled her fingers and placed a thick key in her hand. 'I want you to have your own space, to make as much noise as you want out here. You won't bother anyone. And if, at any time, you just need some space to breathe, this is here for you. As yours.'

'You made me a safe room.' Her brow ruffled, and it twisted his guts.

Had he done the wrong thing? 'You said you liked to do bottle cap mosaics. Right?'

'I do. Did. I mean… You did this for me?' Her eyes widened as she turned around in circles.

He nodded. 'I want you to feel safe, Mia. If it's too much—'

She grabbed his wrist. 'You made this for me.'

He nodded. 'I know it's not romantic, but I wanted to show you how much I appreciate all your hard work and because I want you to be happy.' He liked her smile and it had taken her a long time to find it after what her ex had done. Cap just wanted her to keep smiling.

And there it was. That beautiful, glorious, chin-lifting, nose-wrinkling, sparkly smile that plumped her rosy cheeks. He was such a sucker for that smile.

Mia flung herself at him, hugging him around the neck to shower his face with kisses. 'This is amazing.'

'So, you're okay with this?' He held his breath.

'Thank you, Cap. Seriously, though, you didn't have to do this for me.' She opened the small fridge again, full of her favourite treats and drinks. 'No one has done anything like this for me. You shouldn't have.'

'I wanted to.' Now it had him thinking of other ways to spoil her. 'It's my way of thanking you for helping me achieve my dreams.'

These past few weeks working side by side with Mia had become a part of his daily joy. Sharing lunch together, sitting on the roof of his Tojo, their legs swinging over the edge as they'd eat sandwiches and talk of plans for the paddock they were working on. They'd spend afternoons planting seeds in the nursery, and some days they'd trample through the fresh morning dew, foraging for seeds together. Then at the end of the day they'd sit on his deck to silently watch the sunset, with the dogs at their feet. It was his kind of paradise because Mia was a big part of it.

'Won't your brothers want this space for something?'

'No. They know this is your office, or art room, or whatever you want to call it.' Dex had warned him it may backfire, while helping Cap to find some tools and the key for the door. Ash had recommended the sugar stash, was now hunting for new ideas to do something special for Harper. As for Ryder—he just nodded and went on his way when Cap asked about giving this space to Mia. But Ryder's silent message was loud and clear about not getting too attached.

But Cap was attached. Big time.

It also scared him that Mia could leave at any time.

'Are you sure? I, um…' She twisted her fingers. Mia only did that when she was worried about something. 'I, we should, um— I should tell you something.'

'Sure, go ahead. You can tell me anything.' He waited.

And he kept waiting because he was a very patient man.

She sighed. 'Forget it. What were you going to say?'

'Hey, are you worried about my brothers and this room? Don't be.' He covered her hands with his. 'It's a gift, Mia. You've helped us all out, especially with the data. It wasn't easy teaching us how to use those sampling kits.' Mia had taught all his brothers how to test the water and soils, where each of his brothers kept a testing kit in their vehicles, collecting data to give to Mia.

Mia had helped Harper simplify their data reports using her templates, and the two women were now a big part of their nightly discussions at the outdoor table, and on their cooking roster making hearty meals that they all enjoyed.

With the bruises long gone, Mia's personality truly shone through. She was a part of this place, and he wanted her to feel like she belonged.

Although, he hadn't quite plucked up the courage to say the L word yet, but he'd fallen deeply, madly in love with Mia. He just didn't know how to say it when Mia only wanted to take it day by day.

Bree was right. He didn't know how to communicate his emotions with words, but with actions like this room, he hoped she'd got the message.

He just didn't want her to leave.

Well over a month ago, beaten, bloodied and bruised, he'd found her hiding in the dog cage, and tomorrow they were going back to the town Mia had fled from.

Fate may have brought them together, but it was fear that might tear them apart. Mia might have arrived with nothing, but if she left, she would be taking his heart.

Twenty-nine

Excitement filled the air as people of all ages arrived in trucks and assorted four-wheel drives, towing trailers and horse floats. Sturdy stockhorses nickered and neighed, cattle lowed, and dogs yipped and barked as the aroma of barbecued meats scented the air to create a carnival-like atmosphere for the annual Elsie Creek Campdraft, held at the rodeo end of the local sports grounds.

'Have you ever been to a campdraft?' Cap asked Mia, as they unloaded their many trays of seedlings from the Tojo, while Atlas, Fern and Willow waited obediently inside the large cage. Ryder's big ute was parked on one side of the Tojo, and Harper in her Audi was parked on the other.

'No. Are cowboy hats part of the uniform? I've never seen so many hats.' She tugged on her overalls, feeling underdressed. But it was all she had.

'Careful saying the C word with this crowd.' Cap chuckled, loading up the trolley with their best seedlings. They had hundreds, along with the Elsie Creek Station brochures about their various patented products and native nursery, it also included instructions for seedling care while outlining the benefits of native windbreaks, to share with their neighbours.

'Why can't I say *cowboys*?' The place was wall to wall cowboys of all ages. 'Do I call them cowgirls, too?'

'In this region, cowboys are what we call the boys, or girls, who do minor jobs around stations before they train to become stockmen.'

'Oh, so it's…'

'An insult to a stockman.' He nodded.

Tugging on her ponytail, again she felt severely underdressed. 'Maybe I should've brought my hat out.' But it was dirty, and they were supposed to be in a tent all day.

'Feel free to pinch any of my caps, if you want.' He pointed to his vast collection of hats that covered the entire dashboard of his Tojo. The sun sparkled to catch the buckle on Dodge's old dog collar. It made her pause, to realise she'd been through worse and shouldn't worry about the little things.

'I'll be fine.' She then playfully patted his amazing butt in his good jeans. 'But you look nice.' More than nice, her man was sweet sassy malassy hot and sizzling. *Dayum.*

'It's for the show events.' Cap smoothed down his necktie over his checked shirt, in clean jeans, and polished boots. 'I've got a lot riding on today.'

It was her turn to give his hand an encouraging squeeze. 'Hey, you'll be incredible.'

He gave her a wink, the sly kind that always made her smile from the inside. 'Here, you take Willow with you.' He led the kelpie from the cage, her coat gleaming. 'I've got to admit Bree's dog shampoo is fancy. The kelpie looks like one of those polished racehorses at the Melbourne Cup.'

'So do Fern and Atlas.'

'They do look good.' He patted the dogs in the cage. '*Stay*… I'll come back and set them up once I've shown you where the tent is.' Closing the cage, he grabbed the trolley loaded with crates of plant seedlings.

'Do we lock the Tojo up?' Considering they locked nothing at the station.

'Yeah, I forgot.' He chuckled as he walked around to the driver's side and locked the old ute.

'What about the back?'

'The dogs won't let anyone near it.'

She dropped her head at the reminder.

'Hey, my little stowaway, you're okay.' He gave her

shoulders a squeeze and kissed the top of her hair as if he'd read her mind.

Ash closed the boot of Harper's slick Audi. 'Babe, we should've brought my ute for all this stuff.' He juggled with the fold-up tables and chairs. 'Cap? Have you got room on that trolley? I've still got a kid to get out of his seat and they don't travel light.'

'I've got you.' Cap helped his brother with the tables.

'Here, let me.' Mia helped Harper load up the pram with a cooler, a water container, and the many items a toddler needed.

It was like a bucket of cold water being splashed over her good mood. She hadn't told Cap about her not being able to have children. Every time she tried, she chickened out because she didn't want to ruin what they had.

'We good?' Cap asked, while waiting for her like always so he could walk at her side.

'Yeah.' She pasted on a smile, sliding the baby bag over her shoulder, and grabbed the boxes of pamphlets, looking for Willow's lead, following close to Mia's knee, like always. 'Good girl, Willow. Stick close.'

'Anyone see Bree?' Harper pushed the loaded pram like a wheelbarrow.

'Bree is parking Charlie's car up by the vintage cars display near the beer tent,' replied Ash, hoisting his son onto his shoulders.

'Pandora,' said Harper. 'It's says so on the new numberplates Bree got for the car, that Porter helped her get registered. Bree has a nickname for everything.'

'And everyone,' said Ash already looked bothered as the packhorse. 'Where are we setting up?'

'Our tent is on the main thoroughfare. Good traffic, Bree said.' Cap pulled out the mud map Charlie had given them. 'Here.'

'Will your other brothers help us today?' asked Harper.

Cap grinned at Ash, who said, 'Dex, the revhead, has volunteered to watch over Pandora, acting like a proud father. I think he's trying to convince Charlie to make it a black muscle car. Porter thinks it should be a hot rod.'

'I like how it is now. Charlie was up late polishing it.'

'Like you were, polishing dogs. I've gotta say that kelpie's looking good.' Ash tilted his head at the dog. 'Great shine on her coat.'

'Thanks to Bree's dog shampoo,' Mia said.

'Another witchy concoction.' Ash shifted his shoulders to better balance the child, before hooking his arm through the camp chair and cooler.

'Will you be showing the fluffy white bears next year?' Harper asked.

'Babe, those guardian dogs aren't pets.'

'But Lurch and Momma Bear are adorable,' said Harper. The new guardian dogs had settled in so fast they were like part of the furniture, protecting a paddock full of poddy calves.

'Will you guys ever use them for mustering, like your other dogs?' Harper asked Ash as they made their way through the crowded car park of assorted utes, trucks, and four-wheel-drives.

'No. They're not built for that. They're just there to protect our calves.'

'Is that why you put those dogs in the kennel when Mia and I are having horse riding lessons with the calves?'

'Help me out here, bro?' Ash pleaded with Cap, lifting his arms, carrying the camp chairs, while balancing a toddler on his shoulders.

'We're not just training you two to be stockwomen, but we're also teaching the calves to get used to being mustered by stockhorses. And sometimes guardian dogs can be protective, as they aren't used to our processes either.'

'So, it's one big lesson for everyone,' said Mia smiling up at Cap. She loved everything about station living, the pace, the lifestyle and how no two days were the same.

But today she was in town for the first time in over a month, and switched on her mobile phone. In a matter of moments, it displayed over thirty phone messages and another fifty text messages waiting for her.

Most of them were from Gavin.

Thirty

'Our tent is this way.' Cap led Mia, Harper, Ash and Mason through the crowds, past the food stands and stalls selling leather goods, saddles and stockwhips, belts, and hats, as well as displays of tractors, trucks and other large farming equipment.

This wasn't Cap's first campdraft, it also wasn't the first time he'd manned a tent to sell seedlings, or participated in the muster dog trials. But it was the first time he'd done so as a co-owner of Elsie Creek Station, using today's campdraft to show off their goods that didn't involve cattle but the other aspects of the cattle industry.

A lot of the other stations had stalls set up as well. There were display tents with handmade quilts and knitted toys for toddlers, beef jerky, jams and chutneys, and assorted woodwork, jewellery and even clothes—including, strangely, a tutu stall. There was something for everyone, from proper no-nonsense steak sangas, rich aromatic coffee, to boot repairs.

The sweet sugary aroma of fairy floss had him inhaling deeply, as Mason squealed, from high on Ash's shoulders, pointing at a colourful jumping castle in the process of being inflated, with a group of children lining up before the show had even officially kicked off.

On the far side, on a small rise, stood a mechanical bull inside its own fenced arena. It clearly stood out near the beer tent, where assorted classic utes and vintage cars sparkled under the sun. Nearby, a group of musicians were setting up at the bandstand, testing their instruments, ready to party late into the night.

'Here we are.' Cap steered the loaded trolley under the shade of the simple tent, that was a large rectangular area with simple canvas walls on three sides. He brushed the dirt spilling off a seedling tray from his shirt. 'I should've brought a spare shirt out. Or just worn my station clobber like you.'

'I should have worn something else.' Mia twisted her fingers, as she shifted uneasily in the overalls she lived in at the station. He loved her in those overalls, because she loved them.

'You look comfortable.'

'Are you?'

He shrugged. It wasn't often he wore a tie.

'When are the dogs on?' Ash held one end of the sheets for Harper as she set up their display tables like they were a fine dining restaurant about to seat royalty.

Cap checked his watch. 'Not for a while. The gymkhana for the kids is on first, then the junior stockhorse events. The muster dog trials will be on before the senior events.'

'Jump? Uncle. Jump?' Mason's little hands reached up.

'Not here, mate.' Cap picked up his nephew.

'Is he talking about the obstacle course?' Mia asked.

Cap nodded. 'I've rescued this guy from the dog's tunnel a few times.'

'Or plucked him off the high beam when he'd crawled on top.'

'What?' Both Ash and Harper stopped and stared in horror.

'All good. It's just the dogs' agility set that Mason uses as a playground.' And it had been used a lot these past few weeks.

Cap always used whatever scrap he found at stations, from spare tyres, old boards, and empty oil drums to create an obstacle course. Working dogs needed to work, or they'd get into mischief, and he found the obstacle course was the best way to keep them active and stimulated, while fine-tuning their skills in their downtime.

But now he owned a permanent obstacle course. Coming home one afternoon from planting trees with Mia, they found Dex and Bree bantering with each other in a competition to see who could weld up the frames quicker.

In no time they had built him an entire obstacle course with the proper placings you'd find at any fancy dog trials. That pair never said who won. And Bree dragged her welding gear away refusing to accept anything more than thanks.

Harper opened the boxes containing their station's brochures and set them out in a fancy fan on the display table in their tent. 'We should have bought balloons.'

'What for, babe? It's not a kid's party.' Ash playfully tapped down the brim of his son's cowboy hat. Mason giggled and started playing peekaboo.

'This reminds me of a political campaign, where we'd shake a few hands, talk the talk, and win a few votes,' said the daughter of a federal minister.

'None of us are politicians, Harper.'

'I know. But this is what I do. So, Ash, you can take Mason and go find Ryder and get the okay from the organisers for using the drone. Cap, you go see to your dogs and let me and Mia do our jobs.'

'Don't worry, we'll be there to see the dog trials. I can't wait.' Mia kissed his cheek and pushed him out of the tent.

Cap hesitated. Not only was he beginning to feel the pressure of representing the station in the competitions, but he also didn't want to leave Mia behind.

'Go, I'll be right here while you get the dogs settled in.'

'Promise?'

Thirty-one

Mia could feel Cap's nervousness. For a man who was normally so calm, it wasn't often she saw any nerves. She had no doubt it was about the dog events they'd been practising for. She was a little nervous herself, hoping it all went perfectly for them.

'Stop searching, the party has arrived.' Bree pushed up her sunglasses as she dragged her large cart into their tent. Her long loose curls had a glorious shine. Dressed in a cute summer dress and western boots, even wearing make-up and jewellery.

'You look so different, Bree,' Ash said.

'Town clothes. But I'll take that as a compliment, thank you.' She propped a hand on a generous hip. 'Aren't you meant to be somewhere, Cap?'

Again, Cap hesitated as he turned to Mia.

'I'll watch over the girls. You boys go do what you do while we set up. You'll just get in our way.' Bree shooed them away.

'Thanks, Bree.' Cap squeezed her upper arm before leaving. Cap went left, Ash and Mason went right, leaving the three women to organise the tent.

'Right, ladies, let's do this.' Bree rubbed her hands together. 'We'll set it up to suit the crowd. If I know Territorians, they like to chase the shade and will come inside just to get out of the sun. And when they find a suitable spot,' she said, dragging a large floor fan from her cart, complete with extension cords, 'they tend to stay and have a chat as they cool off. Which gives you more time to talk the talk. There should be a plug back here.' She lifted the tight back of the tent flap that had no room to wriggle under. 'Stop looking. I found it.' And in a matter of minutes, they had a fan circulating the air, plus a water station with a stack of paper cups cleverly placed near their glossy brochures.

'You're a genius, Bree.' Harper with her immaculate polished appearance, nodded with approval. 'What are you selling?'

'The usual cattle brands, fire pokers, and some of my herbal products.' Bree snapped out a black cloth over her table, pushed to the far side of the tent, where she pulled out her laptop and a very comfy camping chair.

'I hope you brought your sunscreen,' Harper said, helping Bree with the corners of the tablecloth to make it perfectly symmetrical. 'I love that stuff, as well as your hair products.'

'I did.' Bree pulled out some boxes and started sorting out the small bottles. 'The way that kelpie looks, I should have brought some dog shampoo, too.' She patted Willow's nose. 'Don't you look pretty, Willow? We should talk your owner into buying you a new collar.'

'Cap is with the dogs,' said Mia.

'I wasn't talking about Cap.' Bree rolled her eyes as she sorted out the small vials that Dex called her witchy potions.

'Did you bring out any of your cooking oils?' Mia asked. 'Everyone loved your chilli oil when I used it the other night.'

'I make them for the Station Hand's Daughter. It's the brand name for Lucy's food van parked near the grandstand. Normally she has it parked by the train station in town.'

'But it's your oils.'

'Lucy provides the herbs, and she pays me to do the distilling. If I didn't need a liquor licence that gives the government a chance to steal tax from me, I'd be selling my gin, too. I like how you did your displays, Harper.'

'Dad would drag us out to all the local shows in his electoral district to listen to the locals' concerns. Normally, we'd have balloons for the kids to entice the people to come near us. And buttons and stickers.'

'We're not chasing votes, Harper.'

'Well, not exactly…' From her laptop bag, Harper removed some paperwork. 'I've still got this petition for the government, to protect farmers' water rights and our zoning.' She held up the paperwork. 'Is it okay, if I put this out today? I don't want to step on any toes.'

'We're selling to the same people, the landowners and those involved with the industry.'

Mia brushed down her overalls, really feeling underdressed now. 'Is the station going to be okay? With all of us here today?'

'Yep.' Ryder strolled in, scrolling on his satphone with one hand while carrying a tray of coffees in the other.

It was another reminder for Mia to deal with the messages on her own mobile phone, which she'd been avoiding.

'I can see our cameras. Ash can, too, on his new satphone. Sarge is on duty. Besides, Leo and his cronies are here. Grab a coffee each, my treat.'

'Where is Leo?' A chill brushed over her scalp, sending a squirrel of goose pimples down her spine.

'At the beer tent. Bree, don't go stirring up any trouble.'

'Cupcake, it's not my fault that trouble tends to want to cosy up to me.' She clipped up her wide banner that said *Master Brand Maker—built to last lifetimes.* 'This isn't our first campdraft.'

'But it is our first as station owners.'

'Want me to move away and pretend we don't know each other? I'm quite happy to set up shop closest to the ladies' loos. I'll sell out in an hour and can hang out in the beer tent for the rest of the day.'

In a rare moment, Ryder grinned at her. It was brief, but it was surprising enough to Mia, she looked at Harper suppressing a smile.

'If you play nice,' he said, passing Bree a coffee, 'I'll buy you a beer later.'

'I always play nice, cupcake. And you're on.' Bree's focus

switched to three middle-aged cattlemen walking along the main thoroughfare. 'Hey, Jimmy Anders, has your lovely wife let you out to play? And you're hanging out with these two troublemakers? Barney and Mike, aren't you two on probation or something?'

'Bree, always a pleasure.' Jimmy removed his hat to kiss Bree's cheek, as did the other men, positioning themselves near the fan, just as Bree had predicted.

'Have you guys met the Riggs brothers? They're the new owners of Elsie Creek Station. Ryder, this is Jimmy from Amber Downs Station, and Barney and Mike are partners in The Lazy N Station.' This was a whole new Bree, who played the perfect hostess, introducing Ryder to other cattle station owners.

Throughout the morning it became obvious that Bree knew everyone. She would call out to people as they walked past the tent and they would stop to say hello, stand in the shade, and soak up the cool fan and drink some iced water. That gave Ryder and Ash the opportunity to talk about the newly patented cattle tags and the prospects of muster dogs and revegetation processes.

It was a hustle in a whole new way.

Then Willow started whimpering as she hid behind Mia's seat.

'What's wrong with Willow?' Harper straightened up their presentation table for the thousandth time, always ensuring it was perfect.

'I'm not sure. It's okay, Willow.' Mia crouched down to hug the dog, who was visibly trembling when a shadow came over them, as if someone had blocked the sun.

'Where the hell did you get that dog?' It was Leo, towering over them. Leo with his jet-black hair and fine flecks of grey, a three-day growth peppered across his strong jawline, without wearing a suit and tie. He was handsome, rich, but he also had that whole dark dangerous mobster vibe to him that was enough to render Mia helpless.

'Hello, devil's spawn. Kill any babies today?' Bree shifted

from her table to stand in front of Leo.

Leo's lips tugged into a devilishly handsome grin, as he stepped back. 'Wow, Bree.' He patted his hand over his heart, but his eyes had a dark, sinful look focused entirely on Bree and her generous curves. 'Don't you look exceptionally fine today. Best in show. How about a private—'

'Careful, Leo.' Bree's tone was loaded with warning, as she narrowed her green eyes at him.

He held her gaze for a beat too long before giving a deep, low chuckle. 'You know, that offer to have dinner with me still stands. We'll fly to Melbourne to do dinner and a show much bigger than this one. Or we could do a private show.'

'I've already told you, I've cancelled my subscription to romance. But if you're here to steal our oxygen, may I suggest you get some fresh air at the stables?'

'I'm not a horse person, but I know you look good in the saddle.' Leo had a hard and hungry glint in his eyes aimed at Bree, where the air between them held a blend of tension and electric chemistry.

To Mia, it was unclear if Bree and Leo hated each other or liked each other.

'Are you spying on us again?' Bree asked Leo.

'I have cameras, just like the Riggs brothers. And you do check our boundary fence regularly.' His eyes crawled inch by inch over Bree's curves. Mia felt for Bree under that intense scrutiny, which only got worse when his voice got low, husky, and heavy. 'I'd happily watch you all day—'

'About that.' Bree wiggled her finger at him. It only made him smirk more as if enjoying their game. 'Lose any dogs lately?'

'I did. That one.' Leo narrowed his ink-black eyes at Willow then at Mia. 'That's my kelpie. You stole it from me.'

'No, I...' Mia shook her head, her eyes wide, and looked to Bree for help.

Bree stepped in. 'Oh, please. You're more suited to carry a purse pooch in your man bag than keep a working dog. It'd destroy your furniture and your fancy city suits from boredom.'

Leo's lips curled into a grin, keeping those dark and sultry eyes on Bree. He should have been insulted, but he seemed to enjoy this game. 'Bree, my darling, I'm more than happy to buy you one of those dogs, and the entire wardrobe to go with it, anytime. But that is my kelpie.'

'Prove it.' Bree blocked his path with her chin raised.

Mia couldn't escape. With the dog cowering in the corner, she had to do something to defend them. But Mia hated any form of confrontation. She just couldn't bring herself to do anything, except cower in the corner with the dog.

'Ash, go find Porter.' Ryder's deep voice was a much welcome presence as he entered the tent with Ash carrying his son on his shoulders.

Ash passed Mason to Harper. 'Back in a second.' He turned and bolted.

'How can you tell it's your dog, Leo?' Ryder asked, casually tucking his phone into the pocket of his jeans.

The two men made their tent seem small.

'Kelpies in this town are rare, and that one has no white on her.' Leo scowled at Mia. 'Where did you get that bitch from?'

'How did you lose her, is what I want to know.' Bree crossed her arms over her chest, still refusing to budge, effectively blocking Leo from going anywhere near Mia and Willow.

'I didn't lose her. That farm girl stole her.' Leo pointed at Mia.

'Says the man who's taken up the occupation of playing water thief.'

'It's just business, Bree. And I'm a man who knows how to keep business and pleasure separate. But I'll take my dog back first, and then I'll ask you for a dance later.'

'I've told you my dance card is full, cowboy. Especially to you.'

And there it was. Finally, Leo's eyes flared with annoyance.

'What's going on?' Policeman Porter rushed in with Ash.

'That farm girl stole my dog.' Leo pointed at Mia.

Again, Bree blocked him. 'If you're going to point fingers at anyone, why not point them at me?'

'Well, the way I'd heard it, you and Charlie were rather upset over losing your cattle dogs, swearing to never take on another dog.'

Bree's eyes went dark, and her hands curled into fists, while gritting her teeth. 'I know your balding gorillas did that.'

'Easy, Bree.' Ryder held her back.

'Good luck controlling your caretaker, Ryder. Bree's all fire, it's one of the things I admire about her, and her outlaw attitude.' Leo chuckled. 'Now that Charlie is no longer the caretaker, what is your job title these days, Bree?'

'Chief shitkicker. Allow me to demonstrate with my boot and your butt!'

'Bree, calm down.' Ryder physically corralled Bree to the other side of the tent and held her there. 'Let the police do their job. Think about it...'

Bree glowered at Leo, shrugging off Ryder as she stepped back, only to pace like a wild animal trapped in a cage.

'Officer, that dog is mine.'

Porter adjusted his police cap, his expression calm while he spoke with a deep formality, 'Can you prove ownership of the animal, sir?'

'I brought her up from Adelaide. The breeder owns a sheep station, and I paid eight hundred for that kelpie.' Leo scrolled through his phone. 'I can call him up and I'll email you the details.'

'Do you have any breeding papers, or microchip details?'

'Who's got a microchip wand out here?'

'The vet does, some stock inspectors have them, and I carry one in the police van to use whenever I pick up strays. So, I'll ask again, can you prove the dog is yours?'

'And I said I'll email you the papers.' Leo looked bored talking to Porter. 'I'll have to search my office first.'

'Giving you enough time to create a set of dog papers over the internet,' called out Bree from the side. 'Want me to show you my internet qualifications as a brain surgeon, before I offer you a full lobotomy?'

Ryder grabbed her arm to hold her back. 'Bree, let the police deal with this.'

Again, Bree shook him off, stepping towards Leo. 'You can't have the dog. She's not yours.'

'It's my dog. She stole it from me. And I detest anyone stealing my stuff.' Leo's dark eyes, along with his tone, made Mia shiver with fear. Gavin may have scared her, but Leo was terrifying.

Their raised voices, and the police presence, had drawn a crowd. There was no way Mia could scoot past them with Willow. They were trapped.

'Here's an idea…' Bree became eerily calm, while effectively blocking Leo from getting anywhere near Mia and Willow. 'Why don't we ask the dog who her owner is?'

Leo stepped back, arching an eyebrow as if coolly calculating Bree's next move.

'That's a good idea.' Ryder stood beside her. Now both were protecting Mia and Willow. 'What do you say, officer?'

'What's going on, Porter?' A large police officer, with the arms of a bodybuilder, entered the tent. He wore two pistols strapped into his chest holsters the same way the Riggs brothers wore their radio harnesses. This was a cop who meant business. '*Back up, you lot*. Give us some space.'

The crowd did, but only a few steps; they weren't going anywhere, killing any hope of Mia sneaking past them.

'Sarge, it seems we have a dispute over the dog's ownership. The kelpie.' Porter pointed to Willow.

'I can prove she's mine. I've got the papers, and I can call the breeder for photos. Porsche? Porsche, come here, girl.' But the dog only cowered from Leo, with her tail tucked under as she hid behind Mia.

'Don't dog breeders usually have a way to identify them, like the cattle?' The beefy sergeant pointed to Bree's cattle brand display.

'The local vet told me they'll either have a microchip or a tattoo, some both, but puppy farms don't like to have any id,' said Porter. 'Sarge—'

'I know, Porter.' The Sergeant held up his hand to silence the younger officer as he looked at the dog. The man was as big as Ryder in the shoulders, both sharing an expressionless nod of strangers.

'Porsche is mine. She cost me twelve hundred.'

'You said eight hundred a minute ago,' said Bree.

'I didn't include transport costs.'

'So, you can't count, is what you're saying? Or are you making that up, too?'

'Bree.' This time the Sergeant glared at her.

She shrugged. 'I'm just making an observation, Detective Senior Sergeant Moore.'

Finally, Mia found her voice. 'I know Willow has been microchipped and…'

Porter, who had Willow microchipped, slyly shook his head at Mia to stop.

'You did that *after* you stole her from me. It's my dog.' Leo went to grab the lead, but the dog cowered. 'Come on, Porsche.'

'Back off, mate, or I'll pop your arm clear out of your shoulder socket, to dislocate it permanently.' Ryder's voice was low and loaded with warning. It even had Bree backing away.

'Is this a good time to repeat that we get the dog to pick her owner?' It was Harper, timidly standing on a stack of empty boxes, to raise her hand in the air. 'I believe the idea was tabled earlier, and I'd like to second the motion.'

'All right, everyone, back up. You too, Leo.' The sergeant's authoritative tone had everyone's attention. He held out his large hand to Mia. 'If I may?'

'What are you going to do, Sarge?' Porter asked.

'Let the dog choose.'

'Go with him, Willow.' Mia handed the lead to the

sergeant, who trotted the dog out of the tent and into the main thoroughfare.

'*Everyone, clear a path.*' The crowd eagerly split up along the main walkway from the Sergeant's stern voice. 'I want you, Porter, you—' He pointed at Mia.

'That's Mia,' said Bree.

'Porter, Mia and Leo make a line along here.' He flicked out his police baton, it had Willow cower. 'Easy girl, I won't hurt you.' He then dragged the baton along the dirt to form a line. 'You lot line up here. And I want two volunteers from the crowd to join that line. Not you, Bree, or anyone else who knows these people. I want two complete strangers who have never seen the dog before.'

A woman with an umbrella that matched her glamorous fifties outfit, and another stockman volunteered. Mia didn't know either of them.

'Are you doing a police line-up, Sarge?' asked the volunteering stockman.

'Something like that.' The Sergeant walked the length of a cricket pitch with the dog, then he turned and faced everyone. 'To make this fair, I want all those in the line to face the other way and keep their backs to the dog and not move. You will not coerce the animal. There will be no signalling. No whistling. No calling any names. And we will let the dog choose of her own free will.'

Ryder stood in front of Mia. 'If you want the dog, Mia, you'll have to do this. If Cap was here, he'd do it.'

But Cap was nowhere in sight.

'I don't do public speaking or stand in front of a crowd. I get stage fright.' And she hated confrontations that scared her so silly that she needed to pee.

'You have to, or you'll lose the dog. Who do you want Willow to be with?'

Thirty-two

The breeze barely blew as the heat rose from the soil, making Mia's brow break out with beads of sweat. With unsteady legs, she struggled to walk in a straight line to stand beside Porter. 'Is this going to be okay?' For her, the dog, and everyone else.

'Stand at the other end, Mia. Furthest away from Leo if you can. I'll stand in the middle. I want arm's length apart, to give the dog plenty of room to roam.' Porter positioned the two strangers and Leo. Then he leaned over and whispered to Mia, 'I've got my fingers crossed she'll go to you.'

'But the crowds? All these people?' She hated the attention.

A warm hand squeezed hers. It was Cap, and her heart flooded with warming relief. 'You've got this, Mia.' He walked her to the end of the line, gave her hand a squeeze, and let her go.

She didn't want him to go. 'But—'

'Don't worry. I'll be right over there, standing with the rest of the family. I'm not going anywhere.'

Every time he said *family*, her heart twinged with guilt that she hadn't shared her secret yet. 'You could take my place.'

'She's not my dog.' Cap gave her a sly wink before standing beside Ash and Ryder, along with Harper and Bree.

'We're rooting for *Team Willow*,' called out Harper, holding little Mason. The mother and son duo gave her the double thumbs up, just like they did from the viewing platform in the drafting yards.

Mia swallowed hard, brushing her hair down around her face to avoid all those eyes watching her. Feeling even more underdressed.

'All right, no one move. And no one says a word,' called out the sergeant, and a hush washed over the crowd. 'I'll unclip the dog's lead and the dog will choose where to go. No coercion.'

Mia heard the distinctive click of the dog lead.

She held her breath, shutting her eyes, and dropped her head with hands at her sides. Her heart leaped with panic at the thought of actually losing the friend who'd shared the dark with her when Mia had first arrived at the station. Those mornings when her wet nose nudged Mia's cheek when she didn't want to get out of bed, to then share the joy of the day's adventure. There was Willow's wide smile as she raced alongside the ute with the other dogs. How she'd splashed around in the troughs, or effortlessly moved a herd, or zipped around the obstacle course, happily listening to Mia commands. And then she'd curl up in her corner of the nursery to watch Mia work, or at the end of the day on Cap's outdoor deck to watch the sunset.

Was this the last time Mia would see her friend?

Willow could choose Porter, who'd spent months nursing her back to health.

She could choose Leo.

She could run to Cap, standing next to Bree, who too spoiled the dog.

Or Willow could run for the hills, just like Mia did to become a stowaway at the station.

When a moist nose pressed against her fingers. She opened her eyes, and there was Willow sitting at her feet.

'*Willow.*' Mia's heart nearly burst from her chest as she hugged the dog that was more than a dog, she was family.

'Looks like we have a winner,' called out the sergeant. The crowd clapped, and soon dispersed.

Cap hugged them both. 'Congratulations. Willow is all

yours now.'

Through her hot happy tears, Mia couldn't wipe the smile off her face.

Until Leo leaned down and said through gritted teeth, 'The luck was with you this time, farm girl, or should I say, little Mia?'

'Back off.' Cap scowled as he jumped to his feet.

Leo just tilted his head to narrow those cold ink-black eyes at Mia. 'To think I almost didn't recognise you, Mia. You're Gavin's *little Mia*.'

The pet name put her on her arse. Leo stepped closer, pointing at Mia as she scrambled on her knees in the dirt, desperate to get to her feet.

'Mia, it's okay.' Cap lifted her up.

'Gavin's been searching everywhere for you. Yet here you are, shacked up with the neighbours.' Leo sneered at Cap like he was trash, then dragged out his phone. 'I'll text him, shall I?'

'H-h-he's here?' Terror made her blood freeze as Leo's thumb swiftly moved over his phone's keypad. 'You didn't tell him—'

Sliding his phone away, Leo smirked at her. The look he gave her was like opening that dark cupboard filled with all of her worst nightmares. Her ex knew she was here.

'Leave her alone.' An angry Cap pushed Leo back.

'Well, look at this.' Leo gave an evil chuckle. It made the hair crawl on the back of Mia's neck. Leo casually brushed over his shirt, glancing at Cap as if he were no challenge for a man of his stature.

Where did the police go? Where was Ryder? Or Dex? Cap could use the backup of his bigger brothers about now.

'I said leave her alone.' But the calm Cap she adored gritted his teeth. His hands fisted so tight they shook with rage, and he stepped right up to Leo. 'I will clobber you.'

'Behave. There are children present.' Leo stepped back, adjusting his shirt, all cool and collected. Again, he smirked as if this whole scene was a joke. 'What is it with you, Mia?

Sending perfectly passive men mad like some infectious disease, to make them want to lash out in anger.'

Mia gasped. Leo knew!

But he was right, too. Cap was livid—just like Gavin had been.

'Easy, brother.' Ash rushed over and patted Cap's chest, dragging him back to calm him down. 'He's not worth it.'

'That's one thing we can agree on. None of you are worth my time, except Bree. And your petty petition won't save your station.' Leo flicked at the paperwork neatly stacked on the table sending the pages, containing all those signatures, to float like falling autumn leaves that landed in the dirt.

Mia had to leave.

Right. Now.

Thirty-three

'*M*ia?' Cap ran after her, pushing his way through the crowds as she rushed with Willow to the car park. 'Mia, it's okay.'

Mia weaved through the cars, the trucks, the utes. He followed, hating that she'd run from him.

But then she turned a corner around a large truck and was gone.

'Aw, come on, Mia. I won't hurt you.' He called out to the empty lot filled with assorted vehicles. His heart squeezed in his chest as if wrapped in fiery steel bands. He struggled to breathe.

'I'd never hurt you. And I hate how that animal hurt you so much that you don't trust me.' He gripped his head, as the thought of losing her tore through him and his brain went into overload.

Then he spotted her reflection in one of the cars. She was at the Tojo, hiding behind the cage. He walked around to the side of Ryder's ute, parked next to his Tojo, worried that if he got any closer, she'd run.

'I'm so sorry that this happened to you, that you feel the need to run.' He sighed, leaning against the side of Ryder's large ute. 'I'm so sorry that you gave so much of yourself to someone who truly didn't deserve you or know how precious you are to this world. It's so wrong that you experienced pain at the hands of someone who said they loved you. Love may be painful at times, but it should never leave bruises.'

In the reflection of Harper's Audi, she was just around the

corner at his ute, listening, with head down, while Willow lay calmly at her feet.

It gave him hope.

'I'm not going anywhere, Mia.' He waited, and he'd keep waiting, for as long as she needed, for he was a very patient man.

'I'm here.' Mia's voice was too quiet.

He stepped around the corner then stopped short, fighting the urge to hold her. She looked so fragile and flighty as if ready to run again. 'Don't listen to Leo. He doesn't know what he's talking about.'

'But you got so angry.'

'Because I wanted to protect you and Willow.' He stepped in closer.

'Why? I'm a nobody. I'm a stray, like Willow.'

'Don't *ever* say that to me. You know I never turn away a stray, not when they become a part of my family, like you are to me—we are a family. And in my family, we protect our own.'

Her face fell, as she twisted her fingers. 'But you deserve better.'

'No, I... *For fate's sake.*' He ripped off his cap, raking fingers through his hair.

'Leo said—'

'This has nothing to do with Leo. It's how I feel about you. This isn't anger. This is frustration. And before you say it, it's me who's frustrated with myself.'

'Why?' This time she approached him with concern in her eyes.

'Isn't it obvious?' He sighed, pressing his hat against his chest. 'I love you, Mia Dixon.'

She gasped. 'You can't.'

'I can, and I do.' He fought himself to stop his own frown for fear of her rejection. 'Falling in love with you was the easiest most pleasurable experience of my life, that I've found every moment I spend with you has been an absolute blessing to me. I truly believe fate brought us together.' Even if it was her fear that was now threatening to tear them apart.

Yet, he refused to give up on this, on her, and on them.

'I'm sorry that love didn't give you that safe space you are more than worthy of receiving. But I can show you a love that can be gentle, a love that can be kind, a love that can be your safe space. It's the right kind of love everyone deserves, especially you.' He slowly approached, wary that if he touched her, she'd run. 'I'd never hurt you, Mia, just like I've never hurt my dogs. And I am nothing like that animal who made you want to run from me.'

'I was running to help you.'

He double blinked at her. 'How?'

'Because I thought if I got away from you, Leo and I can't hurt you.'

He arched his eyebrows. 'You were trying to protect me?'

Mia twisted her fingers as she meekly screwed up her face. 'I panicked.'

'Yes, you did.' He gently gathered her fingers and gave them a tender squeeze. 'But that's okay. It's our first trip to town since the incident.'

'And I had to ruin everything.'

'No, Mia,' he said, lifting her chin with his fingertips. 'You finally accepted that you and Willow are partners. And I saw how far Bree and my brother Ryder were willing to go to protect you. And for someone like Ryder, that's a big deal.' Considering how Ryder was quite clear about Mia's place on the property.

He crouched down and patted the dog. 'You're a good girl, choosing the right family.'

Mia gave a slight gasp, only to bite on her lower lip.

'What's wrong?'

'I can't—'

'What is it, Mia? Tell me.'

Thirty-four

Mia squeezed her eyes shut, her whole body in knots but it barely stopped her trembling. 'Please don't hate me when I tell you something. You may not like it, or me.'

'Mia, look at me.' Cap tenderly stroked her hair.

Slowly she opened her eyes to face Cap, the beautiful, kind and caring man.

'You can tell me anything.'

Even if it meant losing him.

'Go on.'

He deserved to know.

She took a deep breath and whispered, 'I can't have children.'

Cap stepped back, eyes widening.

'I know it's early to say these things, but you can't love me, not when you have the chance to be with someone else who can give you a family. I can't get pregnant.'

'Why? How long have you known?'

'Since I was a child. I had such severe cramping on my first period that my mother took me to the hospital. That's when they learned I had underdeveloped ovaries and was infertile. It's a birth defect.'

'How do you feel about that?'

'Right now, not so good.'

'Why not?'

'I mean, I accepted it when younger, but now I've met someone like you... So, I'll understand if you want to end this, I get it. I'm—'

'Are you serious?' For the first time Cap scowled at her as he stepped in closer. 'Do you really think that little of me.'

'You deserve to have someone who can give you everything.'

'Who said I wanted children?'

'But you're so good with Mason.'

'As his uncle, and I like babysitting him.' He stepped back, rubbing his palm down his face. 'That's why you've been holding back from me.'

She couldn't tell if he was mad with her or not. 'I'm sorry I didn't tell you sooner.'

'Why didn't you?'

'Because I didn't want you to...' She struggled to swallow past the thick knot in her throat. 'To reject me.'

He dropped his head low, hands on hips.

'I'm sorry.' Hot stinging tears trickled down her cheeks. 'I'm sorry.'

'Why? Because of something that you were born with that was beyond your control?' He tilted his head at her. 'Most of my muster dogs were rejected because they weren't purebreds or had a fault. And how do I treat them, Mia?'

She sniffed hard, the tears trickling off her chin as she wiped her runny nose with the back of her hand. 'Like family.' That only spurred on more tears.

'Family comes in many shapes and forms, especially when least expected.' He tapped the Tojo's cage where she'd found him, or he'd found her. 'With those dogs, I don't see their faults or imperfections.'

Yet she felt full of imperfections.

'I only see perfection.' He dropped his head, using his finger to lift her chin. 'And I see you.'

She lifted her eyes to meet his, and her world was full of the handsome man, with his warm malt-whisky eyes.

'I see your happiness when I see your heart fill with hope. I see joy when you're kinder to yourself, learning to love yourself for who you are and not at the hands of others, but you. And I see you. For you.' His hand tenderly stroked her hair. 'I love you, Mia Dixon. And if you want, I'd love for you to be a permanent part of my family. I don't expect you to say anything, yet. I know you'll need time.'

Her lips trembled, desperate to stop blubbering at the words spoken by this perfect man.

'Hey, I told you from the beginning, I'm a patient man who'll wait for you until you are ready.' He hugged her, swallowing her in his arms, and she felt safe there, where the outside world's ugliness fell away to the soothing sounds of his heartbeat.

'*Cap? Oi!*' A huge whistle ripped through the air. It came from Dex standing at the far end of the car park. 'There's something wrong with your dogs.'

Thirty-five

'What happened?' Cap raced over with Mia and Willow hot on his heels.

'Charlie said something's not right with Atlas,' said Dex. 'It's got the old man worried. He told me to find you, Bree, and Harper.'

'Why?'

'Charlie said Bree's got her witch's bag with her, and I want Harper to call her boss, the vet. I wish I had their numbers to call them. Have you got their phone numbers, Mia?'

'No.' She patted her overall's pocket. 'I only switched my phone on today.'

Cap didn't have Mia's number, either. They didn't need them at the station, only using shortwave radios. 'I have Ryan's number. But I'm not calling him until I see what's wrong.'

'When this is over, we're all swapping numbers.' Dex ran off towards the show displays.

Cap led Mia by the hand into the large display tent where they passed the other assorted animal pens. On one side, half a dozen dogs paraded on leads in the shady arena for the judges. It was the show dog category.

'Shouldn't your dogs be a part of that presentation?' Mia pointed. 'That's what my mum did.'

'No. Atlas isn't pretty enough for that. He's enrolled in the agility trials, and then him and Fern are doing the muster dog trials.' He looked at his watch. 'We've only got an hour.'

He spotted Charlie inside the pen, squatting down to pat the dogs.

'Charlie, what's wrong?' Cap flicked back the handle to swing open the gate, as an icy wash of dread trickled over his scalp. Atlas was on his side, panting as if short of breath. 'What happened?'

'He threw up and then fell over, and started panting like this,' said Charlie. 'He can't get up.'

Atlas tried to get up, but his limbs were trembling.

'Easy... I'm here, mate. Lie down.' He gently coaxed his best mate to lie still as he dialled the local vet. 'Come on, pick up. Pick up.'

'Elsie Creek Vets.'

'Ryan, are you at the campdraft? Or are you at your surgery?' Over the phone Cap heard music and a crowd in the background.

'I'm near the mechanical bull, trying to talk Cowboy Craig into a bet to ride the thing and not spill a drop of his beer.' Ryan chuckled. 'Where are you?'

'As much as I'd love to be in on that action, I've got a dog down. I'm in the dogs' tent. Other side of the stables.'

'I know where it is. I'm on my way.'

'Vet's coming.' Sliding his phone away, Cap patted his dog while checking out Fern, who was leaning against him. 'It's okay, Fern.'

'It looks like lead poisoning to me,' said Charlie.

Cap's worry heightened, as his frown deepened. 'Lead? How is that even possible? I only know of lead that builds up but that takes time. The only lead I know is in old paint.'

'Liquidised lead, given in a sudden dose causes trembling limbs, panting, vomiting, and frothing at the mouth. I know the signs.' Charlie's grey eyes were adamant, that Cap believed the old stockman.

'Pop, what's wrong?' Bree ran up with her large leather handbag.

'Lead poisoning. Look at him.'

Bree rushed into the pen and checked over Atlas. 'How

could this happen? They've all been here.'

'It doesn't matter how, we've gotta race the clock, kid. Have you still got that turmeric on you?'

Bree began rummaging through her bag. 'Never leave home without it.'

'What does turmeric do?' Mia hovered over their shoulders. 'I've only used it for cooking.'

'Turmeric has lots of health benefits, including anti-inflammatory and antioxidant properties for humans and dogs.' Bree rummaged through her bag and dragged out a simple spice jar containing orange powder. 'May I, Cap? It's only a short-term solution until you can get the dog to Ryan.'

'What will you do?'

'I'll rub it on his teeth. It'll make him lick it, hopefully ingesting it quicker to slow down the poisoning process. I swear it helps.'

'How do you know this?' Dex stood outside the pen, leaning against the rails with Ryder beside him.

'Because we lost our dogs to lead poisoning.' Charlie ripped off his hat. 'Not again. We can't go through this again, Bree.'

'It's okay, Pop. Atlas is healthy. He's young, and we've caught it quickly.' Bree sprinkled the bright orange powder into her hands and brushed it against the dog's teeth and upper lip. The dog sneezed, but she did it again. 'Good boy.'

He licked at her cupped hands holding cold water from her water bottle. 'There you go, Atlas. What about Fern?'

Cap checked over Fern, her eyes clear, her nose moist and cool. 'No obvious signs.'

'That's the problem. Lead poisoning can affect a dog in a day or an hour. Do you want to dose Fern?' Bree held out the spice jar. 'I swear it won't hurt them. In fact, they recommend a small daily dose in their food to improve their overall health. I used to put it in the dog stew I'd make for ours. Ask Ryan. He was the one who recommended it to us as a bush medicine.'

'And I know plenty of bushies who swear by it.' Charlie

worried his bottom lip.

Cap let Bree sprinkle the powder into his palm, then applied it to Fern's teeth. 'I'm so sorry, girl.'

The cattle dog sneezed and gagged.

'Use one of these water bottles. They're filtered.' Bree passed him a large bottle she dragged from her large leather handbag.

The water was cool in his hand that Fern eagerly lapped up.

'How did this happen?' Cap poured more water. 'My dogs only eat on command, and only our family knows those commands. It's the first thing I teach all new dogs, so they never get poisoned by dingo baits.'

'It can't be the water at the station. We've been testing it regularly.' Dex shrugged, looking at Ryder beside him.

Ryder leaned closer, with his voice low. 'Listen, if it gets out that we've got a dog suffering from lead poisoning, it'll ruin our reputation for cattle. No one will touch any of our projects—the tags, the dogs, or the nursery products we've all been promoting today. And if we're not careful, we'll also have the environmental department on our backs and our land value will drop.'

Cap felt his stomach plummet, sending a scurry of spiky prickles over his skull and down his spine.

Dex mirrored the look, obviously feeling the same.

Their home, their livelihood, their entire lifestyle, and their dreams were under attack.

'I bet Leo did this.' Dex scowled at the crowd as if searching for their neighbour.

'But Leo was with us, arguing over Willow,' said Bree, feeding water to Atlas.

'So how did my dogs get sick?'

'Cap, you don't think anyone could've put something in there?' Bree pointed to the water bowls. 'Have any of you got your testing kits in your car?'

'We have. Mia?' Cap handed her the Tojo's keys.

'Got it. Here, watch Willow.' She passed the dog lead to

Dex. 'I'll be right back, Cap.'

He didn't like her running off, but Atlas started hacking a hearty cough. 'It's okay, mate… Bree?'

'Good boy, Atlas, get it all out.' Her voice was calm, even her hand on his arm was calming. 'Give him more water, Cap. We need to dilute the toxin.'

'Where is that flamin' vet?' Charlie ripped off his hat, searching the crowd in all directions.

Dex scooped up the small spice bottle. 'Why carry turmeric around?'

'I made Bree do it,' replied Charlie.

'Why?'

'Because if we'd had some with us, we might have saved our own dogs.' Hat in hand, Charlie slowly shook his head, inhaling deeply as he watched over Cap's dogs. The worry made the sun-hardened crinkles deepen around his grey eyes. 'It was a slow and terrible death I wouldn't wish on anyone.' Charlie's voice cracked and his bottom lip quivered. 'They were in such pain that… She… Bree…'

'I had to put them down. All of them.' Bree's voice was so cold. She then inhaled deeply and leaned down to cup Atlas's furry chin and kissed his nose. 'But we won't be doing that today, Atlas. You hear me? We won't be doing that today.'

Thirty-six

With her heart in her throat, trying not to panic for Cap and his dogs, Mia raced to the mustard-coloured Tojo that shone like a beacon of hope in the dusty car park.

At the driver's door, she fumbled with the keys, dropping them in the dirt. When she scooped them up, footsteps crunched behind her. She peered over her shoulder and gasped. 'Gavin!' She stepped back into the Tojo, trapped.

'Leo said you were here.'

She froze. The last time she'd seen him, he'd been so angry at her.

'I've been looking for you everywhere.'

A car door slammed, another ute rumbled past, and some dogs barked. It was enough to wake her out of her trance, to remind her of Atlas. Of Cap.

'I can't talk to you right now.' She unlocked the driver's door and rummaged around the back of Tojo's cab. It's where Cap kept the toilet paper, the first-aid kit, and the testing kit, which she dragged out by the handle and slammed the door.

If they could pinpoint what toxin caused the dog's sickness, then the vet could administer the right medicine to cure Atlas quicker. So she had no time to waste talking to Gavin. Confrontation avoided.

'Hey, stop and talk to me. I haven't seen you for a month.' He blocked her off, and gripped her upper arms.

'I can't. I've got to go. It's over.'

'No. We are not over until I say so.' His frown was dark.

It's the one she remembered from her nightmares.

She pulled her arm free. 'I have to go. We can talk about this later.' Not if she could help it.

'No, we're doing this now.' He pulled her back with an iron grip on her arm. 'Leo says you've shacked up with the neighbours who've stolen his water access and stopped his mine from getting off the ground. They're bad people.'

'No. Leo is the bad guy. Not the Riggs brothers. They're the good guys.' It was the first time she'd spoken to anyone like that. It was like this foreign feeling of courage surging inside. If nothing else, this confrontation helped her recognise that she had no feelings for the man standing before her. She'd never loved Gavin. She'd just been desperate to be with someone because she only saw her faults and didn't think she deserved someone special. She had to get back to Cap.

Mia struggled to get out of his grip. *'Let. Me. Go.'*

'No, my little Mia, remember you belong to me.' Gavin tightened his grip, cutting off the circulation in her arm.

She froze with terror.

'Is everything all right there, miss?' Nearby, two stockmen closed the door of their black monster-like truck, its back tailgate covered in stickers.

'It doesn't concern you.' Gavin scowled at them. 'Move on, mate.'

But they didn't, instead the pair of stockmen casually sauntered towards them as Mia struggled to get her arm free.

Before she'd moved into Cap's place, one night while huddled on Bree's couch, sharing a tub of ice cream, Bree had told Mia if she ever got into trouble while in the small town of Elsie Creek to go find a stockman. Most of them were gentlemen who'd help anyone in need. Bree had said stockmen might look calm on the outside, but they played with cattle for a living and were a lot tougher than the miners in this town realised.

Mia hoped Bree was right.

'We weren't talking to you, mate.' With a deep tan, dark hair under his black hat, the young stockman hooked his thumbs through his jeans belt loops, wearing a long-sleeved shirt that displayed *Danbunnan Station* on the pocket. 'Josh, did you hear who I was talking to?'

The younger stockman, wearing a matching shirt, gave a cheesy grin as he scratched his chin. 'Oh yeah. I'm a hundred per cent sure my friend, Tyson here, was talking to the lady. Not you, mate.' Josh was so young, nineteen if that, wearing a cheeky grin. 'Just so there's no confusion, I'll ask... Are you okay, Miss? We both heard you telling this fella to let you go.' His eyes showed concern as they landed on the grip Gavin still had on her arm.

Tyson, the stockier offsider, nodded at her. 'I know I did. It's why we're being nosy, when we'd rather be holding up the bar inside. So, mate, the lady made her request clear for all of us to hear. Let her go. *Now*.'

Thank the heavens for stockmen, who proved chivalry was not dead. Mia's arm was freed from Gavin's burning grip.

'Ease up, we were just talking.' Gavin stepped back, yet he was still too close. 'We live together.'

'No. We don't. We're done, Gavin. It's over.' She rubbed at her arm, scowling at the enemy as she stepped clear of him.

'Were not finished talking, little Mia.'

'It looks like she has, mate.' Tyson said, as the Danbunnan Station stockmen blocked Gavin from getting near her.

'You okay, miss?' asked the one called Josh.

'Yes. Thank you, gentlemen. You're my heroes.' She scooped up the testing kit.

'Hear that, Tyson, I'm a hero. Wait till I tell Sienna back at the station. I reckon she'll make me custard slice as my reward.' Josh tapped his mate's chest. He tipped his hat at Mia, giving her a charming yet boyish grin. Only to scowl at Gavin and block his path from following her.

It was enough for her to bolt free, with that feeling of leaving her past behind as she wove her way through the car park to help Cap.

Thirty-seven

By the time Mia made it back to the dogs' tent, Cap and his two dogs were gone. Only Ryder and Dex were there, along with Bree and Willow. 'Where did they go?'

'The vet has them. Charlie and Cap went with,' explained Bree, packing up the leads and brushes that belonged to Cap's dogs.

'Did you get the testing kit for the water?' Dex pointed to the dog bowl.

'Yes. I'll use the strips. They'll tell us the results straight away.' Her fingers trembling from her confrontation with Gavin, Mia struggled to open the lid on the plastic bottle, wishing Cap was here to open the cap for her.

That's when the first of her tears fell.

That arsehole Gavin ruined everything, reducing her to a blubbering mess. She sniffed heavily, roughly wiping away her hot stinging tears.

'What happened to you?' Bree's warm hands encased hers.

'Gavin grabbed me in the car park.'

'What the hell!' Bree's eyes widened, then swapped to a furious frown. 'Where is he?'

'These two stockmen stepped in.'

'Mia, pass me the kit.' Ryder stepped inside the pen and held out his hands.

'No. I can do this. I will *not* let Gavin beat me.' Mia gritted her teeth and finally unscrewed the lid. She took out a swab and dropped to her knees, placing it in the dog bowl. Dex, Ryder, and Bree were watching her every move.

She pulled out the swab and watched the colours change.

'Oh, no. It's positive.' Her stomach knotted in fear for Cap and his dogs as she showed them the swab's results.

'You and Charlie were right.' Dex shook his head.

'We didn't want to be.' Bree covered her mouth, her green eyes so dull and sad.

'Dex, ring Cap with the results so the vet can fix it,' ordered Ryder. 'Mia, give us all some swabs, we'll need to test all the water bowls in this tent.'

As streams of people walked around them, there had to be over fifty muster dogs attending today's events. The thought nearly paralysed her.

'Bree, you know everyone,' continued Ryder, as Mia handed him some testing strips with trembling hands. 'Can you tell the kennel master what's going on? But we need to keep this quiet, guys.'

'Why? Because of the station's reputation?' Mia passed some swabs to Bree and Dex.

'We don't want people to panic and ruin the campdraft's reputation. There are a lot of good people involved in these events.'

'Do we call Porter about this?' Dex asked.

'I vote we do, even if I have no voting rights for your family's business,' said Bree.

'Agreed.' Ryder dragged out his phone. 'I'll call Marcus.'

'Who?' Mia asked.

'The sergeant you met earlier.'

'I thought you were strangers.' They'd acted like it earlier when she was fighting for Willow's ownership.

'We're good mates.' Ryder scrolled through the phone. 'I'll take the west side of this tent. Bree the north, Dex the south, Mia the east. We'll meet back here to work out the next step.'

'What do we say to the dog owners?' Mia asked.

'The truth,' replied Bree. 'We're conducting a test on the water to ensure it's safe. You're in overalls, they'll think you're working for the campdraft. And if anyone gives you any trouble, say I sent you. And let's hope no other dog is affected.'

Thirty-eight

'Thanks, Dex.' Cap ended the call with his brother, then spoke to Ryan, inside the local veterinarian surgery that Cap was far too familiar with. 'It's confirmed, they found concentrated lead in my dogs' water bowls. They're checking the rest of the water in the tent to see if any other dogs have been exposed.' It made him sick to the stomach at the thought of all those muster dogs in danger.

'Gawd, I hope not.' Charlie ripped off his hat, screwing it up. 'That's a proper mongrel act that, poisoning dogs.'

'At least we know what it is, so I can treat the dogs properly. Otherwise, it would be a week for lab results.' Ryan opened one set of cupboards, then another.

Cap stroked Atlas's coarse fur. 'It's okay, mate. It's gonna be okay.' This was a nightmare crashing down on them.

What sort of soulless sociopath did that to dogs?

But to poison them in such a public place was a deliberate attempt to shut him down for what he was trying to achieve. Not only to hurt the station's reputation, but his goal of showing the benefits of using muster dogs at the campdraft was nothing but dust left lying on a deserted track after being trampled by a herd of cattle.

But none of that mattered now. Not when he desperately wanted his mate to survive.

Cap patted his dog that lay deathly still on the examination table.

'Now that I know it's lead, I can use the correct chelating agent to remove it from Atlas's blood. Bree did the right thing with the turmeric, it should give us a head start.' Again, Ryan rummaged through his many glass cabinets. 'I'll need to do it intravenously to get the agent straight into his bloodstream.'

'Will it work?'

'We'll have to wait and see.'

'Do we need to treat Fern, too, doc?' Charlie squatted to pat Fern, who'd been abnormally quiet, with her eyes on her mate.

'Fern hasn't shown any symptoms, but I'll check her over, once I've started the treatment for Atlas. Get her to drink, Charlie.' Ryan pushed the water bowl closer. 'Then we'll need her to pee and we'll monitor her for the next few hours.'

'How did they poison your dogs?' Cap asked Charlie, as they sat in the large examination room at the vet's, while he slowly stroked his dog Atlas, on the IV. 'We found no traces of lead in the water on the station. Thanks to Mia, she has us testing our water regularly.'

'It was in our own water tank, the one behind the cottage. We all started feeling funny, I got headaches and stomach cramps. That's when Bree twigged that something was wrong. Next thing I know, Bree bundles me into the Kombi, dumps me at the hospital doors with a bottled water sample from our tanks, telling them our water's been poisoned. Only problem was, she'd left me there, to bolt back home to...' Charlie heaved slow breaths, his bottom lip quivering. 'Bree won't let us drink nothin' now unless it's filtered. She got us one of them fancy towers for drinking water, like you'd see in some city office. It sits next to the hat rack in the kitchen. She's also put filters on all the tanks and taps around the homestead. I know she tests 'em and cleans 'em regularly with this smancy testing kit she keeps in the smithy's shed, and she keeps a note on the calendar as a reminder to swap them filters out every few months, but she'll spot check the water at random times.'

'Where?' Cap stared wide-eyed at Charlie, astounded that the cheeky redhead was doing all this in plain sight.

'Farmhouse, the sheds, yours and even Dex's place. I know she put one in the kennels too, when she made you them special dog-watering troughs.'

'I didn't know that.' Bree surprised him all the time when it came to the dogs, like with the dogs' obstacle course.

But there were lots of little things being fixed at the kennels, too. There was the day he'd come home to find the kennel's frames all reinforced, and new hinges on the doors. The next day they had new roofs. While out digging his new wildlife corridor with Mia, they'd come back to find shade cloth stretched over the kennels to protect them from the outback's harsh elements. And just last week, a row of shiny steel, custom-made water troughs were welded to each kennel, to never have to fill a bucket again.

He'd asked his brothers if they'd done it, all of them shaking their head. Only now realising how watchful Bree had been over his dogs. And also his family, and all she'd done for Mia, too.

Mia adored Bree, who'd helped Mia settle in. Especially when Mia would attend Bree's cooking lessons up at the cottage with Harper—which everyone knew was code for long liquid lunches where you could hear the ladies laughing, singing and dancing late into the night. Lucky ladies, he'd never had a lunch last that long.

That's when it twigged. Ryder was right, Bree did know more about the station than she let on. Cap could see it now.

Not only through the women, but he'd have quick ten-minute conversations with Bree at least once a day, whenever she breezed by going to or from somewhere. Dex and Ash did, too. The three of them had individually sought out Bree's brutally blunt, but honest, opinion when planning something new at the station.

Not only that, but he also now realised Bree had been dropping subtle hints to him, too.

It was Bree who'd suggested that he pick the paddock beside Ash's as the best place to start his wildlife corridors, to start containing the sandstorms through the Stoneys.

It was Bree who'd suggested using one of the kennels for a nursery, before he'd even met Mia.

It was Bree who had shown Mia the best places to forage for seeds and told her how easy it would be to build a native nursery. On what had seemed like a simple drive to check the eastern border with Cowboy Craig, they'd filled up the Razorback full of seeds, using the sacks and shovels Bree just happened to have with her. At that stage Mia hadn't even thought about it, until Bree showed her how easy it could be.

Everything Bree did was for a reason.

That sneaky, big-hearted, sassy-mouthed redhead was like the fairy godmother of Elsie Creek Station. She'd done so much for all of them, and he'd be willing to bet none of his brothers had realised it either. Especially Ryder who argued with Bree the most.

What else had Bree done for them behind the scenes that they didn't know about?

'Why didn't you say anything to us, Charlie? About your dogs, and the water?' Acid burned in Cap's chest, was his family in danger too?

'We didn't want to worry you none. I was hoping them nasty shenanigans were done and dusted when you mob bought the place. But it isn't, is it?' Charlie's grey eyes were as pale as his skin, sick with worry. 'Now you lot blocked his mine, Leo's still gunning for the station, isn't he?'

The acid rolled again, sending hot sparks to rise like a bad case of indigestion. Cap picked up his phone and started texting Ryder to alert his brothers to protect their family. They had to protect their home.

Ryder was right again: Leo was a lot more dangerous than Cap realised.

Thirty-nine

'What now?' Mia patted Willow as Dex, Ryder, and Bree returned to the empty dog pen after testing all the water troughs inside the dogs' tent, even the tanks and troughs for the horses. None of them came back positive for any toxins. Only Atlas and Fern's water bowls had, that Policeman Porter had taken for evidence.

Mia fingered the keys to the Tojo in her pocket, keen to drive around to the vets already.

'We pack up and go home. Ash and Harper are packing up our displays in the tent as we speak.' Ryder scowled as he read something on his phone. He glanced up, narrowing his eyes at Bree, collecting Cap's dog supplies.

'Even you, Bree?' Mia asked.

'I sold out hours ago, and was planning on partying, but I'm not in the mood now. Pity, I was really hoping to see Cap and his dogs. You've both worked so hard for this.'

'You know, we have one more dog.' Dex nodded at Willow, lying quietly on her lead near Mia. 'You could go in Cap's place in both the agility and the muster dog trials.'

'Dex, sometimes your brain amazes me with your ideas.' Bree patted Dex's shoulder and faced Mia. 'One of Cap's goals was to show how easy it was to connect rehabilitated muster dogs, with people who have never used them before, like new farmers.'

'And we know you've only been doing it what, three weeks?' Dex nodded along with Bree.

Mia had to step away from Bree and Dex ganging up on her. 'Yeah, but in fun. Only when Cap was training his dogs. And Cap was going to compete against others who have been doing this for years and years. I'm only learning.'

'Yeah, but Willow has been training right alongside Atlas and Fern,' said Dex. 'I saw you train with Cap. You two have been inseparable since my brother brought you home. You both walk in sync and talk your own language even when you're not speaking.'

Was that true? 'I don't do public events. I'm a behind-the-scenes kind of person. I hate being in the spotlight. I don't do confrontations.' *Like this!*

'Let's put it this way,' said Ryder, taking a step closer, his presence powerful. 'If Cap were in your position, I know he'd do it for you. No questions asked.'

'I-I-I… I can't. I'm barely holding it together after seeing Gavin—who might still be out there.' She pointed to the car park. 'I just want to see Cap and the dogs.' But the guilt trip they were laying on her was like hot steel pressing across her shoulders for not having the courage to face a crowd.

'Can I tell you a story, Mia?' Bree took her hands.

'Does it come with a happy ending?' She could do with one about now.

'Now, let me see if I remember it correctly.'

'Bree?' Ryder frowned. 'It's not the time for stories.'

'Cupcake, please. This matters.' She playfully rolled her eyes at Mia, and said, 'Once upon a time—'

'Are you flippin' kidding me?' Dex groaned, dragging a hand over his face.

'There was this little princess.'

'Right, next it'll be dragons and castles and white knights who can't see squat out of their ridiculous tin helmets. Have you been sneaking into my goodies stash, Bree?'

'Dex, let it play out.' Ryder nodded at Bree to continue.

'As Pop would say, Anyhoodle...' Bree bobbed her eyebrows up and down, making Mia smile a little. 'This princess, who had her own white horse, found her prince and moved to a faraway land.'

'Seriously,' mumbled Dex under his breath.

'They got married, had a child, and all was blissfully perfect. Until…' She paused.

'Until?' Mia grinned at the game.

'Her prince went dark and hit her.' Bree's smile fell, as did the fun mood. 'The princess thought she could save him, fix him, make the home better for him, but he only got darker and darker.'

'What happened?'

'The princess remained loyal to the prince she loved. Thinking no one else could help her, that it was all her fault that the prince was like that, believing she could save her prince.'

'Lost cause, she should've dumped that prince on his ass,' mumbled Dex.

'Maybe she might have, if they didn't have a child.'

The air got heavy as if everyone paused, the brothers who went to extra lengths for family were silent.

'Was the child safe?' Mia whispered.

Bree nodded. 'The princess built this special cupboard just for the child, who thought it was part of a special secret game. The princess told their child to hide inside this teeny, little cubbyhole, where the child would find new toys to play with, along with promises of ice cream and trips to the zoo if the child stayed quiet. Because they both knew that the prince would become the perfect husband and the perfect father *after* his black moods had faded and the bruises disappeared. Until the next time the black moods returned.'

'What happened to them?'

'He killed the princess. Murdered her before breakfast.'

Mia gasped, holding her stomach. Beside her, Dex sucked air through his teeth with a hiss.

'The princess thought her family couldn't help, when all she had to do was call them and they would have been there in an instant.'

Mia dropped her head, the guilt of not calling her family

now making her ill.

'However, the princess's child did get the support of the princess's loving family, they helped her heal so she could grow up stronger, to not hide from the world. They gave her the support and the confidence to be anything she wanted to be.' Bree squeezed Mia's hands like a sister. 'The reason I'm telling you this is that you have your family to help. And there's also us. Ryder and Dex won't let anything happen to you. You've got me and Charlie as your support group, Harper too, that we know you'll handle anything, and we'd be willing to help you. Especially Cap. But do you think your family would have helped you out?'

Mia nodded. 'My family would have caught the first plane out to take me home. But I don't want to go back there. At first I was just ashamed to tell them, but now I don't want to go back there at all.'

'Because you have your home, with Cap, at the station.' Bree cradled Mia's hands, lowering herself so Mia couldn't look away from those empathetic green eyes. 'The reason you didn't call them is that you are far stronger than you realise. You knew, deep down, that you were always going to be okay. This past month, you could have left Elsie Creek Station at any time, but you chose not to because you've been proving to yourself that you have that strength to keep moving forward to put all that horribleness behind you.'

'Is that what you do? I know about your son, the dogs...' Mia swallowed.

Bree didn't even react, no frown, no raised eyebrows, nothing. 'It's why I know you can do this, Mia. You are far stronger than you realise. And you deserve a big win after what you've been through. So, by entering Willow and yourself in the trials, you'll not only be helping Cap in the biggest possible way, but you'll be returning that kindness that the Riggs brothers have done in making sure you're kept safe and have a home where you belong.'

Dex nodded, over Bree's shoulders. Ryder didn't react, as per normal.

'More importantly, precious, doing this event will help you.'

'Me?'

'You'll prove to yourself that Gavin hasn't beaten you. No one can, because your past will only make you stronger.'

'Do you really believe that?'

'I do. Now you need to believe that, too. So, what do you say? You in?'

Forty

Mia shook her head. She wanted to run and hide like she always did, but she had no choice. She looked at Willow, sitting patiently by her side, unaware at what they were asking. 'Do you think we can do it?'

'I do,' replied Bree.

'Ditto.' Dex nodded behind her.

'You don't need to win,' said Ryder bluntly, leaning against the rails of the empty dog pen, as the crowds shifted in the display tent.

'Why not?' Dex asked.

'The pressure to try and win might be too much for Mia. She only needs to finish the obstacles as a demonstration of what the dog and handler can do.' Ryder pointed at Mia. 'And that I know you can do.'

'You might even have fun out there.' Bree nodded with that encouraging grin.

'When you two team up, it's hard to say no,' said Mia.

'It's rare for us to agree on anything, but we all agree on this. So, stop with the suspense, precious, and just say *yes*.'

Mia held her breath, shutting her eyes tight to whisper, 'Yes.'

'Good.' Ryder nodded with approval. 'I'll go talk to the organisers and change the names over. Bree, one more thing.' Ryder opened his wallet and held out his credit card. 'Do something with Mia. She is representing the station.'

'You don't judge people by what they wear.' Bree frowned at Ryder.

'They do in these events.' Ryder matched Bree's frown. 'Cap polished his boots and put on a tie for this event.'

'Ryder's right.' Dex nodded at the group of dog handlers standing in line for the judging of the show dog category. They all wore ties, and long-sleeved shirts. 'Cap said all competitors do it out of respect for the sport.'

Mia patted her messy hair, rubbing one of her dirty boots against the back leg of her dust-covered overalls. 'Bree, help?'

Bree's eyes wandered over Mia's appearance. 'Fine… Ryder, while you go see the organisers, how about you give Dex the card to give to Harper where she can use it to buy an outfit for Mia. She knows Mia's size. Tell Harper I want farmer's daughter pizazz with a bit of her politician's polish for the presentation. She'll know what I mean.' Bree hooked her arm through Mia's. 'You're with me, precious. It's makeover time.'

'Bree? Before you go, I have to ask…' Dex took the credit card from Ryder and twirled it in his fingers. 'Who was the princess in the story? A relative?'

'It was my mother.' Bree gave such a casual shrug. 'It's the story of how I came to live with my grandparents. They flew down straight after they got the phone call from the police that every parent dreads.'

Mia gasped. 'That's why Charlie said you'd be an instant friend who'd help me. And how you could relate to my situation in so many ways. All those words of wisdom — they were life lessons.'

'Life lessons? Sure, if that's what you want to call it.' Bree gave a soft smile, barely curling her lips, yet it revealed a wise soul hidden beneath all that brassiness. 'I think everyone needs lessons on how to protect the people they love, to help them become better than how they found them.' Bree tenderly brushed the hair away from Mia's face like a sister. 'Everyone heals their own way. And I know I told you to take as long as you need to heal, by doing it the right way for you. And, as Cap would say, fate brought you out home that day for a reason and I think it was not just to heal, or to find Cap, but to find *you*.' She gently poked Mia's chest. 'You can do this. You are stronger than you realise.'

It gave her hope and that spark of courage. 'Okay, I'm in.'

'Good… Stop looking at me like that, you two.' Bree shooed the two men away and re-hooked her arm through Mia's. 'Now, let's do this makeover. We all could do with a win about now.'

Forty-one

'Fern did the deed.' Charlie was jubilant as he strolled back into the surgery, with the blue heeler trotting beside him on a lead. 'Reckon she'd been holding it for a while. But she looks good to me, Doc. What do you reckon?'

Ryan checked over the dog.

Cap was sitting on the floor of the large cage with Atlas lying alongside, watching the drip-drip-drip of the liquid falling from the plastic bag, the clear tube disappearing under the bandage wrapped around one of Atlas's front legs.

The dog thumped his heavy tail, his worried eyes on Cap.

'All good, mate. I'm right here. You just get better.' He tenderly stroked the animal.

Ryan finished inspecting Fern and stripped off his gloves. 'I don't think Fern got poisoned. Her vitals are fine, and my preliminary blood tests didn't find any toxins in her system. Is it possible she didn't drink any of that water?'

'There were two bowls in their pen. Maybe she didn't. Come here, Fern?' He sat forward. 'Stay, Atlas.'

The blue cattle dog trotted over, her tail wagging, her eyes clear, and lapped up the pats. 'Fern's been known not to drink that much water. She does after a big run, but they haven't run today. I was saving them for…' The events he'd been hoping to make a name in, not only for himself, but for the station, to show his brothers they were a team. Even though his methods may seem unconventional to some for picking up stray dogs or saving them from a farmer's bullet to turn them into muster dogs, he was doing it to help the dogs born for the job, and also to show those farmers how minor changes could make a bigger impact for the better.

But that was all dashed.

And he was never leaving his dogs unsupervised in town again.

'To be on the safe side, Charlie, keep giving Fern water,' said Ryan.

'I'll get Bree to whip up her special chicken dog stew,' said Charlie. 'Cleans 'em out proper, but full of goodies. It'll be safe for all your dogs, Cap, for sure.'

'What about Atlas? Did you find anything in his bloods?'

'Yeah, sorry mate. Sadly, it's only preliminary findings so I can't tell you the concentration level. The police have asked me to do a full blood screening.'

Charlie poked back the brim of his hat. 'Who called the coppers?'

'Ryder, who else?' His big brother was always on the ball. 'If they only found the lead in my dogs' bowls, that's malicious tampering.'

And if the police were involved, it wouldn't take long for word to get out in a small town about the lead poisoning, it could ruin their family's reputation as cattle producers and all their goals as a family. Was this what Leo was aiming for?

It was also a stupid way to do this, because everyone was going to know it happened at the campdraft, ticking off a lot of those dog owners. Stockmen hated anyone messing with their muster dogs. 'Will the police charge them with animal cruelty, too?'

Ryan nodded. 'Porter spent thousands on Willow fixing her up, so he's on a mission to lay charges.'

'Did Porter tell you they found out who Willow's owner was?'

'Who?'

'Leo Travers.' Cap scowled at the name, both dogs perking their ears in his direction. 'All good, Atlas, you chill there, mate. You've earned a few days of R&R. But I'll take you up on that offer for Bree's dog stew, Charlie, if it's okay with Bree. I'll get the recipe.'

'Trust me, that kid will be stoked to make it for them puppies. Bree cooks when she's worried.'

'Bree must worry a lot, because she's always cooking.' Some days the cooking aromas that wafted over from the cottage were torturous, the memory made his stomach grumble, even now.

'Bree enjoys cooking, just like her grandmother, my beautiful Bea. My wife wasted nothing, always preserving, drying and what-not with food. Me, I just baked the bread or pizza bases.'

'I've heard about your pizza nights,' said Ryan, checking on Atlas's IV bag and vitals. 'Do I get an invitation one day?'

'Sure. I'll talk to the party planner later. Shouldn't the rest of your mob be here, Cap?'

'They're packing up. Ash said they were heading home to wait for the news. We don't want to crowd out Ryan's surgery.'

'Did Ash get to test out his new gadget, that drone thingy?'

'Ryder got permission for him to use it for our dog trials.' But that wasn't happening. 'I'll let Ash know Fern's going to be okay. He can pass on the news.' Again, he tapped out a text message, much shorter than the one he'd shared about the previous water poisoning and warning his brothers how dangerous Leo might be. *Fern is good. Atlas is still being treated. Fingers crossed.'*

It was a few moments later when Ash texted back. The all-night gamer was always quick at texting.

'What the hell?' Cap sat forwards, staring at the text message.

'What's wrong now?' Charlie asked.

'Mia is entering Willow in the muster dog trials.' Did he read that right? Instantly, he pressed the dial button. 'Are you for real?'

Ash chuckled over the phone. 'I know, right? It made me

ask twice when I found out. They got Harper to shop for a special show outfit, and Bree's doing a makeover on Mia. Don't worry, bro, I'm going to film it with the drone, so you'll get to see everything.'

He couldn't picture Mia standing there in front of a crowd. It couldn't be true. Mia would run. It's what Mia did. 'Mia won't do it, brother. Tell the others not to get mad at Mia when she pulls out.'

'Why would she? She's agreed.'

'Because Mia hates being the centre of attention, especially when she knows that her ex is somewhere in that crowd. It was a nice thought, though. Tell Mia that. I appreciate the effort. But be prepared for her to bolt at the first chance she gets.' And then he'd lose her, and his best dog, along with his dreams, and perhaps his family's dreams all on the one day. He should have never left the station, then none of this would have happened. They should have just stayed home.

Forty-two

'That's not me?' Mia gasped at her reflection in the mirror of the sporting grounds' changing rooms. The eyes were hers, but the make-up was new.

She rarely wore any. Working outdoors, she never dressed to impress. But the clothes were new. In a striped collared business shirt, fitted jeans, heeled boots, and a black leather belt. 'I'm dressed like you, Harper.'

'I don't do stripes. But they suit you.' Harper straightened Mia's collar. 'You did a good job on the hair, Bree.'

Mia touched her smooth silky hair. 'I could do with a cap.' Missing Cap, hoping Atlas was okay. She'd heard Fern was fine. But sadly, Atlas was still getting treatment.

'For this event, you get a new town hat to add to your wardrobe.' Bree carefully placed it on Mia's head like a tiara. 'Perfect. You're ready. And so is Willow.' She touched the dog's nose. 'You look good in your new dog collar.'

'I chose the mustard colour because it reminded me of Cap's Tojo.' Harper adjusted the collar that was like a minimalist rope bracelet. 'I think the tiny charms on it are a cute touch. And I've ordered a special name tag for Willow with Mia's number on the back for when they come to town. My dogs are getting one, too.'

'I think you should become a personal shopper, Harper, for both human and canines,' said Bree.

'Willow needed to look as good as her new owner to celebrate their participation.' Harper's phone pinged, and she read the message. 'Ash says they want Mia at the arena now.'

'Let's go.' Bree hooked her arm through Mia's, hustling her out the door and into the bright sunshine.

'Do I have to do this?' Mia swallowed hard, while the dog trotted beside her, with her tail up, her coat gleaming, and her new collar all sparkly.

'You said you'd do it.'

'But do I have to get dressed up?'

'This isn't dressed up, it's smart casual,' said Harper. 'I have plenty of ball gowns and cocktail dresses if you want to get dressed up. Hey, we should do that at our next cooking lesson and make cupcakes while wearing ball gowns and tiaras.'

'Oh, I'm in,' said Bree with a bright smile. 'Mia, didn't your mother dress up when she did her dog shows?'

'Um, yeah… I should call her.'

'Give me that.' Bree snatched the phone. 'You can call her after the events. In the meantime, I'll take photos you can send to your parents and Cap.'

'Cap knows I'm doing this?' She licked her lips, that felt foreign from the lipstick.

Harper nodded. 'I can't wait to watch. Ash is filming it with the drone.'

Mia stumbled.

'I've got you.' Bree clutched her arm tighter.

'Do you think I'm going to run away?' Which is what she wanted to do.

'I think when you give that first command to Willow, the crowd will disappear, and it will be just you and the dog having fun out there. You'll forget we're even here.'

'Can we forget I said yes?'

Bree gave a wry smile as they approached the arena. 'You can back out. Anytime.'

'Really?'

'But then you'll suffer with crippling guilt for quitting, and end up with stomach ulcers—'

'Bree!' Harper motioned with her eyes at Bree to stop.

Bree laughed. 'Let's put it this way, precious, it's just the fear talking. Look, let's picture your fear as black mould that grows in dark, stagnant places. We try to conceal it, ignore it, yet sometimes that fear compounds into something like a phobia,' Bree said, brushing some lint off Mia's shoulder. 'With your fear of standing in front of a crowd you can either trample on it like a weed to make room for the pretty native wildflowers, or you can go hide in a dark corner again. But I know you'll be disappointed in yourself for not trying. Now, get out there and have fun. We'll be here supporting you.'

'One last gift. A bottle of water for you, and this is a portable water bowl for the dog. It matches her collar and lead. *Go Team Willow*.' Harper gave the thumbs up, just like she did at the drafting yards.

They left Mia on the edge of the arena with Willow beside her, holding a lead, a bottle of water, and a portable dog bowl that folded away like a compact grocery bag with a clip.

Ryder approached, carrying a large piece of paper in his hand, it was like a running bib worn by marathon runners with large numbers on it. 'Mia, I'm going to pin this number to your back.'

'Isn't that Cap's number?'

'It's yours too. I've put your name beside Cap's as the team representing Elsie Creek Station.'

Didn't that make her stomach swirl. Did this mean they'd officially made her a part of the team?

'As the last contestant for the obstacle course, you're to stay out in the arena for the next event.'

'Back-to-back events?'

'It's how we got the extra time to allow you to get ready. You'll start there at the jumps. It's set out the same as Cap's obstacle course back home.' He pointed at the small jumps.

'We only did that for fun. Not for show. Cap's dogs did this.'

'Mia, we don't care if you win. We're just proud of you for stepping up in Cap's place. And if Cap were here, I'm sure he'd tell you that you look nice. Good luck.'

Wow! Ryder Riggs said all that. Her jaw fell open

watching the big man walk away.

That's when she noticed the crowd of assorted hats spread around the arena. At one end sat a group of stern-looking cattlemen seated at a long table holding pens and clipboards. Another held a microphone. Above them stood a huge board lit up with red numbers.

'Ready, Miss?'

No way was she ready to stand in front of E.V.E.R.Y.O.N.E.

Willow brushed her moist nose against Mia's hand. It was her dog. Who was a part of her team.

She crouched down to the dog. 'Think we can do this, Willow?'

Willow's tail wagged, her eyes on the obstacle course. Willow loved the course. And this was for Cap, for his family and friends who'd helped her. For a month she'd been searching for a way to thank them all, so this was it.

She unclipped the dog's stylish new lead. 'Steady, Willow…'

The dog crouched down, tail wagging, her eyes on Mia.

She nodded to the adjudicator, who held up his hand.

A buzzer went off. The large clock started.

'*Go, Willow, over to the end.*' The dog ran her heart out, making quick work of the small jumps which represented the differing heights of the cattle rails. She then ran around the top end, through the mesh tunnel to leap effortlessly over another set of jumps, and up to the tall bridge to represent cattle ramps. Then, back through the jumps again and over to the paddle swing.

'*Hold…*' There was a pause as the dog used her weight to lower the board like a seesaw, then through a series of tyre jumps, then the sprint towards Willow's favourite section of the twenty-part obstacle course, the weave poles.

Twelve plastic poles stood over six feet high where the dog had to swing past them going from the left, to right, left, right, left, right, past each pole evenly spaced at sixty centimetres apart.

With her dainty paws doing a swimming step as if dancing on the dust that made up the outback arena, Willow raced through it as if it was a straight line, then over the last hurdles to race back to Mia.

'I've got you, girl.' Mia crouched down with her arms out, and Willow jumped into them for a hug. It was then Mia heard the crowd's applause.

The numbers on the clock showed sixty-nine seconds.

Was that a good time?

Then the ground crew made quick work of putting the obstacles onto a truck, leaving Mia and Willow all alone in the arena. She'd barely had enough time to test out the new water bowl for Willow, when the truck left the arena and a gate opened at the far end allowing three steers to enter the holding pen.

Willow barked, her tail thumping in the dirt, her eager eyes on the cattle.

It was time for the next event.

'*Welcome to the muster dog trials,*' said a male voice over the loudspeakers and the crowd's voices hushed to listen. 'For those new to the muster dog trials, all dogs start with a hundred points. Points will be deducted for errors such as excessive barking, nipping, excessive force, and disobeying commands. The aim is to walk three cattle calmly around the fences then through the gates to represent drafting gates. It's a test to show the skills of the dogs helping the stockman move the cattle where they want them. And competitors have six minutes to complete this trial.'

A sweat bead trickled down the side of her face, Mia swallowed hard wishing they'd just get on with it.

The MC continued, 'First off will be the kelpie, Willow, and her handler, Mia Dixon, from Elsie Creek Station, who recorded an impressive time in the obstacle course. I've been told that Mia and Willow have only been working together for three weeks. They've been trained by Caleb Riggs, co-owner of Elsie Creek Station, who trains handlers and problem dogs in the art of mustering partnerships. Let's begin…'

Mia felt the world fall away. The breeze grew still, as a bird flew past, and a fly flirted with her shoulder.

'Willow, steady.'

The dog crouched down, her eyes alert and shining, focused on the cattle.

The buzzer went off and the three steers were released.

'*Away, Willow.*'

With speed, the kelpie ran in a wide, arching circle towards the cattle.

'*Come round.*'

Willow rushed around them on the right, pushing the trio towards the first rails. One steer lowered its head and Willow barked, getting close enough to almost nip at its nose. Would they lose points for that?

'*Easy, Willow.*'

The dog backed off, weaving back and forth like a western line dancer to push them through the first gate.

But Mia still couldn't breathe, the sun scorching down on her, twisting her fingers, as the time seemed to stretch into hours. '*Come round… Push them through… Steady… Walk up. Walk up.*'

Willow ran side to side, herding the cattle just like she did in the drafting yards to walk them through the open gate. Mia closed it behind them. Five minutes and sixteen seconds, with forty-four seconds to spare.

It wasn't fast like Atlas or Fern would have done, but it was steady, the cattle were calm, and it's what Cap would call *a good clean close.*

'Well done, Willow, well done.' She patted the dog heartily as her reward.

A buzzing noise hovered overhead. She looked up to face Ash's drone. Normally she'd duck and hide, but today she waved, then she waved at Bree and Harper holding Mason where they cheered loudly with Dex and Ryder clapping beside them. Mia had nothing to hide.

Why should she?

After all, there was nowhere to hide in front of everyone in the arena. So what if she mucked up, she was having a go. She even shyly smiled at the crowds who were clapping for them.

Bree was right—Mia might not have won, but this was a win for her. It was also a win for all those who called Elsie Creek Station home.

Forty-three

It was late in the afternoon as Cap steered his trusty Tojo through the wide-open gates of Elsie Creek Station. Willow and Fern gave barks of joy from the back cage. He felt it too. 'It's good to be home.' Especially after the day they'd had.

'When can we pick up Atlas?' Mia asked from the passenger seat.

He liked the way she said *we*. 'Tomorrow. Ryan's giving him another treatment tonight, to be on the safe side.' The dog needed sleep and Atlas wasn't doing that with everyone, including his furry playmates, in the same room.

'Atlas is going to be okay.'

'I know.' It still hurt. 'What about you?' He gave her a gentle smile, his eyes roaming over her face. In make-up, new shirt, and her hair back, showing the world how truly beautiful she was. 'Look at you.'

'I got attacked by Harper and Bree.' She dropped her head humbly.

'You look amazing. If we weren't so beat, I would have taken you out to dinner. But we'll do it soon. Like a date?'

How slack was he, when Mia deserved to be spoiled? He was going to speak to Ash about the romantic stuff. His baby brother was always spoiling his lady, organising with Cap to babysit for their weekly date nights.

'That'd be nice. I'd like that.'

His eyes narrowed at her. She seemed different, more confident. 'Something happened to you, didn't it? During the trials?'

Mia nodded. 'I think I found my confidence again. Did that sound foolish?'

'Hey, remember who you're talking to. All secrets, worries, or any fears we have, we share between us so we can tackle them together. Okay?' He gave her hand a tender squeeze.

'I promise.' She playfully rolled her eyes. 'I don't want to hide anymore.'

'Really?' That sounded promising.

'And I don't want to run either.'

'Does that mean you'll stay here with me?'

She hesitated.

'Hey, no rush.' Even though he wanted to rush her, he was also a patient man. 'I'm not going anywhere.' He steered them around the sweeping bend and the farmhouse came into view.

But there was no shepherd barking from the front porch to greet them.

It was enough to make him slow down.

'What's wrong?'

'There's no Sarge.' The massive shepherd would normally run out and greet him, along with Scout. After what happened to Atlas, it had him worried.

They came around the bend where a large maroon Land Cruiser ute had parked in the yard. 'Who does that belong to?'

'Oh, no, it's Gavin's.' Mia's face paled.

'Are you sure?' His grip tightened on the steering wheel. *That arsehole had better not be here!*

'Maybe. I'm not sure, because it's got a dog cage on the back, and Gavin hates dogs.' She leaned closer, then her eyes widened and she sat back. 'It is his ute. I gave him that footy sticker by the number plate and those are his fancy tyres. I remember the hassle he went through to get those rims.'

It was a fancy ute. 'I can turn us around and go.'

Mia sat tall, shoulders back, chin high, then she tapped

Dodge's collar that hung from the rear-view mirror.

It was his gentle reminder that he'd get through the bad days. And this had been one exceptionally bad day. Yet, it always gave him strength.

Now it seemed to be doing the same for Mia, when she said, 'No. I have to finish this.'

'Are you sure?' He wanted to smile and cheer his girl on. Look out, who knew courage could be so stunning.

'Yes.' She may have said yes, but her head was shaking no. 'I'm guessing Bree would tell me it's time to face my demons.'

'It's been a big day for it.'

'Tell me about it.'

Today, in the arena, Mia didn't win, but she made sixth place. It was a brilliant result for someone who had only just learned how to work with muster dogs.

Cap wished he'd been there to cheer her on. But, then again, if he had been there, she wouldn't have entered.

Did fate have a hand in this? Because through Mia's determination in the arena, not only had she faced her fear of being in the public eye, but she'd also successfully captured the audience's attention. His brothers had been swamped with queries about muster dog training. But more importantly, he had queries about not only about retraining some problem dogs, but to help stockmen rebuild their mustering dog teams. It's what he was hoping for all along.

But right now, this was Mia's greatest threat ahead of her. Did she have the strength to do this? Or was she still riding on some high from today?

Mia gripped his hand. 'Can you please promise me you won't lose your temper?'

He couldn't promise her that, not after what Gavin had done to her. Not when the memory flashed in his mind of her bloodied and bruised. 'I'll try.'

This woman had ignited something so primal inside him that he would protect her at all costs. The fates weren't going to help this Gavin, should he even dare look at Mia the wrong way, because Cap, the peacemaker, was ready to go to war!

Forty-four

As soon as Cap parked the Tojo, and before the dust had settled, Mia jumped out. With the dust kicking up behind her new boots, this was the first time she willingly walked towards confrontation.

'I'm not leaving until I speak with Mia.' Gavin's determined voice echoed around her. It made her skin crawl.

At the farmhouse, she spotted Harper on the other side of the screen door with young Mason, Ruby the labrador, and Scout the beagle beside her. So where was Sarge the shepherd?

She approached the front of the vehicles to find Gavin standing before Ryder, Dex, Ash, and Charlie. Sarge calmly sat beside Ryder, yet the muscular dog still looked lethal, especially in his harness.

'There's my little Mia.' Gavin approached.

But Cap blocked him off. 'Back off! You can talk to her from there.'

'Who is he, Mia?' Ryder asked. 'He claims to be a friend of yours.'

'This is the mongrel who hurt Mia.' Cap's voice rang out, and Sarge emitted a low growl.

'Control your dog.' Gavin backed away from the dog. 'This is intimidation.'

'No, this is trespassing.' Dex stepped closer to Gavin, wearing a menacing scowl. He looked positively lethal. 'How about you and me go a few rounds? Right here, right now, in a fair fight. Or are you just a coward who hits women?'

'Mia?' Gavin turned to her, looking so innocent. 'What lies have you been telling these people? They don't know me or you.'

'You're the one who lies.' She finally found her voice and, with it, her fury, effectively pushing away her fear of confrontations.

It was on.

'*You* were the bully who stopped me from ringing my family. *You* stopped me from socialising. *You* controlled me, and *you hit me.*' She jabbed at the air between them as she took a step closer.

'Admit it, you never liked those people and used me as your scapegoat because you'd rather hide at home.'

'You knew I was scared of being in the public eye and how much I hated confrontations.' Up until today she'd always done her best to avoid them. 'Instead of supporting me, or helping me to get past them, you deliberately used those fears of mine to control me. Where you beat me up!'

'It was an accident. I hit that bump on the road and my elbow—'

'LIAR!' Mia trembled with rage as the word echoed a dozen times in the open air. 'It's over. I wasn't living a life with you, I was just existing in a shell. And it's only since I came to this place, that I've learned the true value of friendships, and how friends support and encourage each other while accepting their faults, like a family—even if they're not actually related. But some faults are unforgivable, especially when it comes to physically harming another member of that family.' Thinking of Bree's father, and what Gavin had done to her.

She exhaled, untangling her fingers and flexing them free. 'Some of the kindest souls are those who have come from an unkind world. Bree and Cap taught me that.'

She turned to smile at Cap, and his brothers, even the charming stockman Charlie. 'That even if they may argue, they're still tight as friends, as family, who'd back each other up when someone is in trouble, without question. These people showed kindness to a stranger.'

She turned to face Cap, lacing her fingers through his and squeezing his hand. 'Here I finally understood what actual love is, and what a real man is, because they weren't afraid to show their kindness. A real man isn't afraid to show his love for his family, to animals, or to me. Finding your soulmate does more than complete you—it magnifies the spirit that only makes you shine.' And Cap did make her shine from the inside, that she'd felt her courage grow inside her to face her fears.

'Loving the right people has shown me that love can be gentle, love can be kind, more importantly love can be that safe space everyone deserves.' And she got all that with Cap, who was the man of her dreams, now that she was wide awake to the world.

'I should thank you, Gavin, because without you, I would have never met these people. And I would never have fallen in love with someone as amazing as Cap.'

Cap smiled at her as he tenderly reached out to cup her cheek.

'Oi, get your hands off her.' Gavin scowled as he pointed at Cap.

Mia faced him, chin up with nothing to hide. 'I don't belong to you anymore.' Her voice was no longer meek and mild; she felt the force behind everything she said because she believed in them, because she believed in herself. 'There is nothing left for you here, Gavin. Go. And never come back.'

Then there was the distinctive click of a double barrel shotgun loading behind them.

'Hello, chopped liver.' It was Bree aiming her shotgun at Gavin. 'I've got a watering hole with some big crocs dying to meet you.'

'Oh, crap. You're in trouble now. You've unleashed the kraken.' Dex grinned as he stepped back from Gavin with hands up. 'Bree, take your shot. Or we could tie him up with some rope, drag him behind the Razorback and take him on a special sunset tour to meet those snapping handbags.'

'I've done nothing to you.' Gavin held his hands up, taking a step back from the redhead.

'Yes, you did.' Bree scowled, taking a step closer, the shotgun rock-steady against her shoulder. 'I absolutely abhor any man who dares to hit a woman. Just so you know, I have a tonne of unresolved daddy issues that need sorting out, starting with you as my golden therapy pill.' She then aimed, with finger on the trigger. 'Any last words?'

'Mia?' Gavin went white as a ghost.

Mia could only shrug, because Bree was serious. And scary.

Forty-five

Cap looked at his big brother for help. There was no way he was going to tackle the redhead holding a shotgun, because they all knew Bree wasn't afraid to use it. 'Ryder?'

Ryder rolled his eyes. 'Bree, you will not spend the rest of your life in prison for murdering this douchebag.' He stepped forward and in some seriously fancy military move, he'd removed the shotgun from her hands and unloaded it in a matter of seconds.

'Hey, that's my shotgun. Give it back.'

'No.' Ryder rested it on his shoulder. 'The first rule of murder club is *no witnesses*.'

'I'll back you up, Bree,' said Dex. 'I'll supply the rope.'

'Stuff the rope, let's use the chain,' said Charlie, poking at Gavin's chest. 'We don't like anyone hitting women round here, boy.'

'No one is murdering anyone.' Cap stepped up, playing his part as the family's peacemaker, and put himself in front of Gavin.

'Can I at least hit him?' asked Dex. 'Just one punch, or five.'

'Oh, me too. I've always wanted to play dentist.' Bree tried to push past Ryder.

'No.' Ryder held her back. 'Dex, stop stirring up the redhead.'

Ash calmly strolled up to Gavin with a grin on his face. 'You know what would work in this situation?'

'What?'

'If you were to leave.'

'Fine. No problems, I'm happy to go.'

'Nah, mate, I don't think you're getting me,' said Ash. 'You need to leave the Territory. Because Bree and her grandfather know everyone, and the Territory is a small place. None of the locals like women-hitters, which is what you are.'

'Mia lied. It was just an accident.'

'We all saw the damage you did.' Cap's fire instantly refuelled, to hiss through gritted teeth. 'The bruises.'

Sarge growled and Cap gripped his halter. 'Easy, boy.'

'Get that dog away from me.' Gavin stepped away with his eyes widening.

'It was you!' Mia made stabbing motions at Gavin with her finger. 'You poisoned Cap's dogs.'

'Mia? Is that true?' Cap was so stunned by her words, he nearly let go of the dog.

'I've got him, Cap.' Ash took control of the shepherd's halter.

Charlie poked up his hat's brim. 'Girlie, are you saying this mongrel who hit you, also poisoned Cap's dogs?'

'I wish I'd thought of it sooner, but it only made sense now.'

Dex stepped right behind Gavin. 'Don't move, arsehole. It seems we have some unfinished business.'

Gavin struggled to swallow. 'Mia?' His voice was strained.

'What makes you think this mongrel poisoned my dogs?' The thought made Cap's blood boil.

'Gavin is a diesel fitter for the mines,' said Mia, facing the man who'd plagued her nightmares. 'Lead is everywhere. I know lead is used to line the tanks that hold corrosive liquids that are commonly found on mine sites. It's also in the big batteries for their machinery, and there are stacks of them in Gavin's workshop at the mine.'

'Why would he do that, girlie? He doesn't know us.'

Charlie squinted at Gavin like he was rotten meat. 'I've never met the bloke until today.'

'Because Gavin is working for Leo. It's why he hasn't left the Territory, because Leo was going to pay Gavin double what he was getting at his old job if he didn't mind getting his hands dirty.' Mia wagged her finger at him. 'Leo is your boss. He's paying you, isn't he?'

'It's a job, that's all.' Gavin shrugged. 'Easy money to buy that farm you always wanted.'

Mia shuddered, holding up her palm to make him stop talking. 'You confronted me in the car park at the campdraft because you'd *followed* me back *from* the dog tent. It's why Leo made such a fuss over Willow at our display tent about owning her. It was a distraction, so Cap would come running, leaving his dogs unattended, where you poured the poison into their water bowls. I watched Leo text you when it was all over after I'd won Willow. He was texting you to warn you that Cap might come back!'

She then pointed to the back cage of Gavin's ute. 'That dog cage on the back of your ute, I know it's new. Which doesn't make sense when you hate dogs!'

'So? Some people don't like cats.'

'I bet it was you who let those wild dogs out on this property.' She shook her head. 'I was there when Cowboy Craig told me about the tyre treads on the vehicle used to dump those wild dogs on this property. He said they were special all-terrain tyres commonly bought by concrete cowboys.' She pointed to his car's tyres. 'I remember the fuss you made in getting these and how it took ages for them to arrive. Bree would recognise the tread. She was there.'

'Me, too,' said Charlie. 'And Craig took pictures on his phone.'

'It was you who hurt the dogs. YOU.' Mia stood right before him stabbing her finger at him. 'Leo paid you, didn't he? Go on, be a man and admit it.'

'Yeah, alright. As soon as Leo told me he'd seen you here, shacking up with these mongrels, I did all of it —'

'You arsehole.' Cap saw red. His hands squeezed tight into fists, and he lashed out at Gavin. *Bang bang.* Two quick punches into Gavin's right eye, in the same spot Mia wore her black eye. 'That's for Atlas.'

And he was just warming up, to let loose with another flurry of lightning-quick punches that smashed into Gavin's nose, the gristle and bone no match for Cap's fists. 'And that's for all those wild dogs we had to put down, too.'

But Cap wasn't done; he still needed to dish out some justice. Yet, he waited a beat for Gavin to take a swing, just like they'd all been taught.

Gavin swung.

Cap ducked, deflected Gavin's punch, to hit hard with his elbow, clipping Gavin's lips in the same place Mia had her fat lip.

Gavin collapsed to the ground, and Cap booted him right in the ribs. 'And that's for Mia.'

Even though Gavin was a bloody mess kissing the dirt floor, Cap dragged the cretin up by the shirtfront. 'If I ever see you again, I will play by the rules of murder club, and I will take you to that watering hole to meet those crocodiles myself, and I will watch them tear you limb from limb.'

'Cap, please stop.' Mia tugged on his arm, pulling him away as Gavin fell back to the ground.

Dex leaned down and checked over Gavin. 'You'll live.'

'Good. Time to leave.' Ryder roughly dragged Gavin like a rag doll, shoving him into the driver's seat of the maroon ute. The big man then said something quietly to Gavin that made her ex's eyes widen in terror, before he quickly drove away.

'Well done, brother.' Dex patted Cap on the shoulders. 'We taught you well.'

'I've never seen you fight, Cap.' Ash arched his eyebrows at his brother. 'You're always stopping the fights as our peacemaker.'

'Sometimes you have to make war to get peace,' said Ryder, watching Gavin's ute drive away.

'I'm sorry, Mia. I know you told me to keep my temper, but after what you said about the dogs, I couldn't let him get away with that. Not after what he did to Atlas, and especially to you. I want you to be free from him, to live without fear.' With his sore, bloodied hands, he cupped her cheeks, only to pull back. 'I'm getting your good clothes all dirty.'

'Dirt never bothered me. I know I'm all about saving the environment and being a peace lover, but that was hot. *The rush* of the whole confrontation, and you, you're so nasty.' She giggled.

He chuckled, slinging his arm around her shoulders, using the crook of his elbow to bring her close. 'I'd do it for you again in a heartbeat. But Bree?' He showed the redhead his fists. 'Have you got anything in your witchy kit for knuckles?'

'Come on, you big bad hero, I've got a freezer full of ice and a jug of gin with your name all over it, we'll fix up those cuts in no time. If your brother gives me back my shotgun?' She narrowed her eyes at Ryder.

Ryder peered down the empty barrel. 'This shotgun is a mess. It looks like it's been buried in the dirt somewhere.'

'So what, if it has? It would've worked.'

'What are you worried about, kid? You've got plenty of shotties stashed all over the place.' Charlie grinned at his granddaughter, as the Riggs brothers raised concerned eyebrows at each other. 'But I reckon you boys have earned yourself another invite to pizza night. We can celebrate Mia's win.' Charlie hooked his arm through Bree's. 'What do you lot say?'

'I'm in,' Dex said. 'I'll get the beer and we can spend the night convincing you to give us our cattle brand back.'

'You can try.' Charlie gave a coy grin, his grey eyes sparkling.

'Harper, get Mason. It's pizza night over at the caretaker's cottage.' Ash jogged after Dex and Ryder, heading for the farmhouse.

Beside his Tojo, Cap hugged Mia, admiring her lively

aroma of orange blossoms. 'You do realise you told me you loved me, in front of everyone?'

'I did. I've never done that before.'

'Are you sure it's not too soon for you?'

'I knew the second I saw Gavin earlier today that I didn't love him. I never loved him. Not like I love you. I settled for him because Gavin desired me, when I didn't think I deserved better, and then I came to fear him and that fear made me fear everything. But since coming to Elsie Creek Station, I've learned to push past my fears to find true love, like I have with you. Because of you I found my courage to try to do more, live more, and to take the centre stage in my own personal arena.'

'I'm sorry I missed your event.'

'Maybe next year?' She grinned at him. 'And we'll see which one of us gets the higher points.'

'You're on.' He cupped her cheeks and lovingly kissed her. He might not know how to be a romantic, but he sure as hell knew how to show her how much he loved her in one kiss.

As the sun set over Elsie Creek Station, the campdraft might not have gone to plan, but in the end, he got the girl. And that's what mattered to him.

Forty-six

With her heart hammering in her throat, Mia used the sleeve of her crusty work shirt to wipe away the sweat stinging her eyes.

'Hit it.' Dex held the punching bag, and Mia swung hard with the cumbersome boxing glove.

'Come on, harder than that. You hit like a girl.'

A giggle escaped, sapping all her energy she barely managed to give the punching bag a feeble tap. 'I am a girl and I'm done for today.' She removed the gloves that had been a gift from Dex, who'd set up the punching bag beside a proper boxing ring, complete with assorted gym equipment that was part of the stockman's shack, where Dex lived.

'Your turn, brother.'

'Nah, I'm a lover, not a fighter.' Cap showed his knuckles that were almost healed. Atlas, Fern and Willow lay near his boots, with the rest of the muster dogs stretched out under the shade of the nearby tree.

'Nothing wrong with getting fit.'

'I dig holes and plant trees for cardio.'

'Who's been digging holes?' Mia wiped down her sweaty face with a towel and guzzled on some water.

'I wanted to, but you wouldn't let me.' Cap hadn't held a shovel for days, not after punching out Mia's ex. She'd told him she didn't want his grazed knuckles to get infected. And he told her he wasn't a wimp. But he could never refuse her requests.

From the farmhouse, the shepherd gave a deep bark,

warning them of an incoming vehicle.

'*Oi, it's Porter.*' Ash waved from the back of the sheds that stored their various vehicles.

'What is Porter doing here?' Cap waited to walk beside Mia.

'He's probably going to charge you with assault for recalibrating the bone structure on Gavin's face.' Dex smirked at him.

'That sounds like something Bree would say.'

'She did. We're very proud of you, brother.' Dex patted Cap's shoulder as they headed to greet the police paddy wagon.

Cap tried to hide his smile, slinging his arm around Mia's shoulders. 'I'd do it again to protect you,' he whispered in her ear, sending shivers down her spine. She matched his grin.

Climbing out of the police wagon, Porter adjusted his police cap and smiled. '*Willow.*'

Willow gave a yap of recognition and bolted across the yard to jump straight into Porter's arms for a hearty hug.

'You didn't bring another dog out, did you?' Ryder crossed over from the farmhouse to meet them, with Charlie and Bree leaning over the front fence of the caretaker's cottage.

'No. But we got Atlas's blood test results.' Porter pulled out a folder and flicked open the cover. 'It was a high concentrate of lead commonly found in industrial batteries used in mining machinery.'

Ryder slid his hands into the pockets of his jeans. 'Any clues who did this?'

'I was hoping one of you guys might know. I'm aware you're having issues with the neighbours over the new lithium mine, and now Willow.'

'Did Leo ever show you the paperwork proving Willow's ownership?' Cap squeezed Mia's hands, ever so gently. She knew they weren't going to say anything about Gavin, to protect Cap for hitting him, and Bree for pointing a loaded shotgun in his face.

'No,' replied Porter, his brow shifting. 'Leo said he got rid of it. Didn't see the point if he couldn't keep the dog. Said he lost the dog off the back of his ute when he was pig shooting.'

'Do you think he ever owned the dog?'

'Willow reacted to him like she knew him, which wasn't good,' replied Porter, his brow furrowing into a frown as he looked at the kelpie. 'And Leo would have contacts to access lead, especially if he was opening a mine. And rumour has it, Charlie, you'd lost all your working dogs to lead poisoning. Is that true?'

'Can't prove nothin'.'

Porter narrowed his eyes at everyone as if he saw straight through them. He was a lot smarter than Mia had realised.

'And before you ask,' said Charlie, waving his hand at the officer, 'it was in the tank. Not the soil.'

'Pop. Stop.' Bree hissed, as Dex rolled his eyes, even Ryder shook his head.

'What?' Charlie shrugged. 'The dogs are long buried in the dog cemetery.'

'Right. When did this happen?' Porter dragged out his notebook.

Oh, no. Mia froze, while trying not to look guilty.

'You lot do want justice?' Porter pointed at Willow, who he'd cared for. 'Don't you want it too, Cap?' His gaze dropped down to Cap's hands, the knuckles still bruised.

Cap slid his hands in his pockets.

'Alright, let's kill the suspense, shall we...' Bree opened the gate and approached the officer. 'As a good and close personal friend of the family,' said Bree quietly, sliding her arm over Porter's shoulders, 'will you trust me when I say justice has been served for Willow and Atlas.'

Porter frowned. 'I have a job—'

'That I would never *ever* put you at risk of getting into trouble over. I know you love your job, and I have respect for you and your job, which is why I won't tell you. The technicalities would've just gotten in the way of justice being served, Territory style.'

Porter stared at her for a long beat, then gave her a short sharp nod.

'There's a dog cemetery here at the station?' Cap shrugged at his brothers, hoping to clear the tension in the air.

'Yeah. Pleasant spot on the side of the hill, looks over the Mitchell Plains. A good spot for muster dogs as their eternal long paddock. Just don't ask me to show you. Bree can.' Charlie turned to head back inside.

'Before you go, Charlie, I need to ask you something.'

Everyone froze.

'It's about your brother, Harry.' Porter approached the old man.

'Please don't build his hopes up, Porter,' muttered Bree.

'Charlie started this by putting in a missing person's report. As frustrating as it has been, sadly, I've found nothing. I wish I could give you more, Charlie, which is why I'm here. You said Harry allegedly ran off with another man's wife?'

'Yeah, that's right.' Charlie thumbed up the brim of his old Akubra with the hatband made from crocodile leather. His squinted eyes deepened the sun-tanned creases of a man who'd lived a long life under the outback sun. 'Pen was her name. Penelope Price. She was wife to the head stockman, Jack Price.'

The Riggs brothers frowned as if some unspoken stockman's code had been broken for someone sleeping with another stockman's wife—especially the wife of the head stockman.

'I could search for Penelope Price, hoping she might point us in the direction where your brother may have gone. But I technically can't.'

'Why not? You're the copper driving that paddy wagon around like you stole it. Or are you wearing that uniform for fancy dress?' Charlie waved the callused hands of a master brand maker who'd refused to retire in his eighty young years.

'If I do, I'll have to reopen the murder case.'

'Why?'

'My boss said so. It's procedure. But I won't do it, not without your permission. Yet, I think we should, Charlie, because with today's technology we can look at it from a completely different viewpoint.'

'Are you using this as some case study?' Bree asked.

'No. I mean, it is a cold case, and I am going for my detective's certificate and want to—'

'Use it like some school project.' Bree crossed her arms over her chest, arching an eyebrow at him.

Ignoring the redhead, Porter lifted his chin to face the old man. 'Do you want answers or not, Charlie? You're the one who asked me to start this. I want to take it to the next level, but only if you say so.'

'Pop, I warned you, this was wrong; it's like opening Pandora's Box—'

'Pandora's Box also held curiosity and hope in there too, kid. I know my Greek mythology.'

'If Harry is still alive, do you really want him spending his last days in prison? And if you were in Harry's situation, would your brother do that to you if he knew you'd done the Harold Holt and bolted after a murder? Don't you think you should let sleeping dogs lie?' Bree asked.

Charlie squinted his grey eyes at Porter, then turned to the Riggs brothers. 'What would you mob do, if one of your brothers went missing?'

Dex and Cap shrugged.

'I'd wanna know.' Ash thoughtfully rubbed his jaw. 'Because I'd be like you, Charlie, always wondering where my brother went.'

'You'll be opening old wounds, Pop.'

'I know, I know.' Charlie then faced Ryder. 'What would you do?'

'Not my choice, mate,' said the man who'd practically disappeared for ten years. 'But I know if I had to leave in a hurry, I'd make sure I'd leave some sort of message to say goodbye to my brothers, to stop them looking for me.' And Ryder always did send messages to their mother.

'That's what I'd do, and Harry, too. We were close. But he left me behind without a word.'

'And you copped a lot of hell for it too, Pop. Not only from the cops—'

Policeman Porter cleared his throat.

'Not you, Porter, the investigating officers hassled Pop about the murder.' Bree sighed heavily, her eyes softening as she spoke to her grandfather. 'You also got hassled about Harry running away with the stockman's wife. A head stockman at that. And we all know that's a line a stockman does not cross—especially on a station. And because they couldn't get Harry, they took it out on you. I saw the newspaper clippings.'

'I know, I was there.'

'Well, why would you want to stir up the dust of the past, when you can live the rest of your days doing what you love by annoying these boys?'

'Maybe Bree's right.' Charlie poked up the brim of his hat, but then he squinted up at the policeman. 'What do you think I should do?'

Find out in
STOCKMAN'S STORMCLOUD

I HAVE A GIFT FOR YOU!

Learn more about
ELSIE CREEK STATION
The family tree
Behind the scenes
Plus so much more

Free & Exclusive!
Simply go to:
https://melarowe.com/the-stockmen-series-gifts/

Want more from the Elsie Creek World?

Binge-read all the bestsellers found in:

The Elsie Creek Series

&

The Station Series

Find them at your favourite online bookstore.

ACKNOWLEDGEMENTS

Look out, we are now at the halfway mark in this four-part series that continues to twist and turn, with a smattering of dog hair, and the ever-continuing battle with misplaced semicolons. Believe me, the struggle is real, my friend. But hey, you're still here reading this, so let me say a big: *Thank you*.

I'd also like to give a big Charlie-nod of gratitude to those amazing muster dogs and their owners. As a fan of the heeler, having owned a few in my time, I've seen how incredibly fearless and faithful these amazing cattle dogs are. It's any wonder I've included them in my stories.

I'd also like to thank the many amazing people within the Northern Territory cattle industry. Like I've said before, there are too many to put on one page. I'd also like the thank those retired ringers who are always keen for a chat as they share their history over a cold beer on a hot day. Thank you to the campdrafters and their families that made those weekends so worth the travel. Thank you to my friend, Vicki, for helping me brainstorm this story while on a random road trip down the track. Thank you all for being a part of the real-life outback story, where I am truly humbled to share some of our adventures within *The Stockmen Series*.

Thank you to the amazing Handbrake, who will be sighing with relief that this series is almost over. And I forgive you for writing off my car.

Thank you to the amazing arc readers, your reviews about my stories not only motivate me, but they make me want to hug you all. Thank you to the epic editing Deb team at DP Plus, what more can I say but: 'love your work!' (Even if they are cringing at the mistakes I've made on this page.)

Lastly, to you, dear reader, thank you so much for giving up your spare time and for the courage to be a part of this adventure romance series. It means the world to me, and I look forward to sharing more with you in that romantic *'Escape to Happily Ever After'*.

Until next time,

A. ROWE

Also by MEL A ROWE

THE STOCKMEN SERIES:
Stockman's Sandstorm
Stockman's Stowaway
Stockman's Stormcloud
Stockman's Showdown

ELSIE CREEK SERIES:
The Art of Dust
Diamond in the Dust
Caked in Dust
Xmas Dust
Muster in the Dust
Rolled in Dust
Written in Dust
Doctoring Dust
Buffalo Dust

OASIS OF THE OUTBACK DUOLOGY:
The Station, Volume One
The Station, Volume Two

STANDALONE STORIES:
Avoiding the Pity Party
Unplanned Party
The Football Whisperer
Winter's Walk
Run Beautiful Run
The Sister Trip

For story exclusives & more visit MelAROWE.com